商務英語
BUSINESS 必備指南

金利 主編

英文是世界共通語言，但在學校學了十幾年的英語，
除了會讀、會寫，你確定自己會講了嗎？
在企業中，舉凡與外國客戶的會議、產品介紹與發表、
商務接待等等都離不開英文，不敢開口大聲說英語，
如何成為獨當一面的商務人才？

崧燁文化

目錄

Chapter 1
商務往來

Chapter 2
工作會議

Chapter
3
商務談判

Chapter 4
貿易往來

Chapter 5
市場行銷

前言

　　這是一個全民開口說英語的時代。為了提升溝通品質，盡享旅行樂趣，變身面試達人，促成大筆交易，你必須能說一口漂亮的英文！本書囊括了必備詞彙及地道表達，旨在幫助讀者在實際情境中將英語運用自如。

　　和老外交流時，我們通常會先想到中文，然後再去想對應的英文表達。這是我們臺灣人學習英語的思維方式。比如訂機票時，我們肯定先想到「單程票」，再去想對應的英文說法。本書在編排單字和句子時，都是先提供中文，後提供英文。並且按照這種思維方式，本書設計為詞→句→會話的學習流程。針對每一情景，設定了「必備表達、句句精彩、情景線上」三個部分，讓讀者由淺至深、循序漸進、環環相扣的學習，打牢基礎！

1.　必備表達

　　我們對商務場景中經常使用的漢語說法進行歸納，整理出單字和片語，引導讀者學習對應的英語表達，並加以解析。

2.　句句精彩

　　與單字理解方式一樣，我們整理了商務場景中經常使用的漢語句子，將其放入對話場景，提供對應的英語表達，並對重難點問題加以解析。

3.　情景線上

　　本書針對每一個情景，設計了情景會話。這部分用於實戰演練。我們提供了漢語表達的句子，要求讀者說出對應的英文。這些內容均在之前的環節學習過，旨在為讀者提供一個鞏固與提高的機會。這樣，讀者既可以鞏固所學知識，又可以進行自我檢測，力求做到學以致用。我們相信，透過將單字、句子與會話合為一體，一定能為讀者帶來意想不到的收穫。

透過閱讀本書，你將體會到：只要方法用對了，想要流利開口說不再是難題。
商務英語，志在必得。你準備好了嗎？

編者

Chapter

1

商務往來

Scene 1 建立聯絡

Step 1 必備表達

發電子郵件	send an e-mail：對應的「接收電子郵件」就是 receive an e-mail。
名片	business card：business 商業；此外，「名片」還可以用 calling card 或 visiting card 來表示。
聯絡方式	contact information：contact 聯絡；information 資訊；還可以用 contactway 來代替。
擴展業務	expand business：expand 擴展，擴大；而 business 在這裡表示「生意；業務」。
有空	available：除了指「有空的」，還可以指「可用的」。
分銷商	distributor：動詞形式是 distribute，表示「分配」。
銷售網	distribution networks：network 網路。
合作	cooperate：cooperate with 與……合作，該片語還可以表示為 be incooperation with。
商業往來	business relationship：relationship 關聯；還可用 commercial intercourse 表示「商業往來」。
傳真號碼	fax number：fax 傳真。

Step 2 句句精彩

① 我曾給您發過一封電子郵件，告訴您我要來這裡。

A： Nice to meet you, Mr. Zhang. I sent you an e-mail about my trip here. 張先生，很高興見到您。我曾發過一封電子郵件給您，告訴您我要來這裡。

B： Oh, nice to meet you. So you must be Mr. Li from Hongyun Company. 哦，很高興見到您。那麼您一定是鴻運公司的李先生了。

Tips

Have you made a reservation? 您預約過嗎？

Have you made an appointment in advance? 您提前預約過嗎？

I called you last week about my visit today. 上週我打過電話給您說今天要來拜訪。

② 我們公司營運有 50 多年了。

A： We've been in business for over 50 years. 我們公司營運有 50 多年了。

B： I've known about your company for a long time. 我久聞貴公司大名了。

Tips

be in business 經商；營業。

We've had a good reputation over these years. 這些年我們公司累積了很好的聲譽。

Our company has established representative office in New York. 我們公司在紐約設立了代表處。

③ 能給我一張您的名片嗎？

A： Could I have one of your business cards? 能給我一張您的名片嗎？

B： Sure. Here you are. 當然，給您。

Tips

Do you have a business card? 能給我一張您的名片嗎？

Can I have your business card? 能給我一張您的名片嗎？

Let me give you one of my business cards. 給您一張我的名片吧。

④ 與您聯絡的最佳方式是什麼？

A： What is the best way to contact you? 與您聯絡的最佳方式是什麼？

B： You can call this number. 你可以打這個電話。

Tips

Can I get your contact information? 可以告訴我您的聯絡方式嗎？

May I have your phone number if you don't mind? 如果不介意可以把您的電話號碼告訴我嗎？

When is the best time to contact you? 什麼時間聯絡您最合適？

⑤ 我們公司希望擴展與你們的業務。

A： Nice to meet you, Mr. Wang. What can I do for you? 很高興認識您，王先生。有

什麼可以為您效勞的？

B： Our company hopes to expand our business with you. 我們公司希望擴展與你們的業務。

Tips

■ I'm sure you're our best choice to cooperate with. 我相信貴公司是我們合作的最佳選擇。

■ I'm sure your company could benefit from our cooperation. 我確信我們的合作會使貴公司受益。

■ Our company hopes to cooperate with you. 我們公司希望與貴公司合作。

---

⑥ 打電話給我辦公室。

A： Give me a call at the office if you're free at 10 a.m. tomorrow. 如果明天上午十點你有時間，打電話給我辦公室。

B： It's a deal. I'll call you tomorrow for detailed information. 那就說定了。明天我打電話給你再詳談。

Tips

■ Would you call me at 3 p.m. this afternoon, please? 今天下午三點可以給我打電話嗎？

■ We can keep in touch by phone. 我們可以通過電話保持聯繫。

■ You can contact me by e-mail. 你可以通過電子郵件和我聯繫。

---

⑦ 能告訴我您的傳真號碼嗎？

A： Can I have your fax number? 能告訴我您的傳真號碼嗎？

B： Sure. It's 010-88099999. 當然，010-88099999。

Tips

■ Would you like to tell me your fax number? 可以告訴我您的傳真號碼嗎？

■ I need to fax our quotation to you. So can I have your number? 我需要傳真給您我們的報價。可以告訴我您的傳真號碼嗎？

■ Is it convenient for you to take down our fax number now? 你現在方便記下我的傳真號碼嗎？

Step 3 實 戰 對 話

① 初次見面

A： Good morning. Is Mr. Kevin Jobs here? 早上好，請問凱文‧約伯斯先生在嗎？

B： Yes, I am. Good morning. 我就是。早上好。

A： Nice to meet you. I sent you an e-mail about my trip here. 很高興見到您。我曾發過一封電子郵件給您，告訴您我要來這裡。

B： Oh, nice to meet you. So you must be Mr. Wang. Welcome to our company. 哦，很高興見到您。那麼您一定是王先生了。歡迎您來到我們公司。

A： Thank you. Our company hopes to expand our business with you. 謝謝。我們公司希望擴展與你們的業務。

B： Have a seat, please. Let's have a talk for more details. 您請坐。我們詳談一下。

② 介紹公司情況

A： I'm very glad to meet you, Mr. Wang. 王先生，很高興認識您。

B： Glad to meet you, too. When did your company set up? 我也很高興認識您。貴公司是什麼時候成立的？

A： We are established in 1963. We've been in business for over 50 years. 我們公司成立於 1963 年。我們公司營運有 50 多年了。

B： That's quite a long history. 那時間真的很長了。

A： Yeah. And now our company has established representative office in New York. So We'd like to cooperate with you. 是啊。現在我們公司在紐約設立了代表處。所以我們想和貴公司合作。

B： Glad to hear that. We have been looking for a suitable partner in your industry. 我們很高興聽到這個消息。我們一直都期待在您這個行業找到一個合適的合作夥伴。

③ 索要名片

A： Could I have one of your business cards? 能給我一張您的名片嗎？

B： Why not? Here's my card. 當然，給您。

A： Zhang Yuan. ABC Company. I got it. 張元，ABC 公司。我知道了。

B： Can I have your business card? 能給我一張您的名片嗎？

A： Oh, sorry. I forget to bring my business card. Could you write down my phone number? 哦，對不起，我忘帶名片了。你可以記一下我的電話號碼嗎？

B： OK. Just tell me. 好的，您說吧。

Scene 2　商務預約

Step 1　必備表達

預約	set an appointment：set 安排；appointment 預約，也可以說 make an appointment。
當面談	discuss in person：in person 表示「親自、當面」；face to face 也可表達此意。
方便的時間	convenient time：convenient 方便的。
詳細地	in detail：detail 細節。
來訪	stop by：也可用 visit 或 come by 來表達「拜訪」的意思。
日程表	schedule：a full schedule 表示「排得很滿的日程表」。
確認	confirm：confirm 表示「確認」，reconfirm 表示「再次確認」。
取消	cancel：也可用 call off 來代替。
晚點	behind schedule：還可以用 late 來代替。
提前	ahead of schedule：也可用 ahead of time 來表達「提前」的意思。
準時	punctual：還可以替換為 on time。

Step 2　句句精彩

① 我想和你們經理約個時間。

A： What can I do for you, sir? 先生，有什麼事嗎？

B： I'd like to set an appointment with your manager. 我想和你們經理約個時間。

Tips

■ 出於禮貌，拜訪客戶之前都應提前預約，並至少提前一天，較正式的會談則需給客戶更多時間準備。

■ I'd like to arrange an appointment to visit your company. 我想安排個時間去拜訪貴公司。

■ Should I make an appointment in advance? 我需要提前預約一下嗎？

②　下週到你辦公室當面詳談這筆交易好嗎？

A：Why don't I come by your office next week so we can discuss the deal in person? 下週到你辦公室當面詳談這筆交易好嗎？

B：That's fine. How about next Tuesday? 非常好。下週二如何？

Tips

■ May I make an appointment with you sometime this week? 這周可以跟你約個時間嗎？

■ Are you free tomorrow or the day after tomorrow? 你明天或後天有時間嗎？

■ Is it convenient for you to discuss the deal tomorrow? 你明天方便來談這筆生意嗎？

③　我們何時會面會比較合適呢？

A：When is a good time for us to meet? 我們何時會面會比較合適呢？

B：How about this Friday? 這週五怎麼樣？

Tips

■ 出於禮貌，可以讓對方提出見面時間。

■ When is it convenient for you? 您什麼時候方便？

■ When are you free? 您什麼時候有空？

④　我想盡早在您方便的時候與您見面。

A：Let me check my schedule and call you back. 讓我查查我的日程表，然後回電話給你。

B：Fine. I'd like to see you at your earliest possible convenience. 好的。我想盡早在您方便的時候與您見面。

Tips

■ I'd like to meet you as soon as possible. 我想盡快與您見面。

■ I'm eager to see you at an earlier time. 我十分期待盡早見到你。

■ I'd like to see you when you are convenient. 我想在您方便時見您。

⑤　我們可以見面詳細討論一下這件事情嗎？

A：Could we meet and discuss the matter in detail? 我們可以見面詳細討論一下這件事情嗎？

B：No problem. 沒問題。

Tips

I was hoping to discuss about the details of the plan with you. 我想和你討論一下這個計畫的細節。

There are still some details undone. Can I discuss with you right now? 還有很多細節都沒解決，我現在能跟您一起討論一下嗎？

⑥ 我大概上午九點半過來。

A： When will you come over next Tuesday? 下週二你什麼時間過來？

B： I'll stop by around 9:30 a.m. 我大概上午九點半過來。

Tips

Shall we make it two o'clock? 我們兩點見可以嗎？

Is ten convenient for you? 十點你方便嗎？

定好具體時間後，就可以說一句「It's a date.」（那就定那天了）。

⑦ 明天早上你可以來一趟嗎？

A： Can you come by tomorrow morning? 明天早上你可以來一趟嗎？

B： Sure. How about nine o'clock? 當然，九點怎麼樣？

Tips

Could you come over after lunch? 午飯後你可以過來一下嗎？

Can you stop by after 3:00? I have a meeting before that. 你可以三點之後過來嗎？那之前我有個會。

You'd better come by after 4:00. I have plenty of time to talk with you after that. 你最好是四點之後來。那之後我有足夠的時間跟你聊聊。

Step 3　實 戰 對 話

① 與客戶經理預約時間

A： What can I do for you, sir? 先生，有什麼事嗎？

B： I'd like to set an appointment with your manager. 我想和你們經理約個時間。

A： Hold on please; let me check the schedule of our manager. 請稍等，讓我查一下我們經理的日程表。

B： Thank you. 謝謝。

A： Well, he's free after 3 o'clock tomorrow. 嗯，他明天下午三點之後有空。

B： I see. So I'll visit after 3 o'clock tomorrow. 我明白了，那我就明天下午三點之後拜訪。

A： I got it. I'll tell him. 知道了，我會告訴他的。

B： Thank you so much. I'll be punctual. 多謝。我會準時到的。

② 約定詳談時間

A： We're very interested in your proposal and want to cooperate with you. 我們對你們的提案很感興趣，想和你們合作。

B： That's awesome. Thank you for your appreciation. 太棒了，謝謝你們的賞識。

A： Why don't I come by your office next week so we can discuss the deal in person? 下週到你辦公室，當面詳談這筆交易好嗎？

B： That's fine. I am looking forward to talking with you. 好。我也一直期待著跟您聊聊。

A： So how about next Tuesday morning? 那下週二上午怎麼樣？

B： This time fits me. 這個時間很好。

A： I'll stop by around 9:30 a.m. 我大概上午九點半過來。

B： It's a date. See you then. 說定了。那就到時候見。

③ 期待盡早見面

A： Our company hopes to cooperate with you. 我們公司希望與您合作。

B： Me too. We'd better set an appointment to meet.
我也是。我們最好約個時間見一面。

A： When is a good time for us to meet? 我們何時會面會比較合適呢？

B： Let me check my schedule and call you back. 請讓我查查我的日程表，然後回電話給你。

A： Fine. I'd like to see you at your earliest possible convenience. 好的。我想盡早在您方便的時候與您見面。

B： I'm looking forward to that, too. 我也很期待。

Scene 3 客戶拜訪

Step 1   必備表達

介紹	introduce：introduce sb. to sb. 把某人介紹給某人。
同事	colleague：也可用 workmate、co-worker 來代替。
客戶	client：client 多指進行商務合作的客戶，customer 多指購買商品的顧客。
拜訪	visit：作動詞後面直接加拜訪對象，作名詞則是 visit to 後面加拜訪對象。
進行得很順利	run smoothly：run 持續；smoothly 順利地。
考慮	consider：也可用 think about 來代替。
正式的	formal：反義詞是 informal「非正式的」。
搭檔	partner：partnership 合夥人身分；合夥經營。
握手	shake hands：在商務場合，握手只需輕搖一兩下就鬆手。
請坐	take a seat：也可用 have a seat、be seated 來代替，通常需要加上 please 以示禮貌。

Step 2   句句精彩

① 我的朋友都叫我湯姆。

A： Nice to meet you, Mr. Blunt. 布朗特先生，很高興見到你。

B： Nice to meet you, too. All of my friends call me Tom. So you can just call me Tom.
我也很高興見到你。我的朋友都叫我湯姆。所以你也叫我湯姆就好了。

Tips

■ Just call me Tom. 叫我湯姆就可以了。

■ My name is Tom Jones. 我叫湯姆‧瓊斯。

■ May I have your name, please? 請問怎麼稱呼你？

② 這是我的老闆。

A： Mr. Wang, this is my boss David Lee. 王先生，這是我的老闆，大衛·李。

B： Oh, Mr. Lee, It's my honor to meet you. 哦，李先生，很榮幸能夠見到您。

Tips

■ This is my secretary / colleague. 這是我的祕書／同事。

■ This is David from the PR Department of IBM. 這是 IBM 公關部的大衛。

③ 讓我把你介紹給我的同事，傑克。

A： Hello, Tommy! It's great to see you again. 嗨，湯米！能再次見到你真是太好了。

B： Hello, Jerry. Let me introduce you to my colleague, Jack. 你好，傑瑞。讓我把你介紹給我的同事，傑克。

Tips

■ I want you to meet my colleague. 我想讓你認識下我的同事。

■ I'd like to introduce you to my colleague. 我想把你介紹給我的同事。

■ Allow me to introduce my colleague. 請允許我介紹一下我的同事。

④ 事情都進行得很順利。

A： How's everything with your new project? 你們的新項目進行得怎麼樣？

B： Everything is running smoothly. 事情都進行得很順利。

Tips

■ Everything is fine. 一切都不錯。

■ Everything is getting well in my business. 生意上一切順利。

⑤ 我們為何不詳細討論一下呢？

A： I call you to ask how you think about our proposal. 我打電話來是想問您覺得我們的提案怎麼樣。

B： It's great. Why don't we talk about it in detail? We can meet sometime to talk about it. 很棒。我們為何不詳細討論一下呢？我們可以找個時間見面談談。

Tips

■ Could you explain it to us in detail? 你為何不讓我們詳細解釋一下呢？

■ Please tell me the details. 請告訴我詳情。

■ I'm interested in more detailed information. 我對更詳盡的資訊比較感興趣。

⑥ 我們考慮邀請你們和我們合作。

A： We are considering inviting you to work on it with us. 我們考慮邀請你們和我們合作。

B： I'm very glad to hear that. I'll tell my boss right away. 聽到這個消息真是太高興了。我馬上就告訴我們老闆。

Tips

■ We're considering inviting you to cooperate with our company. 我們考慮邀請你和我們公司合作。

■ We're wondering if you'd like to cooperate with us. 我們在想你們是否願意和我們合作。

■ I hope to have the chance to work with you. 我希望能有與您一起共事的機會。

⑦ 這個地方好找嗎？

A： Welcome, Mr. Zhang. Did you have any problem finding this place? 張先生，歡迎你。這個地方好找嗎？

B： No, your directions were very clear. 好找，你指示得非常清楚。

Tips

■ Did you have a smooth flight? 飛行還順利嗎？

■ We hope you'll enjoy your stay here. 我們希望在您停留的這段時間過得愉快。

■ you'd better have a good rest. We don't stand in your way. 您最好好好休息一下，我們就不打擾您了。

Step 3　實戰對話

① 初次拜訪客戶

A：Hello, are you Mr. Blunt from Microsoft? 你好，你是微軟公司的布朗特先生嗎？

B： Yes, good morning. 是的，上午好。

A： Nice to meet you, Mr. Blunt. I'm David Smith. 布朗特先生，很高興認識你。我是大衛‧史密斯。

B： Nice to meet you, too. All of my friends call me Tom. So you can just call me Tom. 我也很高興認識你。我的朋友都叫我湯姆。所以你也叫我湯姆就好了。

A： Welcome, Tom. Did you have any problem finding this place? 歡迎你，湯姆。這

個地方好找嗎？

B： No, your directions were very clear. 好找，你指示得非常清楚。

A： You must be tired. Take a seat, please. 你肯定累了，快請坐吧。

B： I'm OK. Thank you. 我還好，謝謝。

② 介紹老闆、同事給客戶

A： Hello, Lucy! It's great to see you again. 嗨，露西！能再見到妳真是太好了。

B： Hello, Jerry. This is my boss, David Lee. Mr. Lee, this is Jerry Cooper. 你好啊，傑瑞。這是我的老闆，大衛‧李。李先生，這是傑瑞‧庫伯。

A： Oh, Mr. Lee, It's my honor to meet you. 哦，李先生，很榮幸能夠認識您。

C： Great to meet you, too. 能見到你也太棒了。

A： Mr. Lee, Lucy, let me introduce you to my colleague, Jack. 李先生，露西，讓我把妳們介紹給我的同事，傑克。

C： Nice to meet you, Jack. 很高興認識你，傑克。

B： Nice to meet you, Jack. 很高興認識你，傑克。

D： Welcome to our company. 歡迎你們來我們公司。

③ 專程前來邀請合作

A： How are you, Tom? 湯姆，你最近怎麼樣啊？

B： Fine, thank you. 還不錯，謝謝。

A： How are things going on business? 生意上怎麼樣啊？

B： Everything is running smoothly.How about you? 事情都進行得很順利。你呢？

A： Fine. We're running a new project now. We are considering inviting you to work on it with us. 還不錯。我們現在在進行一個新的專案。 我們考慮邀請你們和我們合作。

B： I'm very glad to hear that. I'll tell my boss right away. 聽到這個消息真是太高興了。我馬上就告訴我們老闆。

A： Yeah, and we need to talk about more details with your boss. 是的，而且我們需要跟你們老闆談談具體情況。

B： I see. 我明白。

Scene 4　企 業 互 訪

Step 1　必 備 表 達

公司	company：還可以用 corporation 表示「公司」。
建立	found：注意這裡不是 find 的過去式，而是單獨一個詞，其過去式為 founded。
資本	capital：capital assets 資本資產。
員工	employee：「雇主」則是 employer。
產品	product：high-quality product 高品質的產品。
年營業額	annual sales volume：annual 年度的；volume 數量。
與……做生意	do business with：business 買賣，生意。
製造	produce：well-produced 製造精良的。
價值	be worth of：如 one million dollars' worth of products 價值 100 萬美元的產品。
經濟特區	special economic zones：zone 區域。

Step 2　句 句 精 彩

① 他初次拜訪我們公司。

A： This is Mr. Blunt. He visits our company for the first time. 這是布朗特先生。他初次拜訪我們公司。

B： Welcome, Mr. Blunt. 布朗特先生，歡迎您。

Tips

■ It's my first visit to your company. 這是我第一次到貴公司拜訪。

■ I have visited your company for several times. 我已經拜訪過你們公司好幾次了。

■ Thank you for your visit to our company. 感謝您來拜訪我公司。

② 我們成立於 1970 年，當時的資本額只有 6 萬美元。

A： We were founded in 1970 with a capital investment of only sixty thousand dollars. 我們成立於 1970 年，當時的資本額只有 6 萬美元。

B： It was a hard time. 那時候很艱難啊。

Tips

■ Our company was established in 2000. 我們公司成立於 2000 年。

■ We were set up in 2005 with a turnover of 5 million dollars in the next year. 我們成立於 2005 年，第二年完成了 500 萬美元的營業額。

■ We were founded in Shenzhen, the special economic zone. 我們成立於深圳經濟特區。

③ 你們當時有多少員工？

A： How many employees did you have at that time? 你們當時有多少員工？

B： Nearly 50 people. 差不多 50 人。

Tips

■ How many people do you employ now? 你們現在雇了多少員工？

■ We have 112 employees in the workshop and 30 employees in the office. 我們在工廠有 112 名工人，辦公室有 30 人。

■ We now employ over three hundred people. 我們現在僱用超過 300 名員工。

④ 我們的產品銷往幾個大洲的二十幾個國家。

A： Do you export your products? 你們出口你們的產品嗎？

B： Yes. We distribute our products in more than twenty countries on several continents. 是的。我們的產品銷往幾個大洲的二十幾個國家。

Tips

■ We export our computers to many countries, mainly European countries. 我們出口電腦到許多國家，主要是歐洲的國家。

■ Most of our business deals in exports and imports. 我們的業務主要是進出口方面的。

■ We mainly do business with domestic companies. 我們主要是和國內的企業合作。

⑤ 你們的年營業額是多少？

A： May I ask, if you don't mind, what is your annual sales volume? 如果你不介意，我可以問一下，你們的年營業額是多少嗎？

B： 46 million dollars in the previous year. 上一年度是 4600 萬美元。

Tips

We have a turnover of 100 million dollars. 我們的營業額是 1 億美元。

We currently produce about 60 million dollars worth of products each year. 我們現在每年製造價值相當於約 6000 萬美元的產品。

Can you tell me your net profits last quarter? 你能告訴我上個季度的淨利潤嗎？

⑥ 那是相當可觀的成長。

A： We have a turnover with a 20% increase per year. 我們的營業額每年成長 20%。

B： That's substantial growth. 那是相當可觀的成長。

Tips

It's impressive. 這很可觀。

Our sales are up every year. 我們的銷售量每年都增加。

We project growth to be around 5% a year. 我們預計每年大約成長 5%。

⑦ 我希望這一切可以說服你跟我們合作。

A： I hope all of this will convince you to cooperate with us. 我希望這一切可以說服你跟我們合作。

B： We will surely consider it. 我們肯定會考慮的。

Tips

convince 說服，常用在片語 convince sb. of sth. 「說服某人……」中。此外，還可以用 persuade 來表示「說服」。

I believe working with our company is the best route for you to take. 我相信與我們合作是您的最佳選擇。

We're looking forward to cooperating with you. 我們期待著與你們合作。

Step 3　實戰對話

① 客戶初次來訪

A： Hey, Jack! The guest arrives. 嘿，傑克！客人到了。

B： Good afternoon! Nice to meet you. 下午好！很高興見到您。

A： This is Mr. Blunt. 這是布朗特先生。 He visits our company for the first time. 他初次拜訪我們公司。

B： Welcome, Mr. Blunt. 布朗特先生，歡迎您。

C： Thank you. I'm very glad to visit your company. 謝謝，我很高興能來你們公司拜訪。

B： Let's have a seat. What would you like, coffee or tea? 我們坐吧。您想喝什麼，咖啡還是茶？

C： Coffee, please. Thank you. 咖啡吧，謝謝了。

② 簡介公司發展史

A： We were founded in 1970 with a capital investment of only sixty thousand U.S. dollars. 我們成立於 1970 年，當時的資本額只有 6 萬美元。

B： It was a tough time then. How many employees did you have at that time? 那時候很艱難啊。你們當時有多少員工？

A： Just 12 people. 只有 12 個人。

B： I see. How many people do you employ now? 我明白了。你們現在僱了多少人？

A： We now employ over three hundred people. 我們現在僱用超過 300 名員工。

B： That's impressive. 真了不起。

A： We believe all sufferings have their reward. 我們相信苦盡甘來。

B： That's true. 沒錯。

③ 介紹公司業務情況

A： We mainly produce computers and related fittings. 我們主要生產電腦和相關配件。

B： Do you export your products? 你們出口你們的產品嗎？

A： Yes. We distribute our products in more than twenty countries on several continents. 是的。我們的產品銷往幾個大洲的二十幾個國家。

B： Great. Well, may I ask, if you don't mind,what is your annual sales volume? 很棒。嗯，如果你不介意，我可以問一下嗎？你們的年營業額是多少？

A： 100 million dollars in the previous year. And we have a turnover with a 20% increase per year. 上一年度是 1 億美元。我們的營業額每年成長 20%。

B： That's substantial growth. 那是相當可觀的成長。

A： So I believe your company could benefit from our cooperation. 所以我確信貴公司可以從我們的合作中獲利。

Scene 5　商務合作

Step 1　必備表達

投資	investment：investment in... 在……上的投資。
合併	merger：a merger between... ……和……之間的合併。
收購	acquisition：acquisition 的本義是「獲得」。
完美的組合	excellent match：match 相匹配的人或物。
擴大為……	expand into：expand 擴大。
代理	represent：representative 也很常用，表示「代表，代理人」。
合資經營	joint venture：joint 共有的；venture 工作專案或事業。
研發	research and development：公司的「產品研發部」通常簡寫為 R&D Department。
協議	agreement：reach an agreement 達成協議。
營運	operation：operation management 營運管理。

Step 2　句句精彩

① 你們進行了相當大的投資。

A：We have invested one million dollars in this project. 我們在這個專案上投資了 100 萬美元。

B：You have a substantial investment. 你們進行了相當大的投資。

Tips

■ The amount of investment we used is more than what we planed. 我們使用的投資額比計畫 的要多。

■ We made a 10% increase on investment. 我們在投資上增加了 10%。

■ We spent 5.5 million dollars on research and development. 我們在研發上花了 550 萬美元。

2 讓我們開個會討論一下各種可能性吧。

A： What do you think of my proposal, Mr. Cooper? 庫伯先生，您覺得我的提議怎麼樣？

B： In my opinion, It's feasible. Let's set up a meeting to discuss the possibilities. 在我看來是可行的。讓我們開個會討論一下各種可能性吧。

Tips

■ Let's have a meeting to discuss your plan. 我們開個會來討論下你的計畫吧。

■ We'd like to discuss the possibility of this acquisition. 我們想要討論下這次收購的可能性。

3 我們一直在尋找合併的夥伴。

A： We want to merge with you to set up a larger company. 我們想與你們合併成立一個更大的公司。

B： That can't be better. We have been looking for a merger partner. 那再好不過了。我們一直在尋找合併的夥伴。

Tips

■ The best way is actually to merge with our rival. 最好的辦法其實是與我們的對手合併。

■ We can merge our two small companies into a larger one. 我們可以把我們兩家小公司合併為一家大的。

■ We're wondering if you're willing to merge with us. 我們在想你們是否願意與我們合併。

4 這會是一個全方位的計畫。

A： We plan to look for a suitable acquisition to create a comprehensive group and then to widen the customer base. 我們打算尋找一家合適的公司進行合併以便打造一個綜合性的集團公司，然後再擴大我們的消費群體。

B： It would be an all-around plan. 這會是一個全方位的計畫。

Tips

■ I think It's a feasible plan. 我認為這是一個可行的計畫。

■ We've come up with a good plan. 我們已經想出一個好計畫。

■ All our plans are still very much up in the air. 我們所有的計畫都還沒有確定。

⑤ 那是一個我們想要進入的市場。

A： I heard our company decided to cooperate with a company in China. 我聽說我們公司決定要與中國的一家公司合作。

B： Yes. China has a big market. It is a market we want to enter. 是的。中國是個很大的市場。那是一個我們想要進入的市場。

Tips

It is a market we want to expand. 那是一個我們想要開拓的市場。

We are very interested in doing business in Japan. 我們對於到日本做生意很感興趣。

The total market is growing. 總的市場在成長。

⑥ 我們想成為貴公司的獨家代理。

A： We would like to be the exclusive agent for your company. 我們想成為貴公司的獨家代理。

B： Show me some details, such as your advantages. 具體談談吧，比如你們的優勢。

Tips

We would like to represent your company in China. 我們想在中國代理貴公司的產品。

We'd like to offer one company the exclusive rights to sell our products in China. 我們想授予一家廠商在中國販賣我們產品的獨家代理權。

Our company is the exclusive distributor for NEC mobile phones in South Korea. 我們是 NEC 手機在韓國的獨家代理商。

⑦ 合資經營的好處很多。

A： You know, there are tremendous advantages to a joint venture. 你知道，合資經營的好處很多。

B： I see. I hope we can be an excellent match too. 我明白。我也希望我們成為完美組合。

Tips

A joint venture can propel us to climb to greater heights. 合資經營可以驅使我們再創新高。

I think our company would be a good match for you. 我認為我們公司與你們會是完美搭檔。

Our company owns the advantage of advanced technology. 我們公司的優勢是擁有先進的技術。

Step 3 實 戰 對 話

① 投資專案

A：To be honest, we have invested two million dollars in the previous project. 老實講，我們投資了 200 萬美元在之前的專案上。

B：You have a substantial investment. 你們進行了相當大的投資。

A：And We're also getting a high return on our investment. 但同時這項投資也得到了很高的報酬。

B：I got it. 我明白了。

A：So we plan to invest three million dollars this time in your project. 所以我們計畫這次投資 300 萬美元在你們的專案上。

B：That's great. Let's set up a meeting to discuss the possibilities. 太好了。讓我們開個會討論一下各種可能性吧。

② 尋找合併夥伴

A：We're wondering if you're willing to merge with us. 我們想知道你們是否願意與我們合併。

B：We have been looking for a merger partner. 我們一直在尋找合併的夥伴。

A：We plan to merge with a suitable company to create a comprehensive group and then to widen the customer base. 我們打算尋找一家合適的公司進行合併以便打造一個綜合性的集團公司，然後再擴大我們的消費族群。

B：It would be an all-around plan. 這會是一個全方位的計畫。

A：Right. Here is our plan. Just tell me if you have any questions and suggestions. 沒錯。這是我們的企劃書。有什麼問題和建議，儘管告訴我。

B：OK. We'll think about it carefully. 好的。我們會認真考慮的。

③ 商議合資經營

A：After a detailed research, we found that China has a big market. 經過詳細的研究，我們發現中國具有廣闊的市場。

B：It's true. It is a market we want to enter. 確實。那是一個我們想要進入的市場。

A：I think a joint venture would be beneficial to both of us. 我認為合資經營對雙方都是有利的。

B：Agreed. There are tremendous advantages to a joint venture. 我同意。合資經營的好處很多。

A：I hope we can be an excellent match. 我希望我們成為完美組合。

B：I hope so. Let's talk about the details of a joint venture. 我也這麼希望。讓我們談談合資經營的細節吧。

Scene 6　相 互 競 爭

Step 1　必 備 表 達

勢均力敵	neck and neck：neck and neck with... 與……勢均力敵。
併購戰	takeover battle：takeover 收購，接管；take over 也有「接管」的意思。
符合要求	meet the need：need 也可換為 demand。
競爭	compete：compete with sb. for sth. 為了某事與某人競爭。
對手	rival：have no rivals 無可匹敵。
有能力的	competent：competent to do sth. 有能力做某事；capable 也可表示「有能力的」。
合格的	qualified：qualified for a job 能勝任工作。
數據	figure：sales figures 銷售數位；statistic 可以表示「統計資料」。
激烈的	fierce：fierce competition 激烈的競爭。
打敗	beat：老外常說的一句口語是 It beats me. 這難倒我了。

Step 2　句 句 精 彩

① 我想我們不會再跟你們合作了。

A：You disappointed us many times. I don't think we can work with you anymore. 你們讓我們失望很多次了。我想我們不會再跟你們合作了。

B：Allow me to explain it... 請允許我解釋一下……

Tips

■ We are frustrated with the big mistake you've made and won't continue our cooperation. 我方對你方所犯的嚴重錯誤表示非常失望，不會再繼續我們的合作了。

■ I'm sorry that we won't finance you anymore. 很遺憾我們不會再提供資金支持你們了。

■ I'm not sure if It's worth cooperating with you. 我不確定與你們合作是否值得。

② 這家公司以前比那家更成功。

A： This company used to be much more successful than that one. 這家公司以前比那家更成功。

B： But they're neck and neck with each other now. 但現在兩家公司勢均力敵了。

Tips

The product quality of this company is much better than that one. 這家公司的產品品質比那家的好很多。

These two companies are rivals in IT industry. 在 IT 界這兩家公司是對手。

They have been competing with each other for many years. 他們已經競爭多年了。

③ 這是一場激烈的併購戰。

A： I've heard the news that ABC Company and BCD Company are fighting to take over Wanhong Electronic Technology Company. 我聽新聞說 ABC 公司和 BCD 公司正在搶著併購萬巨集電子科技公司。

B： It's a bitterly fought takeover battle. 這是一場激烈的併購戰。

Tips

It's really a fierce battle. 真是一場殘酷的戰爭。

This company beat all its rivals at last. 這家公司最後擊敗了所有對手。

This company managed to acquire that company after a fierce takeover battle. 在經歷過一場激烈的併購戰後，這家公司成功收購那家公司。

④ 沒有這個必要。

A： Are we planning to get involved in the takeover battle? 我們計劃參與併購戰嗎？

B： That won't be necessary. 沒有這個必要。

Tips

It isn't necessary, is it? 這沒必要，不是嗎？

We'd better start to find another company if necessary. 如果有必要的話，我們該開始尋找另外一家公司了。

⑤ 我們已經知道有另一家公司可以滿足我們的需求。

A： We'd like to cooperate with you. 我們想與你們合作。

B： I'm so sorry. We've known of another company who will be able to meet our needs. 真抱歉。我們已經知道有另一家公司可以滿足我們的需求。

Tips

- We have decided to cooperate with another company instead of you. 我們已經決定由另一家取代你們來與我們合作了。
- We're likely to choose A company. 我們可能會選 A 公司了。
- It looks like A company will be better for us. 看來 A 公司對我們來說比較適合。

⑥ BSC 公司正在考慮選擇 A 或 B。

A： BSC is trying to decide whether to go with A or B. BSC 公司正在考慮選擇 A 還是 B。

B： Anyway, BSC has to give mature consideration to all aspects. 無論如何，BSC 必須

深思熟慮各個方面。

Tips

- It's hard to make a decision since the two companies are all competent to do the work. 兩家公司都能勝任這項工作，真是很難抉。
- We'll consider all options carefully. 我們會仔細考慮各種選擇的。
- We were considering doing more business with you. 我們曾考慮跟你們多做些生意。

⑦ 很遺憾聽到這個消息。

A： We decided to choose Fenjin Company rather than you. 我們決定選擇奮進公司而不是你們公司了。

B： I'm sorry to hear about that. But may I ask why? 很遺憾聽到這個消息。但我可以問下是為什麼嗎？

Tips

- It's a pity to hear about that. 聽到這個消息太遺憾了。
- It's too bad to hear about that. 聽到這個消息太糟糕了。

Step 3　實戰對話

① 決定不再合作

A： We are frustrated with the big mistake you've made. 我方對你方所犯的嚴重錯誤表示非常失望。

B： I'm so sorry for that. But I think We're just having a problem with communication. Next time We'll... 對此我真的很抱歉。我想我們只是溝通上出了問題。下次我們會……

A： Now We're not sure if It's worth cooperating with you. The mistake caused a huge loss, as you know. 現在我們不確定與你們合作是否值得。你知道，這個錯誤讓我們損失很大。

B：I'm wondering if there is a way to make it up. 我在想有沒有什麼可以彌補的辦法。

A： I'm sorry. I don't think we can work with you anymore. 對不起。我想我們不會再跟你們合作了。

B： I'm sorry to hear about that. 很遺憾聽到這個消息。

② 討論併購戰

A： I've heard the news that ABC Company and BCD Company are fighting to take over Wanhong Electronic Technology Company. 我聽新聞說 ABC 公司和 BCD 公司正在搶著併購萬巨集電子科技公司。

B： I've heard that too. The two companies are rivals in IT industry. 我也聽說了。在 IT 界這兩家公司是競爭對手。

A： Actually ABC Company used to be much more successful than BCD Company. 實際上 ABC 公司以前比 BCD 公司更成功。

B： But they're neck and neck with each other now. 但現在兩家公司勢均力敵了。

A： you're right. It's a bitterly fought takeover battle. 你說得對。這是一場激烈的併購戰。

B： Let's wait and see. 我們拭目以待吧。

③ 另選別家

A： Shall we meet sometime this week to talk about the cooperation between us? 我們這週找個時間見一下談談我們合作的事，可以嗎？

B： That won't be necessary. We've known of another company who will be able to meet our needs. 沒有這個必要了。我們已經知道有另一家公司可以滿足我們的需求。

A： It's a pity to hear about that. We are competent to do your job. 聽到這個消息很遺

憾。我們有能力做你們的工作。

B： I just think that company will save us much time and money. 我只是覺得那家公司能讓我們省下更多的時間和金錢。

A： I got it. 我明白了。

B： I'm hoping to cooperate with you in the future. 希望以後能跟你們合作。

A： We're always willing to. 我們一直盼望著。

Scene 7　客戶投訴

Step 1　必備表達

有問題的	faulty：faulty product 瑕疵品；fault 是 faulty 的名詞形式，表示「毛病，錯誤」。
投訴	complain about：complain 投訴，抱怨；complain to sb. about sth. 向某人投訴／抱怨某事。
投訴率	complaint rate：complaint 是 complain 的名詞形式，表示「投訴」；rate 比率，率。
解決	work out：例如：I'll work it out. 我會解決的。另外 work out 也可用 handle 來代替。
處理	deal with：deal with sb. 處理某人提出的問題；deal with sth. 處理某事（如問題、任務等）。
失望	disappointed：be disappointed about/with sth. 對某事感到失望。
服務	service：at sb.'s service 隨時為某人服務；聽候某人吩咐。
滿意	satisfaction：動詞形式是 satisfy，表示「使滿意」；do the work to the satisfaction of the client 工作做得讓顧客滿意。
技術支援	technical support：technical 技術的。
在保修期內	under warranty：注意介詞要用 under；warranty（商品的）保證書，保單。

Step 2　句句精彩

① 出現了一個系統問題。

A：I can't visit your website now. What happened? 我現在訪問不了你們的網站，有什麼問題嗎？

B： There's a system's failure. We're repairing it. I'm sorry for that. 出現了一個系統問題。我們正在維修。很抱歉。

Tips

- failure 除了表示「失敗」還可以表示「故障」。problem 也可以表示「問題，故障」。
- There is a problem with the system. 系統出問題了。
- The system is broken. 系統出故障了。
- THere's something wrong with the system. 系統有一些故障。

② 出故障了。

A： The machine can't work. THere's a breakdown. 機器無法工作，出故障了。

B： don't worry. I'll send someone to your place to repair it right away. 別擔心。我馬上派人去您那裡修理。

Tips

- This machine is on the brink. 這機器有問題。
- The machine is out of order. 機器壞了。
- The computer crashed. 電腦當機了。

③ 我打電話投訴產品問題。

A： Hello, may I help you? 您好，請問有什麼需要幫助的嗎？

B： I'm phoning to complain about the product. 我打電話投訴產品問題。

Tips

- 接到客戶投訴，先要表示抱歉，可以說：I apologize for that. 我為此表示抱歉。
- I've come to figure out how you are going to settle our complaints. 我來這裡是想弄清楚你們打算怎樣處理我們的投訴。
- I wonder if you can send someone to my home and help me with the problem. 請問您能否派個人來我家幫我處理一下問題。

④ 到底出什麼問題了？

A： What exactly is the problem? 到底出什麼問題了？

B： I don't know. Could you send your technician to give a check? 我不知道。你可以派個技術員來檢查一下嗎？

Tips

- Why isn't it working? 它怎麼不工作了？

What are your requirements? 您有什麼要求？

Would you check it? 你能檢查一下嗎？

⑤ 顧客對我們的產品系列投訴率很高。

A： The complaint rate for our product line is very high. 顧客對我們的產品系列投訴率很高。

B： We need to make an improvement. 我們需要做出改進。

Tips

Customers' complaints rose remarkably. 顧客投訴量顯著上升。

I received a call from our customer who complained about our product. 我接到客戶電話投訴我們的產品。

Customer satisfaction index rises. 顧客滿意指數上升了。

⑥ 我們需要找到根源來解決問題。

A： The sales in this quarter decreased. The complaint rate is high. 這一季度的銷售額下降了。投訴率很高。

B： We need to go to the source to work them out. 我們需要找到根源來解決問題。

Tips

We've got to get this fixed as soon as possible. 我們必須盡快解決這個問題。

We'll find what's wrong and contact you later. 我們會找出問題，稍後再聯絡您。

We can make some compensation. 我們可以做些補償。

⑦ 感謝您的等待。

A： Let me see... Thank you for waiting. Is it convenient for you tomorrow morning? One of our technicians will visit you. 讓我看看……感謝您的等待。明天上午您方便嗎？我們的技術員會去您那裡看看。

B： It's great. I'll stay at home. 太好了，沒問題，我會在家等著的。

Tips

Thanks for being so patient. 感謝您如此耐心地等待。

I'm sorry for keeping you waiting so long. 很抱歉讓您久等了。

Your call is important to us. Thanks for calling. 您的來電對我們很重要。感謝來電。

Step 3　實戰對話

① 系統出現問題

A： I can't visit your website now. What happened? 我現在訪問不了你們的網站，出什麼問題了嗎？

B： I'm sorry for that. There's a system's failure. 很抱歉。出現了一個系統問題。

A： What exactly is the problem? 到底出什麼問題了？

B： I'm not clear about that. But our technician is repairing it now. 我不太清楚，不過我們的技術人員正在維修。

A： All right. I hope it will be OK soon. 好吧，我希望能快點修好。

B： Thank you. Sorry for the inconvenience. 謝謝，很抱歉給您帶來不便。

② 機器出現故障

A： what's the matter? 怎麼了？

B： The machine can't work. There's a breakdown. 機器無法工作。出故障了。

A： I'm sorry for that. I'll send someone to your place to repair it right away. 真抱歉。我馬上派人去您那裡修理。

B： That's good. When will you come? 太好了。你們什麼時候來？

A： Within one hour. 一個小時之內。

B： That couldn't be better. 那最好不過了。

③ 產品出現問題

A： Hello, may I help you? 您好，請問有什麼能幫您的？

B： I'm phoning to complain about the product. 我打電話投訴產品問題。

A： I apologize for that. Is your product still under warranty? 我為此表示抱歉。您的產品還在保固期內嗎？

B： Yes. I wonder if you can send someone to my home and help me with the problem. 是的。請問您能否派個人來我家幫我處理一下問題。

A： Let me see... Thank you for waiting. Is it convenient for you tomorrow morning? One of our technicians will visit you. 讓我看看……感謝您的等待，明天上午您

　　方便嗎？我們的技術員會去您那裡看看。

B： It's great. I'll stay at home. 太好了，沒問題。我會在家等著的。

Scene 8　客戶業務

Step 1　必備表達

交易	transaction：cash transaction 現金交易。
優惠券	coupon：在國外使用優惠券是很普遍的行為，很多企業會透過發放優惠券來促銷。
支付	payment：payment for... 為⋯⋯的付款。
刷卡	swipe the card：credit card 信用卡。
簽字	sign：刷卡時要簽字確認，收銀員也會提醒說：Please sign here. 請在這裡簽字。
註冊	register：register for a course 註冊學習課程。
申請費	application fee：application 申請；fee 費用；fee 既可指服務費，也可指報名費或會費。
不退的	non-refundable：記住這裡的關鍵字 refund 表示「退還」。
申請表	application form：還有一種常用表達 registration form「登記表」。
填寫	fill out：fill out 是美式英語的說法，fill in 是英式英語的說法，都表示「填寫」。

Step 2　句句精彩

① 你今天用優惠券嗎？

A： It's 68 dollars. Are you using any coupons today? 68 美元。你今天用優惠券嗎？

B： No. Here is my credit card. 不，我刷信用卡。

Tips

■ Do you have a discount card? 你有打折卡嗎？

■ Do you have a membership card? 你有會員卡嗎？

■ How many points have I earned? 我的積分有多少了？

② 你能用其他方式支付嗎？

A： Can I pay for it by card? 我可以刷卡付款嗎？

B： I'm sorry tHere's a system's failure. Would you like to use another form of payment? 很抱歉系統出問題了。你能用其他方式支付嗎？

Tips

We accept money orders, travelers checks or credit cards. 我們接受匯款單、旅行支票和信用卡。

We only take cash. 我們只收現金。

③ 請刷卡。

A： I'd like to pay by card. 我想刷卡支付。

B： No problem. Please swipe your card. 沒問題。請刷卡。

Tips

■ I'd like buy the bill with my card. 我要刷卡結帳。

I'm sorry, but your card has been declined. 抱歉，你的卡無法使用。

Your card is maxed out. 你的卡刷爆了。

④ 請在這裡簽字。

A： OK. I finished filling out the application form. 好了，我填完申請表了。

B： Let me see. I'll need you to sign here, please. 讓我看一下。請在這裡簽字。

Tips

Please enter the password. 請輸入密碼。

Please fill in this slip. 請填一下這張單子。

⑤ 有什麼能幫您的？

A： How can I help you? 有什麼能幫您的？

B： I want to register for your English course. 我想註冊學習你們的英語課程。

Tips

How may I help you? 有什麼能幫您的？

What can I do for you? 我能為您做點什麼？

What would you like to know? 您想了解什麼？

⑥ 如果您有其他問題，歡迎隨時再來電。

A： Please don't hesitate to call again if you have any other question. 如果您有其他問題，歡迎隨時再來電。

B： It's very kind of you. Thanks. 你真好。謝謝。

Tips

■ If there is any more information I can provide, please let me know. 如果還需要我提供資料，請告知我。

■ You can contact us immediately once you find anything wrong. 一旦你發現有什麼問題，可以隨時聯絡我們。

■ We are ready to be at your service. 隨時為您服務。

⑦ 我怎麼把這些材料寄給你呢？

A： How can I send these materials to you? 我怎麼把這些材料寄給你呢？

B： Express delivery is preferable. 快遞比較好。

Tips

■ You can either send the application packet by regular mail or you can fax it. 你可以用平郵寄申請材料，也可以傳真過來。

■ You can fill out our application that is on our website. 您可以到我們的網站上填寫申請。

■ Is there any other material I would need to send in addition to the application form? 除了申請表，我還需要寄其他材料嗎？

Step 3　實 戰 對 話

① 使用優惠券付款

A： How can I help you? 有什麼能幫您的？

B： I'd like to buy this dress and that skirt. How much in total? 我想買這件衣服和那條裙子。一共多少錢？

A： Madam, your total comes to $55. Are you using any coupons today? 女士，總共是 55 美元。妳今天用優惠券嗎？

B： Yes. Here's the coupon. 是的，給你優惠券。

A： All right. $5 off if you use this coupon. 好的。使用這張優惠券可以優惠 5 美元。

B： I get it. So Here's $50. 明白了。給你 50 美元。

② 刷卡支付

A： How will you be paying today? 您要怎麼付款？

B： I'll pay by credit card. 我用信用卡支付。

A： All right. Please swipe your card. 好的。請刷卡。

B： OK. 好的。

A： Please enter the password. 請輸入密碼。

B： There you go. 好了。

A： I'll need you to sign here, please. 請在這裡簽字。

B： Done. 簽好了。

③ 無法使用信用卡

A： I'd like to pay by card. 我想刷卡支付。

B： No problem. Please swipe your card. 沒問題。請刷卡。

A： OK. 好的。

B： Well, try again please. 嗯，請再試一遍。

A： Is there any problem with my card? 我的卡有什麼問題嗎？

B： I'm sorry, but your card has been declined. Would you like to use another form of payment? 抱歉，你的卡無法使用。你能用其他方式支付嗎？

A： Well, I'll pay cash. 那我付現金。

B： Thanks a lot. 多謝。

Scene 9　會展

Step 1　必備表達

攤位	booth：也可用 stand 來代替。
展覽	exhibit：也可用 display 來代替。
在展會	at the show：除了 show 可以表示「展會」，exhibition 和 fair 也可以表示類似意思。
目錄冊	catalog：這是美式英語的寫法，英式英語的寫法是 catalogue；anexhibition catalog 展覽目錄。
會場特惠折扣	special in-show discount：in-show 在會場裡的；10% discount 9折。
詢問產品	inquire about the product：inquire 詢問，打聽消息。
獨特的功能	unique function：unique 獨特的，獨一無二的；function 功能。
宣傳冊	brochure：也可用 booklet 來代替。
展廳	exhibit hall：hall 大廳；display area 指「展區」。
貿易展覽會	trade show：也可用 trade fair 來代替。
展館	pavilion：也可用 showroom 來代替。

Step 2　句句精彩

① 我們公司被分配到 14-A 的攤位。

A： Have you gotten any new information about the trade show? 關於展會有什麼新消息了嗎？

B： Our company has been assigned to booth fourteen- A. 我們公司被分配到 14-A 的攤位。

Tips

■ 很多大型會展都會安排攤位給參展商，assign 表示「分配」。

■ Is there a booth available in the exhibition hall? 展覽大廳還有空餘的展位嗎？

■ We need large room for our products. 我們的產品需要很大的空間。

② 我們明天早上多早可以開始搭建攤位？

A： How early can we begin setting up our exhibit tomorrow morning? 我們明天早上多早可以開始搭建攤位？

B： After 7:00 a.m. 早上 7 點以後。

Tips

We're basically set up for the exhibition, but we need to deal with some loose ends. 展會我們基本已布置完了，但是還有些零星事務需要處理。

We need access to electrical outlets. 我們需要使用電源插座。

③ 您打算在展會上買些什麼嗎？

A： Have you heard that there will be a trade show near the Central Park? 你聽說中央公園附近要開貿易展覽會了嗎？

B： I have. Are you planning on purchasing anything at the show? 聽說了。您打算在展會上買些什麼嗎？

Tips

purchase 購買。

Will you buy anything at the show? 您會在展會上買些什麼嗎？

What stuff do you want to buy at the show? 您想在展會上買什麼呢？

④ 你有目錄可以給我看嗎？

A： Do you have a catalog I can see? 你有目錄可以給我看嗎？

B： Of course. Here you are. 當然，給您。

Tips

Are there any free samples that I can have? 有免費的樣品可以讓我帶走嗎？

Could you show me how to operate the product? 您可以給我展示一下如何操作這個產品嗎？

Your brochures are eye-catching and informative. 你們的宣傳冊引人注目並且資訊豐富。

⑤ 我來看看市場上有什麼新產品。

A： What do you want? 您想買什麼？

B： I'm here to check out what's new on the market. 我來看看市場上有什麼新產品。

- I'd like to ask you a few questions about your products. 我想問幾個關於你們產品的問題。
- Would you please give me some information about this product? 您能否給我一些關於這個產品的資訊？
- I'm just looking around. 我只是隨便看看。

⑥ 請隨意參觀。

A： Welcome. Please feel free to look around. 歡迎。請隨意參觀。

B： Thank you. I'm very interested in your new product. 謝謝。我對你們的新產品很感興趣。

- Thank you for stopping by our exhibit. 謝謝您能留步參觀我們的展位。
- I was wondering if you had the time to come to our booth. 不知你是否有時間來我們的攤位看看。

⑦ 如果您還需要更多資訊，可以與我聯絡。

A： Here is my business card. You can contact me if you need any more information. 這是我的名片。如果您還需要更多資訊，可以與我聯絡。

B： Thank you. Here's my card. 謝謝。這是我的名片。

- Would you like to give me a business card so I can call you after the exhibition? 您能給我一張您的名片嗎？以便我能在展覽會後打電話給您。
- My contact information is on my business card. Let me give you one. 我的名片上有我的聯絡方式，給您一張。
- You can contact me by calling the number on my business card. 您可以打名片上的電話聯絡我。

Step 3　實戰對話

① 攤位布展

A： Our company has been assigned to booth fourteen-A. 我們公司被分配到 14-A 的攤位。

B： I got it. Everyone is busy with the trade fair now. 我知道了。現在每個人都在忙展會的事。

A： We need access to electrical outlets. don't forget it. 我們需要使用電源插座，別忘了。

B： I won't. don't worry. How early can we begin setting up our exhibit tomorrow morning? 別擔心，我不會忘的。我們明天早上多早可以開始搭建攤位？

A： 7 a.m. Thank you for your hard work. 早上 7 點。辛苦大家了。

B： It's OK. We do hope our booth can be attractive. 沒事，我們都真心希望我們的展位能引人注目。

② 歡迎顧客參觀

A： Welcome. Please feel free to look around. 歡迎。請隨意參觀。

B： Thank you. 謝謝。

A： Are you planning on purchasing anything at the show? 您打算在展會上買些什麼嗎？

B： Well, I'm actually just looking around. 嗯，實際上我只是隨便看看。

A： I see. So please feel free. 我明白了。那請您隨意。

B： Thanks. 謝謝。

③ 顧客對產品感興趣

A： Good morning! Welcome to our booth. 早上好！歡迎來我們展位。

B： Good morning! I'm very interested in your new products. 早上好！我對你們的新產品很感興趣。

A： Thank you. So what exactly do you want? 謝謝。您具體想看看什麼？

B： I'm not sure yet. Do you have a catalog I can see? 還不確定。你有目錄可以給我看嗎？

A： Of course. Here you are. 當然。給您。

B： Thanks a lot. I'll take it back to my company and have a look. 太謝謝了。我會帶回公司看的。

Scene 10　介紹產品

必 備 表 達

演示	presentation：give a presentation 做演示。
產品展示	product demonstration：demonstration 示範，解釋。
最大賣點	best selling point：擁有吸引人的賣點對產品來說特別重要，也就是產品最大的「特色」，即 feature。
占有	make up：make up 後面常跟一個百分數來表示占多少比例。
款式	style：fashion 指流行的款式，即 popular style。
打動消費者	hit the customer：hit 原本是「打、打擊」的意思，此處引申為「打動」的意思。
使用壽命	service life：service 服務；服役。
知名設計師	famous designer：design 設計。
賴以維生的	bread and butter：賴以為生的產品也就是最基本的產品，bread and butter 產品的字面意思是「麵包與奶油」，這兩樣食物恰恰是老外吃的最基本的食物。
時尚元素	modern factor：factor 因素。

Step 2　句 句 精 彩

① 我可以到您公司為您解說我們的產品。

A：I could go to your company and give you a presentation on our products. 我可以到您公司為您解說我們的產品。

B：Welcome! We're very interested in your products. 歡迎啊！我們對你們的產品很感興趣。

Tips

■ I'd like to visit your company and give you an introduction on our products. 我想拜訪您公司，

為您介紹我們的產品。

Why don't we make an appointment so that I can show you in detail what service we offer?
我們約個時間見面，以便為您詳細介紹我們提供的服務，好嗎？

Is it available for you to know our product? 您有時間了解一下我們的產品嗎？

② 我想為您做個產品演示。

A： I would like to give you a product demonstration. I'm sure you'll like it after that.
我想為您做個產品演示。我相信之後您會喜歡我們的產品的。

B： All right. You can come tomorrow afternoon. 好吧，你可以明天下午過來。

Tips

Let me show you how to operate the product. 我為您展示一下如何操作這個產品。

Let me tell you how our product is unique. 我向您講解一下我們產品的獨特之處。

Let me show you the specialty of our product. 我為您展示一下我們產品的特色。

③ 這款產品一流的設計是它最大的賣點。

A： What is the selling point of your product? 你們產品的賣點是什麼？

B： The classic design of the product is its best selling point. 一流的設計是這款產品
最大的賣點。

Tips

The top-ranking design of the product is its best selling point. 一流的設計是這款產品最大
的賣點。

We hit our customer with the modern factor. 我們以時尚元素來打動消費者。

Its price is quite competitive. 它的價格很有競爭力。

④ 我們的產品有各式各樣的款式。

A： Could you show me the style of your new product? 你可以讓我看一下你們新產
品的款式嗎？

B： Our products are available in various styles. 我們的產品有各式各樣的款式。

Tips

available 在這裡表示「可用的」，various 在這裡表示「不同種類的，各式各樣的」。

■ Our products are designed in various styles and sizes. 我們的產品設計有各種不同的款式
和尺寸。

Our products are available in various sizes. 我們的產品有各種尺寸。

⑤ 它有很多用途。

A： What feature does your product have? 你們的產品有什麼特色？

B： There are many uses. For example, it can be used for both simmering soup and stewing meat. 它有很多用途。比如，它既可以用來煮湯，也可以用來燉肉。

Tips

- We can use it in many ways. 它有很多用途。
- Our items are superior in quality and reasonable in price. 我們的產品物美價廉。

⑥ 我們的產品在中國的市場占有率約為 36%。

A： Do your products sell well? 你們的產品賣得好嗎？

B： Yes. Our products make up about 36% of the market in China. 好。我們的產品在中國的市場占有率約為 36%。

Tips

- Our products hold about 50% share of the Chinese market. 我們的產品在中國的市場占有率約為 50%。
- The product is mainly sold in Europe. 產品主要銷往歐洲。
- This product sells well in our country. 這個產品在我們國家賣得很好。

⑦ 您會對我們的新產品感興趣。

A： After the introduction, you'll be interested in our new products. 介紹之後，您會對我們的新產品感興趣。

B： I hope so. 希望如此。

Tips

- you'll be touched by our new products. 您會對我們的新產品感興趣的。
- I'm sure that you'll be attracted by our new products. 我相信您會被我們的新產品吸引。
- This kind of product is our best. you'll like it. 這種產品是我們最好的產品。您會喜歡的。

Step 3　實戰對話

① 積極介紹產品

A： Excuse me, sir! I was wondering if you had the time to know about our products.

先生，打擾一下！不知您是否有時間來了解一下我們的產品。

B： Well, what do you produce? 嗯，你們生產什麼？

A： We mainly produce air-conditioners. 我們主要生產冷氣。

B： Could you give me some more specific information? 可以給我些更具體的資訊嗎？

A： The products are all low-cost and of good quality. I could go to your company and give you a presentation on our products. 產品都物美價廉。我可以到您公司，為您解說我們的產品。

B： That's great. Here's my business card. 太好了。這是我的名片。

A： Thank you so much. After the introduction, you'll be interested in our new products. 非常感謝。介紹之後，您會對我們的新產品感興趣。

B： I'm looking forward to your visit. 我期待著你的來訪。

② 介紹產品賣點

A： I would like to give you a product demonstration. I'm sure you'll like it after that. 我想為您做個產品演示。我相信之後您會喜歡我們的產品的。

B： Interesting. What is the selling point of your product? 很有意思。你們產品的賣點是什麼？

A： The classic design of the product is its best selling point. 一流的設計是這款產品最大的賣點。

B： I see. 我明白了。

A： In addition, its quality is fine and the price is acceptable. 另外，產品品質不錯，價錢也可以接受。

B： That sounds great. When shall we start the demonstration? 聽起來很棒。我們什麼時候可以開始演示呢？

③ 介紹產品特色

A： What feature does your product have? 你們的產品有什麼特色？

B： here are many uses. For example, it can be used for both simmering soup and stewing meat. 它有很多用途。譬如，它既可以用來煮湯，也可以用來燉肉。

A： Great. Could you show me the style of your product? 很好。你可以給我看一下你們產品的款式嗎？

B： Our products are available in various styles. 我們的產品有各式各樣的款式。

A： Which one is the best-seller? 哪款賣得最好？

B： Let me show you. 我拿給您看一下。

Scene 11　期待來訪

Step 1　必備表達

給某人叫輛車	get sb. a car：還可用 call a car for sb. 和 have a car for sb. 來代替。
保持聯絡	keep in touch：還可用 stay in touch 來代替，另外 contact 也指「聯絡」。
機會	opportunity：還可用 chance 來代替。
期待	look forward to：注意該片語後面要加 sth. 或者 doing sth.。
參觀工廠	tour a factory：tour 巡迴。
廠房	plant：也可用 factory 來代替。
下次來訪	next visit：想表達「下次見」還可以說 See you next time.。
送行	see off：see sb. off 為某人送行。
方便	convenient：出於禮貌對別人提出建議或要求時經常說 if you're convenient，表示「如果您方便的話」。
出席	presence：Your presence is requested at... 敬請您出席……
保重	take care：Take care of yourself！請您保重！

Step 2　句句精彩

① 我得走了。

A： It's late. I should get going. 很晚了。我得走了。

B： OK. Let me accompany you to the door. 好的。讓我送你到門口。

Tips

■ I've got to go. 我得走了。

■ I'd better go. 我得走了。

■ I have to leave. 我得走了。

② 我幫您叫輛車。

A： I would get you a car. 我幫您叫輛車。

B： It's very kind of you. 您真是太好了。

Tips

- May I give you a lift? 要我送您一程嗎？
- I'll drive you to the airport. 我會開車送您去機場。
- I have arranged a colleague of mine to see you off. 我已經安排好我的一位同事去送您。

③ 我想我很快會再見到你的。

A： I have to leave now. Thank you for your warm reception these days. 我得走了。謝謝你這些天的熱情招待。

B： you're welcome. I guess I'll be seeing you around. 別客氣。我想我很快會再見到你的。

Tips

- I guess I'll see you some other time. 我想我們改天會再見的。
- I hope to see you soon. 我希望很快就能見到你。
- I hope We'll meet again sometime. 希望我們能再次相見。

④ 希望您有機會再來拜訪我們。

A： I hope you have a chance to come to visit us again. 希望您有機會再來拜訪我們。

B： I hope too. And I hope you could come to visit our plant some day. 我也希望。希望您有天可以來參觀我們的工廠。

Tips

- I hope you will get an opportunity to come to visit us once more. 希望您有機會再來拜訪我們。
- Please stop by at any time when you are convenient. 請在您方便時隨時來訪。
- I'll be glad if I can see you again. 如果能再見到你，我會很高興的。

⑤ 我們保持聯絡。

A： Let's keep in touch with each other. 我們保持聯絡。

B： Sure. Take care! 當然。保重！

Tips

Stay in touch! 保持聯絡！

Be in touch! 保持聯絡！

Take care and keep in touch! 保重，常聯絡！

⑥ 很高興能有機會見識你們是如何工作的。

A： It was good having the opportunity to see how you work. 很高興能有機會見識你們是如何工作的。

B： It's a good chance to know about us. 這是一個了解我們的好機會。

Tips

It was nice having the chance to see how you guys do things. 很高興能有機會看你們是如何做事的。

Thank you for letting me know how you work. 謝謝你讓我了解到你們是如何工作的。

I'm glad to have this opportunity to look around your plant. 我很高興能有這次機會參觀你們的工廠。

⑦ 您來這裡我們真的很高興。

A： Your plant impressed me a lot. 你們的工廠給我留下了深刻的印象。

B： It was good having you out here. 您來這裡我們真的很高興。

Tips

Thank you for your presence. 感謝您的光臨。

It was nice for you to come here. 很高興您來這裡。

It's been really nice to know you. 很高興能認識您。

Step 3　實戰對話

① 拜訪完畢告別

A： It's late. I should get going. 很晚了。我得走了。

B： OK. Let me accompany you to the door. 好的。讓我送你到門口吧。

A： It's very kind of you. 你真是太好了。

B： you're welcome. I guess I'll be seeing you around. 別客氣。我想我很快會再見到你的。

A： I think so. See you later. 我也這麼想。再見。

B： See you. 再見。

②　幫客人叫車

A： Well, It's already 7 a.m. It's late. 嗯，已經 7 點了。有點晚了。

B： Just stay for a while. 再待一會兒吧。

A： I have to catch the flight. So I'd better begoing. 我要趕飛機。我得走了。

B： OK. I would get you a car. 好吧。我幫您叫輛車。

A： That's great. Thank you so much. 太好了。非常感謝。

B： This way, please. 請這邊走。

③　期待再次來訪

A： It's time for me to go. 我得走了。

B： All right. I hope you have a chance to come to visit us again. 好吧。希望您有機會再來拜訪我們。

A： I hope too. And I hope you could come to visit our plant some day. 我也希望。我還希望您有天可以來參觀我們的廠房。

B： That'll be great. Let's keep in touch with each other. 那太好了。我們保持聯絡。

A： Sure. Take care! 當然。保重！

B： Take care! See you! 保重！再見！

Tips

■ Would you call me at 3 p.m. this afternoon, please? 今天下午三點可以打電話給我嗎？

■ We can keep in touch by phone. 我們可以透過電話保持聯絡。

■ You can contact me by e-mail. 你可以透過電子郵件和我聯絡。

Chapter

2

工作會議

Scene 12　準備開會

Step 1　必備表達

會議	conference：口語中還常用 meeting 來表示會議。
參加	attend：「參加、出席會議」就是 attend a meeting。
部門	department：section 也可用來表示公司的「部門」。
讓某人失望	let sb. down：disappoint 也表達「失望」。
通知某人	let sb. know：也可用 inform sb. 表達。
留言板	notice board：留言板用於張貼公布公文、告示、啟示等提示性內容。
邀請	invite：invite sb. to the meeting 邀請某人參加會議。
準時	on time：還可以用 on schedule 來代替。
開會	hold a meeting：也可用動詞 have 表示開會。
會議室	meeting room：video meeting room 是指「可視會議室」。

Step 2　句句精彩

① 我會和他們的代表約定時間。

A: What is the time for the meeting? 會議什麼時間開始？

B: I'll set an appointment with their rep. 我會和他們的代表約定時間。

Tips

■ rep 是 representative 的縮寫形式，表示「代表」。

■ I want to confirm my appointment time again. 我想再次確認一下約定的時間。

■ You should schedule appointments and send meeting invitations. 你應該安排好約見，並寄出會議邀請。

② 我會通知他們。

A: Who will tell them the time of the meeting? 誰告訴他們會議時間？

B: I'll notice them. 我會通知他們。

Tips

notice 通知，通告。

I saw a meeting notice on the bulletin board. 我看到留言板上有一張會議通知。

We will have a meeting in the meeting room at 2:00 pm, and all employees should attend. 下午兩點我們將在會議室舉行會議，所有員工都要參加。

③ 會上我必須好好表現。

A： I must do well at the meeting. 會上我必須好好表現。

B： don't stress yourself out. 別給自己太大壓力。

Tips

stress out 過度勞累，緊張；stress oneself out 表示「給自己過大的壓力」。

We have made full preparations for the meeting. 我們為會議做了充分的準備。

Part of my duties as a secretary is to do the preparation work well. 身為祕書，我的一部分職責就是做好準備工作。

④ 我打電話是來確定本週會議的一些細節。

A： I am calling to confirm some details of this week's conference. 我打電話是來確定本週會議的一些細節。

B： I will send you the details by email later. 稍後我會以郵件形式把細節發給你。

Tips

I am writing this e-mail to confirm the meeting time and place. 我寫這封郵件是為了確認會議時間和地點。

The details of the meeting had been sent to you. 會議的詳細安排已經發送給你了。

⑤ 你那邊有誰會參加？

A： Who will be attending on your side? 你那邊有誰會參加？

B： The sales manager and his assistant. 銷售經理和他的助理。

Tips

assistant 指「助理」，如 accounting assistant「會計助理」。

I'd like to invite you to attend our conference. 我很樂意邀請您參加我們的會議。

I have to attend the regular meeting. 我必須參加例會。

⑥ 麻煩你請你們的經理也來開會好嗎？

A：Can you ask your manager to attend as well? 麻煩你請你們的經理也來開會好嗎？

B：OK. I'll tell him. 好的。我會告訴他的。

Tips

■ Well, of course, John will attend. 嗯，約翰當然會參加。

■ Our CEO attends the meeting as well. 我們總裁也參加會議。

■ All department managers are asked to be at the meeting. 所有部門經理都被要求出席會議。

Step 3　實 戰 對 話

① 確定會議時間

A：What time is the meeting? 會議是幾點？

B：I'll set an appointment with their rep. 我會和他們的代表約定時間。

A：It will be better if the meeting can be held on Friday.
如果會議能在週五舉行更好。

B：OK, I will try to fix the time as you wish. 好的，我會嘗試根據你們的意願定時間。

A：Once you set the time, let the managers know at once. 一旦確定了時間，馬上告訴經理們。

B：I'll notice them. 我會通知他們。

A：Thanks for your hard work. 辛苦你了。

B：This is my duty. 這是我應該做的。

② 會議表現

A：You look so nervous. 你看起來很緊張。

B：I must do well at the meeting. 會議上我必須好好表現。

A：You are at full cock. don't worry. 你準備得很充分，不用擔心。

B：I have to triple-check the details. 我還得再三檢查細節。

A：Come on, just relax！拜託，放輕鬆！

B：There will be a lot of big shots at the meeting. 會有很多大人物出席會議。

A： But nervousness doesn't help. 但是緊張也沒用。

③ 確認會議細節

A： I called just to confirm some details of this week's conference. 我打電話是來確定本週會議的一些細節。

B： OK, you can confirm the details with me. I am the organizer of the meeting. 好的，您可以和我確認，我是這次會議的承辦方。

A： Could I see your draft for the meeting? 我能看一下會議的議程嗎？

B： No problem. I will send you the draft via e-mail. Could I have your e-mail address? 沒問題，我把會議議程透過電子郵件發給你，能告訴我您的郵寄地址嗎？

A： 123456@hotmail.com.

B： OK, I will send you now. 好的，我現在發給您。

Scene 13　會議開始

Step 1　必備表達

概略介紹	overview：通常與 brief 搭配，brief overview 意思為「簡單的概述」。
年終會議	end-of-year meeting：也可用 annual general meeting 表示「年會」。
主要問題	main issue：相當於 main / key / major problem。
開始	begin：也可用 start 表達，「開始做……」即：begin / start to do sth.。
簡短報告	brief report：brief 簡短的，也可以替換為 short。
目的	purpose：同義表達還有 objective，aim 及 goal 等。
發言開場白	opening of a talk：opening 開始，開端；相當於 beginning。
展示	present：相當於 show 或 display。
描述	describe：常構成片語 describe as，意思為「講成；描述為」。
解釋	explain：也可用 make clear 表示。
議程	agenda：指會議的議程安排，而日程上的「一項」可以用 item 來表示。

Step 2　句句精彩

①　我來概述一下這次會議。

A：Let's welcome the keynote speaker of the meeting. 讓我們歡迎這次會議的主講人。

B：Let me just give an overview of the meeting. 我來概述一下這次會議。

Tips

■ give an overview 做一個概述。

■ This paper provides an overview of the meeting. 這份文件提供了會議的綜合介紹。

■ At first, I want to give you a general overview. 首先，我想先總體概述一下。

② 我覺得我們應該開始了。

A： I think we should begin. 我覺得我們應該開始了。

B： OK, Let's start. 好的，我們開始吧。

Tips

The meeting is about to begin. 會議要開始了。

After all preparations, our meeting will begin. 一切準備工作就緒，會議就開始。

Correspondents may enter the meeting room only before the meetings. 記者只能在會議開始前進入會議室。

③ 我們來參加年終會議。

A： We're here for our annual meeting. 我們來參加年終會議。

B： Since we are all here, Let's begin our meeting. 既然我們都到了，那就開始開會吧。

Tips

annual meeting 年會；指公司一年舉行一次的聚會。

All the employees presented the annual meeting. 所有員工都出席了年會。

I am pleased to address the annual meeting. 我很高興在年會上發表致辭。

④ 我們有五個主要問題要討論。

A： We have five main issues to discuss. 我們有五個主要問題要討論。

B： Let's get down to business. 我們進入主題吧！

Tips

issue 問題、議題，這裡相當於 topic 或是 subject。

Let's move on to the next topic. 我們進入下一個議題吧！

The meeting will discuss some key issues we face now. 會議將要討論我們面對的主要問題。

⑤ 有什麼意見或建議嗎？

A： Are there any comments or suggestions? 有什麼意見或建議嗎？

B： Yes, I have some different opinions on this issue. 是的，對這個問題我有不同的看法。

Tips

what's your view on this subject? 就這個議題，你有什麼看法？

65

■ Tom put forward a good suggestion at the meeting. 湯姆在會議上提出了一個好點子。

■ Your idea is practical. 你的想法很實用。

⑥ 讓我們從第一項開始。

A： Let's begin with the first item. 讓我們從第一項開始。

B： OK, Let's talk about the new product. 好的，讓我們談談新產品。

Tips

■ To begin with, Let's talk about the salary. 首先，讓我們討論一下薪酬問題。

■ I want to make one thing clear. 我想澄清一點。

⑦ 下面請他來發言。

A： I'll hand the floor over to him. 下面請他來發言。

B： Thanks, Peter. 彼得，謝謝。

Tips

■ hand the floor over to 請……發言

■ What do you think of this idea? 你覺得這個主意怎麼樣？

■ It's your turn to make a statement. 到你發言了。

Step 3　實 戰 對 話

① 開始會議

A：Everyone is here. I think we should begin. 人都到齊了。我覺得我們應該開始了。

B： Now I will call the meeting to order. Let me just give an overview of the meeting. The purpose of this meeting is to discuss about the new product. 現在我宣布會議正式開始。我來概略介紹一下這次會議。會議的目的是討論新產品。

A： OK, Let's get down to business. 好的，我們進入主題吧。

B： Mary will present us the design plan of the new product. 瑪麗將會為大家展示新產品的設計方案。

A： If you have any suggestions about the plan, please feel free to tell us. 如果你對這個方案有什麼建議的話，請暢所欲言。

B： Yes, we need to brainstorm. 是的，我們需要進行腦力激盪。

② 會議議題

A： We have five main issues to discuss. 我們有五個主要問題要討論。

B： Let's begin with the first item. 讓我們從第一項開始。

A： The first item is about the sales plan. The manager gives his green light to this. 第一個議題與銷售計畫有關。經理已經批准了。

B： Great! 太棒了！

A： But he thought we could perfect the details. 但是他認為我們需要完善細節。

B： OK, we will handle it. 好的，我們會處理。

③ 討論意見

A： Are there any comments or suggestions? What are your feelings about this plan? 有什麼意見或建議嗎？你覺得這個計畫怎麼樣？

B： I'm afraid It's impossible for us to carry out this plan now. 恐怕我們現在無法實施這項計畫。

A： Could you kindly explain? 能解釋一下嗎？

B： I had investigated the market, and found that customers may not accept the concept. 我調查了市場，發現顧客可能不會接受這一理念。

A： Can you give us some data to support you? 你能給出具體的資料來支援這一說法嗎？

B： Yes, here is the report. 可以，這是我的報告。

Scene 14 　歡迎與介紹

Step 1 　必備表達

突然通知	at short notice：相當於 sudden notice；short notice 還表示「臨時通知」。
助理	assistant：manager assistant 就是「經理助理」。
董事長	president：當首字母大寫時，表示「總統」。
突發情況	unforeseen circumstance：unforeseen「無法預測的」，與 unexpectable 同義。
缺席	absent：常構成片語 be absent from，表示「缺席」。
介紹	introduce：「自我介紹」可以用 introduce oneself 表示。
感謝	appreciate：appreciate doing 表示「感謝」。
參加者	participant：來自於動詞 participate「參與，參加」。
問候	greeting：來自動詞 greet「問候」。
簡單介紹	brief introduction：introduction 來自於動詞 introduce。

Step 2 　句句精彩

① 麗莎現在休產假，我現在是艾曼達的助理。

A：Let me introduce my new assistant to you Lucy. 讓我介紹一下我的新助理，露西。

B：I'll be acting as Amanda's assistant while Lisa is away on maternity leave.
麗莎現在休產假，我現在是艾曼達的助理。

Tips

■ on maternity leave 休產假；on leave 表示「休假，休假中」。

■ I am the manager assistant. 我是經理助理。

■ Lisa will be absent from this meeting for she is sick. 麗莎因病將缺席這次會議。

② 我們很高興歡迎新的銷售經理。

A：We're pleased to welcome the new sales manager. 我們很高興歡迎新的銷售經理。

B：Thank you very much. 非常感謝。

Tips

Welcome to our company. 歡迎加入我們公司。

I'd like you to meet Jenny. 我想向大家介紹珍妮。

Welcome our new colleague. 歡迎新同事。

③ 經理今天不能參加。

A：Where is Mr. Lin? 林先生在哪裡？

B：The manager cannot join us today. 經理今天不能參加。

Tips

Why were you absent from the meeting this afternoon? 你今天下午為什麼缺席會議？

It is a pleasure for professor Li to come to this meeting. 很榮幸能邀請到李教授參加我們的會議。

We didn't come to a conclusion for our manager's absence. 由於經理缺席，我們沒有得出結論。

④ 由於突發情況，董事長不能參加。

A：The president is absent due to unforeseen circumstances. 由於突發情況，董事長不能參加。

B： It is really a pity. 真遺憾。

Tips

circumstance 表示「情況」時，需要用複數形式。

We apologize that Mike is unable to attend the conference due to unforeseen circumstances. 很抱歉，麥克由於突發情況不能參加這次會議。

I didn't join the meeting for something beyond my control. 由於一些無法控制的事情，我沒能參加會議。

⑤ 謝謝你們的到來。

A： Thank you all for coming. 謝謝你們的到來。

B： It is a pleasure for me to be here. 我很榮幸能夠參加。

Tips

■ I appreciate you for giving me the chance. 非常感謝您能給我這次機會。

■ Thank you so much for being here today. 非常感謝你們今天的出席。

■ I really appreciate that you come here. 真的很感謝你們能夠來這裡。

⑥ 你能站起來介紹一下自己嗎？

A：Would you like to stand up and introduce yourself? 你能站起來介紹一下自己嗎？

B：OK. My name is Katherine and I feel so good to join this team. 好的，我叫凱薩琳，很高興能加入這個團隊。

Tips

■ Tell us about yourself. 向我們介紹一下你自己吧。

■ I'd like to present you to our team. 我要把你介紹給我們的團隊。

⑦ 你們大部分人我都認識，但是有一些新面孔。

A：I know most of you, but there are a few unfamiliar faces. 你們大部分人我都認識，但是有一些新面孔。

B：They will introduce themselves to you later. 稍後他們會向您自我介紹。

Tips

■ I found myself among some unfamiliar faces. 我發現身邊有一些不熟悉的面孔。

■ We should know the participants in any meeting. 出席任何會議時都需要了解與會者。

■ I just know some of the participants in the meeting. 我只認識出席會議的一部分人。

Step 3　實戰對話

① 迎接歡迎

A：Let me introduce you my new assistant, Lucy. 讓我介紹一下我的新助理，露西。

B：Hi, everyone, my name is Lucy. 大家好，我是露西。

A：Lucy will be the assistant. 露西將會擔任助理一職。

B：I'll be acting as Amanda's assistant while Lisa is away on maternity leave. 麗莎現在休產假，我現在是艾曼達的助理。

A：Well, you need to summarize what we will discuss in the meeting. 那麼，妳需要

總結我們在會議上討論的東西。

B： OK. No problem. 好的。沒問題。

② 缺席會議

A： Where is Mr. Lin? 林先生在哪裡？

B： The president is absent due to unforeseen circumstances. 由於突發情況，董事長不能參加。

A： What happened? Is it serious? 發生什麼了，嚴重嗎？

B： Sorry, I don't know the situation. 抱歉，我不了解情況。

A： Can we continue the meeting? 那我們還能繼續會議嗎？

B： Yes. Mr. Lin had given instructions. 可以。林先生已經給過指示了。

③ 感謝到來

A： Thank you all for coming. 謝謝你的到來。

B： I appreciate you for giving me the chance to attend this meeting. 非常感謝您能給我這個機會參加這次會議。

A： I believe that you will bring us breakthroughs in this meeting. 我相信你的到來一定會為這次會議帶來突破性進展。

B： Hope so. 希望如此。

A： So, can we begin our discussion? 那麼，我們現在能開始討論嗎？

B： Let's get started. 我們開始吧。

Scene 15　加入討論

必 備 表 達

討論	discuss：也可用 argue 表示。
暢所欲言	speak out freely：同類表達還有 say one's say 和 speak out，都表示「大膽地說」。
詳述	elaborate：常用片語 elaborate on，意思為「仔細說明」。
觀點	point：表示「觀點、看法」的詞還有：viewpoint、standpoint、opinion 等。
打斷	interrupt：片語 cut / break in on 也可表達此意。
腦力激盪	brainstorm：brainstorm 相當於 group discussion，也可以作動詞。
判斷	judgment：sound judgment 表示「正確的判斷力」。
建議	advise：advise 為動詞，名詞是 advice。
新點子	fresh idea：fresh 新的、新奇的。
嚴肅的	serious：serious about 嚴肅、認真對待。

Step 2　**句 句 精 彩**

① 我想要進一步說明傑克的觀點。

A： Anything else? 還有要補充的嗎？

B： I'd like to elaborate on Jack's point. 我想要進一步說明傑克的觀點。

Tips

■ Could I interrupt you for a minute? 我能插兩句嗎？

■ In my opinion, it is better to draft another plan. 我認為最好還是起草另一個計畫吧。

■ I agree with Jack. 我同意傑克的看法。

② 我可以說句話嗎？

A： May I have a word? 我可以說句話嗎？

B： You can speak out freely. 你可以暢所欲言。

Tips

Please voice your opinions freely. 請大家暢所欲言。

I would welcome the opinion of any people who have experience. 歡迎有經驗的人來發表意見。

Anything else to add? 還有要補充的嗎？

③ 對不起，我打斷一下。

A： Excuse me for interrupting. 對不起，我打斷一下。

B： OK, go ahead. 好的，請說。

Tips

Sorry to interrupt. 抱歉，打斷一下。

Does anyone have anything to add? 還有人要補充什麼嗎？

Can I interrupt for a moment? 我能打斷一下嗎？

④ 你想到什麼就說什麼。

A： I don't know how to say. 我不知道該如何表達。

B： Just say whatever comes to your mind. 你想到什麼就說什麼。

Tips

come to one's mind 想起，想到。

■ You have your opinion and I have mine. 你有你的觀點，我有我的觀點。

They all say what comes into their minds. 他們都暢所欲言。

⑤ 我們將進行腦力激盪。

A： What are we going to do next？我們接下來做什麼？

B： We're going to brainstorm. 我們將進行腦力激盪。

Tips

Is there anyone who wants to share the idea? 有沒有人分享一下看法？

In this point, I join with you. 在這一點上我與你意見一致。

I'd like to make one point. 我想發表一下看法。

⑥ 不要下評判！

A： No judgments! 不要下評判！

73

B： I just speak out my point. 我只是說出了我的觀點。

Tips

■ Your words reflect your judgment. 你的話基於你的判斷。

■ It doesn't make sense. 這沒有意義。

⑦ 我們稍後再談論這個問題。

A： We'll get to that issue later. 我們稍後再討論這個問題。

B： Oh, come on. You can't avoid this anymore. 天哪，拜託，你不能再避開這個話題。

Tips

■ Let's change the subject. 讓我們換個話題吧。

■ I don't want to discuss this topic anymore. 我不想再討論這個問題了。

Step 3　實 戰 對 話

① 闡明觀點

A： what's your point? 你的觀點是什麼？

B： I'd like to elaborate on Jack's point. 我想要進一步說明傑克的觀點。

A： Just say whatever comes to your mind. 你想到什麼就說什麼。

B： OK, I think the project itself is good, but the operation mechanism on it is unpractical. 好的，我認為這個專案本身很好，但是運作機制有些不切實際。

A： Sounds reasonable. Could you kindly explain it in detail? 聽起來有道理，能詳細地解釋一下嗎？

B： OK, please watch the Powerpoint. 好的，請看簡報。

② 打斷對話

A： Excuse me for interrupting. 對不起，我打斷一下。

B： OK, go ahead. 好的，請說。

A： I strongly oppose this marketing plan. 我強烈反對市場行銷企劃。

B： I see no reason why we shouldn't do that. 我找不到我們不這樣做的理由。

A： Here is my market research. 這是我的市場調查報告。

B： OK, I will study it. 好的，我會研究一下。

③ 腦力激盪

A： We're going to brainstorm. 我們將進行腦力激盪。

B： It's a good way to bring in more fresh ideas. 這是想出新點子的好方法。

A： Every time we brainstorm, I learn a lot. 每次腦力激盪時，我都能學到很多。

B： So do I. Back to the point, I think the suggestion is constructive. 我也一樣，回歸正題，我認為這個建議很具建設性。

A： I can't agree more with you. 我完全同意你的觀點。

B： Then we can make a decision. 那麼我們可以做決定了。

Scene 16　集思廣益

Step 1　必備表達

集思廣益	put our heads together：也用可片語 pool the wisdom 表示。
分析	analyze：名詞形式為 analysis。
解決，想出	figure out：也可以用 solve 表示「解決」的意思。
決定	determine：determine to do sth. 決定做某事；同義詞組還有：make up one's mind。
有問題	go wrong：同意片語有 be out of order 和 have a screw loose 等。
想法	thought：同義詞還有 idea 和 concept 等。
有效的	effective：口語中也可用 available 表示「有效的」。
分歧	disagreement：have disagreement 表示「意見不合」；同義詞還有 controversy。
解決方案	solution：加介詞 to 表示「……的解決方案」。
發言	fire away：用於口語中表示「不停地說」，相當於 harp。

Step 2　句句精彩

① 也許我們集思廣益，就能找出我們沒注意到的地方。

A：I wonder if we have missed something. I feel something goes wrong. 我懷疑我們遺漏了什麼，我感覺有什麼地方不對勁。

B：Maybe if we put our heads together, we can find out what we missed. 也許我們集思廣益，就能找出我們沒注意到的地方。

Tips

■ Perhaps if we work as a team, we can find out what we missed. 也許我們進行團隊合作，就能找出我們沒注意到的地方。

■ We need more heads to find out what's wrong. 我們需要更多的人來找出問題所在。

■ We hadn't located the problem yet. 我們還是沒有找出問題所在。

② 我們來分析一下，看看怎麼解決這個問題。

A： Let's run an analysis and figure out how we can get this straightened out. 我們來分析一下，看看怎麼解決這個問題。

B： OK, we may need all the related information and cases. 好的，我們可能需要相關的資訊以及案例。

Tips

straighten out 改正。

Let's find out how this happened and how we can fix it. 我們來分析一下，看看怎麼解決這個問題。

We can take some examples for reference. 我們可以參考一些例子。

③ 究竟哪裡出問題了呢？

A： Where did it go wrong? 究竟哪裡出問題了呢？

B： I haven't figured the problem out. 我還沒有找到問題的癥結。

Tips

We need help to locate the problem. 我們需要幫助來確定問題所在。

I think I know where the problem is. 我想我知道問題出在哪了。

④ 只有時間能證明這樣做是對還是錯。

A： How do you know the decision is right? 你怎麼知道這個決定是對的？

B： Only time can tell whether or not it was the right thing to do. 只有時間能證明這樣做是對還是錯。

Tips

How can we judge the decision? 我們如何評判這個決定呢？

It depends on a lot of things, so it only can be proved by time. 它取決於很多因素，所以只能交給時間來判斷。

This decision is too hasty. 這個決定太草率了。

⑤ 我想聽聽你們的想法。

A： I'd like to hear your ideas. 我想聽聽你們的想法。

B： I think it is a reasonable point. 我認為這個觀點很有道理。

Tips

■ Have you got a better idea? 你有什麼更好的主意嗎？

■ We need to seek some professional advice. 我們需要尋求一些專業的建議。

⑥ 我認為費用上不划算。

A： I don't think it will be cost effective. 我認為費用上不划算。

B： We can have a rough cost estimate. 我們可以粗略估算一下成本。

Tips

■ cost effective 指「成本效率，划算的」，相當於 great deal。

■ We still have a problem, so it can be difficult to calculate the cost. 我們仍然有一個問題，因此很難計算成本。

■ Cost is one of the most important factors that affects our decision. 成本也是影響我們決定的最重要因素之一。

⑦ 現在大家的意見有些不一致。

A： We have some basic disagreements here. 現在大家的意見有些不一致。

B： We have to persuade each other now. 我們不得不說服對方。

Tips

■ It doesn't seem to be practical. 這似乎不是很實用。

■ We must make a decision as soon as possible. 我們應該盡快做決定。

■ I understand what you mean, but I still don't agree. 我明白你的意思，但我還是不同意你的看法。

Step 3　實戰對話

① 集思廣益

A： I wonder if we miss something. I feel something goes wrong. 我懷疑我遺漏了什麼，我感覺有什麼地方不對勁。

B： Maybe if we put our heads together, we can find out what we missed. 也許我們集思廣益，就能找出我們沒注意到的地方。

A： OK, Let's solve it together. 好吧，讓我們一起解決吧。

B： Have you checked the details in the project? 你檢查了專案中的細節問題嗎？

A：Yes, I have checked twice, but I think we need to check it again. 是的，我都檢查兩遍了，但是我認為我們應該再查一次。

B：OK, I will help you. 好，我來幫你。

② 分析問題

A：Let's run an analysis and figure out how we can get this straightened out. 我們來分析一下，看看怎麼解決這個問題。

B：OK, we may need all the related information and cases. 好的，我們可能需要相關的資訊及案例。

A：Where did it all go wrong? 究竟哪裡出問題了呢？

B：We will check it from the beginning and find the reason. 我們會重新開始檢查以便找到原因。

A：Well, Let's start now. Here is the analysis report. 好吧，那我們開始吧。這是分析報告。

B：From the report we can know the problem lies in transportation. 從報告來看，問題是出在運輸上。

③ 決策正誤

A：How do you know the decision is right？你怎麼知道這個決定是對的？

B：Only time can tell whether or not it was the right thing to do. 只有時間能證明這樣做是對還是錯。

A：But this thought is too hasty. 但是這種想法太草率了。

B：Then what should we do? 那我們該怎麼辦？

A：We should hear from everyone. 我們應該徵求每個人的意見。

B：OK, I will ask for a show of hands to determine. 好吧，那麼就用舉手表決來決定。

Scene 17　控制流程

Step 1　必備表達

問題	problem：表示「問題」的詞還有 issue、question、trouble、matter 等。
話題	topic：也可以用 subject 表示同樣的含義。
意見	suggestion：「提建議」可以用 make suggestion 表示，此外 advice 和 proposal 也能表示「意見」。
下一步	next move：相當於 next step。
簡而言之	in a nutshell：nutshell 概括；表示「總之」的說法還有：in short、in brief、in a word、put it simply 等。
基本上	basically：也可用 mainly、on the whole、by and large 表示；用來總結，承上啟下。
目前還不錯	so far, so good：用於階段性的總結，相當於 make good progress by far。
歸根究柢	boil down to：boil down 表示「歸結」。
總結	come down to：該片語與 boil down to 都用於總結。
好點子	a good point：相當於 a cool idea。

Step 2　句句精彩

① 我們可以把那個問題列入下次議程。

A：We still have one problem left. 我們還剩一個問題。

B：We can put that problem on the agenda for next time. 我們可以把那個問題列入下次議程。

Tips

■ on the agenda 在議事日程上。

We are running out of time and the problems left will be discussed next time. 時間差不多了，剩下的問題下次再討論。

These two problems are different and we will talk next time. 這兩個問題不是一碼事，我們下次再說。

② 我們是不是該回到正題上？

A： How can we solve this problem? 我們怎麼解決這個問題？

B： That's not the key point. Shouldn't we get back on topic? 這不是重點。我們是不是該回到正題上？

Tips

Joking apart, we have to continue to discuss about the work. 言歸正傳，我們還是繼續討論工作。

I have to remind you to return to the subject. 我得提醒你回歸正題。

OK, we should get down to business. 好了，我們該進入正題了。

③ 我會採納一些意見。

A： How do you think about the suggestions? I think they are feasible. 你認為這些建議怎麼樣？我認為是切實可行的。

B： I could adopt some suggestions. 我會採納一些意見。

Tips

adopt 採納，接受。

This suggestion will be taken into consideration. 這個建議會被考慮。

They may challenge the proposal as impractical. 他們會認為這個建議不切合實際。

④ 我們必須計劃下一步該怎麼做。

A： We need to plan our next move. 我們必須計劃下一步該怎麼做。

B： I suggest that we redo it. 我建議重做。

Tips

What should we do next? 接下來，我們應該怎麼辦？

All in all, we need to consider about the next move. 總之，我們應該考慮下一步了。

Let's move on to the next step. 讓我們進入下一步。

⑤ 我了解你為何這樣問，但是我們可以稍後再討論。

A：We should attach importance to the matter. 我們一定要高度重視這個問題。

B：I understand where you are coming from, but we can discuss that later. 我了解你為何這樣問，但是我們可以稍後再討論。

Tips

■ attach importance to 重視。

■ It's a good point, but We'd better discuss the issue at hand. 主意不錯，但是我們最好還是討論手邊這項議題。

■ I'm sorry, but this issue is not on our agenda. 很抱歉，但是這個問題不在日程上。

⑥ 輪到你了。

A：You're up. 輪到你了。

B：Thank you. I have two points here, one about the hands wanted. 謝謝。我有兩點要說，第一點是關於應徵的。

Tips

■ hands wanted 字面上表示「需要人手」，實際指的就是「應徵」。

■ Ball is in your court. 輪到你了。

■ I know my turn comes. 我知道輪到我了。

⑦ 第一階段完成了，到目前為止一切順利。

A：The first stage is done; so far, so good. 第一階段完成了，到目前為止一切順利。

B：Wow, finally, all goes well. 哇，總算一切進展順利。

Tips

■ I am glad to tell you that so far everything is going well. 很高興告訴大家，到目前為止一切進展順利。

■ We have reached a number of consensuses in the first phase of the meeting. 在第一段的會議上，我們已經在很多方面達成了一致。

Step 3　實 戰 對 話

① 會議進程

A：We still have one problem left in this round. 這一輪我們還剩一個問題。

B： We can put that problem on the agenda for next time. 我們可以把那個問題列入下次議程。

A： Why? 為什麼？

B： The problem should be treated very carefully, so we have to talk about it alone next time. 這件事情要小心處理，所以下次我們單獨討論。

A： OK, Let's get back on topic. 好的，讓我們回歸正題。

B： The next move is voting on our decision. 下一個環節是對我們的決定進行投票。

② 採納意見

A： How do you think about the suggestions? I think they are feasible. 你認為這些建議怎麼樣？我認為是切實可行的。

B： I could adopt some suggestions. 我會採納一些意見。

A： Could you tell me which one? Sorry to push you, but we have to decide now. 能告訴我是哪一個嗎？很抱歉催促你，但是我們現在就得決定。

B： OK. I need your help to make a decision. 好吧，我需要你們幫助我做決定。

A： I tend to choose the one which supports Mike. 我傾向於選擇支持麥克的那個意見。

B： OK. Let me see. 好的。讓我想想。

③ 控制流程

A： We need to plan our next move. 我們必須計劃下一步該怎麼做。

B： Do you mean we have to restart? 你是說我們要重新開始嗎？

A： I don't mean we should restart; we must face up this situation and find some solutions. 我不是說我們應該重新開始，我們必須面對現在的情況，然後找出一些解決方案。

B： I understand. We must solve the present problems and find a new way. 我明白，我們必須解決目前的問題，然後找到一條新路。

A： Yes, That's it. Everyone can give a solution. 是的，就是這樣，每個人都可以給出解決方案。

B： OK, Let's begin. 好的，那就開始吧。

Scene 18　同意觀點

Step 1　必備表達

絕對正確	absolutely correct：相當於 deadly right 或 exactly right。
支持	support：常用片語 in support of 表示「支持」；同義詞組還有：in favor of、back up、stand by 等。
非常棒	terrific：用於口語中，表示讚揚，相當於 excellent、wonderful。
同意	agree：用於片語 agree with，表示「同意，贊同」。
沒錯	exactly：用來強調，加強語氣。
毫無疑問	without doubt：相當於 well and truly 及 without doubt。
完全同意	in complete agreement：後面接介詞 with。
有效的	valid：表示觀點等是「有效的，可實行的」時與 sound 同義。
可行	doable：相當於 feasible。
贊同	in favor of：注意該片語是 in favor of 而不是 in the favor of。
觀點	viewpoint：相當於 opinion 或 thought 等。

Step 2　句句精彩

① 你說得完全正確。

A： You mean John's plan is the best one. 你的意思是說約翰的計畫是最好的。

B： You were exactly right. 你說得完全正確。

Tips

■ You were absolutely correct. 你說的完全正確。

■ That's exactly the way I feel. 我也是這麼想的。

■ I can't agree with you anymore. 非常贊同。

② 理論上這些聽起來都不錯。

A： I think the ideas are perfect. 我認為這些主意太棒了。

B： All of these sound good in theory. 理論上這些聽起來都不錯。

Tips

sound good 聽上去不錯；in theory 理論上。

You might be right, but it must be under some circumstances. 你可能是正確的，但這必須是在一定條件下。

I partly agree with you. 我不完全同意。

③ 我無所謂，哪種都行。

A： what's your opinion? 你是什麼想法？

B： It doesn't matter to me, either way. 我無所謂，哪種都行。

Tips

I think both of them are pretty good. 我認為都很不錯。

I will reserve my opinion this time. 這次我保留看法。

I don't take any part of it. 我不站在任何一方。

④ 你的建議和他的一樣好。

A： Your suggestion is as good as the his. 你的建議和他的一樣好。

B： Oh, I'm really honored. 哦，真是我的榮幸啊。

Tips

It seems that we really reach an agreement now. 看起來我們終於達成一致了。

We're all of the same mind. 我們想法一樣。

We have the same idea. 我們想法一致。

⑤ 我完全支持這個計畫。

A： Are you for or against? 你支持還是反對？

B： This plan has my full support. 我完全支持這個計畫。

Tips

I am all for it. 我完全贊同。

I'm on your side. 我站在你這邊。

I'm with you all the way. 我一直支持你。

⑥ 這樣安排好極了！

A： Are there any more comments? 還有什麼意見嗎？

B： What an excellent arrangement! 這樣安排好極了！

Tips

■ Well done. 幹得不錯。

■ I think It's out of this world — maybe the best！ 我覺得太了不起了——或許是最好的！

■ Terrific! 棒極了！

⑦ 我正好也是這麼想。

A： I think the plan is good. 我認為這個計畫很好。

B： That's exactly what I was thinking. 我正好也是這麼想。

Tips

■ That's what I thought. 英雄所見略同。

■ We were so much on the same wavelength. 我們總是想法一致。

■ I was just thinking of the same thing. 我們想法一致了。

Step 3　實 戰 對 話

① 完全贊同

A： Do you think so? 你也這樣認為嗎？

B： You were exactly right. 你說得完全正確。

A： I am glad that you agree with me. 很高興你能認同我。

B： I concern about the marketing plan all the time and yours is the best one. 我一直很關心行銷方案，你的這個是最好的。

A： I did a lot of researches and interviewed many customers. 我做了很多研究，也採訪了很多客戶。

B： you've done a good job. 你做得不錯。

② 部分同意

A： I partly agree with this scheme, I still feel something is missing. 我不完全同意這個計畫，因為感覺缺了點什麼。

B： All of these sound good in theory but how about in practical? 理論上這些聽起來都不錯，但實際上呢？

A： Yes, That's the question. 是啊，問題就在這裡。

B： I have an idea; we can try to operate it in a small scale. 我有個想法，我們可以在小範圍內試著運作一下。

A： OK, then we can find out if it is workable. 好的，那樣我們就可以發現它是否可行了。

B： So, we achieve the agreement. 這麼說，我們達成一致了。

③ 志同道合

A： Do you agree with this plan? 你支持這個計畫嗎？

B： This plan has my full support. 我完全支持這個計畫。

A： So, we have reached an agreement. The plan will be carried out next week. 所以，我們達成了一致，這個計畫下週就要開始實施。

B： That would be good. 那太好了。

A： Thank you. Hope you all can support this plan; in fact, there may be some problems during the operation. 謝謝。希望大家能夠支持這個計畫，實際上在操作過程中可能會遇到很多問題。

B： don't worry. We'll offer our help. 別擔心，我們會提供幫助。

Scene 19　反對觀點

Step 1　必備表達

不能接受的	unacceptable：un- 為反義詞綴「不」。
確定	sure：「確定，確保」可以用 make sure 表示。
再次確認	double-check：相當於 double confirm。
不同意	disagree：與介詞 with 連接可以表示「不同意」，相當於 disapprove of。
在某種程度上	up to a point：還可以用 to some extent 代替。
不可能	no way：含義類似於 impossible。
不知道	have no idea：除了 don't know 以外，還可以用 have no idea 表示同樣的意思。
後悔	regret：regret to do sth. 表示「後悔做……」。
一派胡言	nonsense：talk nonsense 可以表示「胡說」。
廢話	rubbish：原意為「垃圾」，這裡指「廢話」。
以……的觀點	in one's opinion：相當於 from one's point of view。

Step 2　句句精彩

① 我無法支持。

A：I want to know your idea about this. 我想了解你對此的看法。

B：I cannot support that. 我無法支持。

Tips

■ I see it differently. 我的看法不同。

■ I can't go along with you. 我不同意你的觀點。

■ I'm afraid I can't agree. 我恐怕不能同意。

② 我完全無法接受。

A： Why are you opposed this? 你為什麼反對？

B： I find that it is totally unacceptable. 我完全無法接受。

Tips

I couldn't accept it. 我無法接受。

That's absolute nonsense. 那完全是胡說八道。

This is way out of line. 這個太過分了。

③ 那是令人討厭的事。

A： Let's vote on the issue. 讓我們投票決定此事吧。

B： That's a rotten thing to do. 那是令人討厭的事。

Tips

This is the least thing I want to do. 這是我最不想做的事。

■ I'm totally against the proposal of closing the department. 我堅決反對關閉這個部門的提議。

I don't think That's the way to solve it. 我認為這不是解決問題的辦法。

④ 我覺得你誤會我了。

A： Why don't you agree with me? 你為什麼不同意我的意見？

B： I think you misunderstood me. 我覺得你誤會我了。

Tips

Sorry, That's not quite right. 抱歉，這不是很正確。

That's not quite what I had in mind. 這不是我的想法。

That's not what I meant. 我不是這個意思。

⑤ 我不確定那件事你是否正確。

A： I'm not sure you're right about that. 我不確定那件事你是否正確。

B： You must have your own thought about this. Just tell me. 你一定有你自己的想法，直接告訴我吧。

Tips

I don't agree with everyone. 我不贊成任何人的觀點。

I maintain a neutral position. 我保持中立的態度。

I think I'll give that a miss. 我放棄。

⑥ 你確定嗎？

A： Are you positive? 你確定嗎？

B： No, I am not sure about it. 不，我沒什麼把握。

Tips

- I'm not sure. 我不確定。
- I can't believe that！簡直不能相信！
- Are you kidding? 你開玩笑的吧？

⑦ 我們應該再次確認。

A： We should double-check that. 我們應該再次確認。

B： OK, I will do it. 好的，我會安排。

Tips

- Please confirm every detail again. 請再次確認所有細節。
- We may not decide it now. 我們也許不該馬上決定。
- Think it over before you make a decision. 做決定之前再好好考慮考慮。

Step 3 　實 戰 對 話

① 反對意見

A： I can not give my support to that. 我無法支持。

B： Can you give me a reason? 能給我一個理由嗎？

A： There are two points. The first one is the price, the other one is the logo. 一共有兩點。首先是價格，其次是標誌。

B： I disagree with you. The result of the survey showed that customers prefer this price. 我不同意。調查結果顯示顧客更願意接受這個價格。

A： I have noticed one mistake in your research report. It is the mediumsized pack but not the small one. 我注意到了你調查報告中的一個錯誤，應該是中號包裝，而不是小號包裝。

B： I will recheck it. 我會再檢查一下。

② 言語誤會

A： Why don't you agree with me? 你為什麼不同意我的意見？

B： I think you are mistaken. The idea is great itself, but I think it can only work under certain circumstances. 我覺得你誤會我了。這個主意本身很棒，但是我想它只有在特定情況下才會有效。

A： I don't understand. 我不明白。

B： The idea is good in theory, but only in theory, because your bases for this idea are too perfect. 這個想法在理論上很好，但也僅僅是理論上，因為這個想法的前提太過完美。

A： I think I know the key reason; I need to modify the idea to make sure it is practical. 我想我知道問題所在了。我需要修改一下這個想法，使之能夠在實際中實施。

B： That would be good. 這樣會好一點。

③ 保留意見

A： I'm not sure you're right about that. 我不確定那件事你是否正確。

B： You must have your own thought about this. Just tell me. 你一定有你自己的想法，直接告訴我吧。

A： I don't agree with everyone. I maintain a neutral position. 我不贊成任何人的觀點。我保持中立的態度。

B： Could you tell me your reason? 能告訴我你的理由嗎？

A： Both the two plans are not objective to me. 對於我來說，這兩個計畫都不夠客觀。

B： I hope you could explain it in detail. 我希望你能詳細解釋一下。

Scene 20　困惑與解釋

Step 1　必備表達

困惑	confuse：也可以用 puzzle 來表示。另外，在表示「困惑」時，confuse 常以 confused 的形式出現。
澄清	clarify：更簡單的說法是 explain。
清楚的	clear：常用片語為 make clear 表示「解釋清楚」的意思。
口誤	a slip of the tongue：slip 錯誤；tongue 舌頭。
講重點	get to the point：該片語還有「言歸正傳」的意思，這時可以用 get to business 替換。
重要的	important：相似的表達還有 significant、crucial、considerable 等。
重複	repeat：在沒有聽清對方所言時，還可以用「Pardon?」（請再說一遍好嗎？）
換句話說	in other words：還可以用 put another way 或 namely 來代替。
假設	suppose：還可以用 assume 來代替。
比……重要	outweigh：也可用 take precedence over 代替。

Step 2　句句精彩

① 你把我弄糊塗了。

A： Do you understand what I mean? 你明白我的意思了嗎？

B： you've lost me. 你把我弄糊塗了。

Tips

■ I got so confused. 我很困惑。

■ you've mixed me up completely! 你完全把我弄糊塗了。

■ I don't get the picture. 我不明白。

② 你的重點是什麼？

A：Sorry to interrupt you, but what's your point? 抱歉打斷你，但是你的重點是什麼？

B：What I want to say is that this project is not workable. 我是想說這個專案不可行。

Tips

What does that mean? 那麼說是什麼意思？

What are you trying to say? 您想要說什麼呢？

Could you get to the point? 你的重點是什麼？

③ 您可以為我解釋清楚那一點嗎？

A：Can you clarify that for me? 您可以為我解釋清楚那一點嗎？

B：OK, I will explain it again. 好的，我會再解釋一遍。

Tips

Could you speak clearly? 你能說得清楚點嗎？

■ Sorry, but I don't get it. 對不起，我沒明白。

④ 再說一次好嗎？

A：Come again, please? 再說一次好嗎？

B：I said you can get some advices from Mr. John who is an expert on it. 我說你可以向約翰先生尋求意見，他是這方面的專家。

Tips

Could you please repeat that? I didn't catch it. 能再重複一次嗎？我沒明白。

Could you go over that again, please? 可以請您重述那一點嗎？

Could you say that again, please? 可以請你再說一次嗎？

⑤ 抱歉，我有點笨，但我不確定我是否明白。

A：I'm sorry if I'm being slow, but I'm not sure I understand it or not. 抱歉，我有點笨，但我不確定我是否明白。

B：You can tell me how you understand. 你可以告訴我你是怎麼理解的。

Tips

I'm not sure whether I make myself clear. 我不確定是不是講明白了。

Sorry, but I don't think I fully understand your question. 抱歉我不太明白你的問題。

Sorry, I don't quite see the point. 對不起，我不太明白這意思。

⑥ 也許我說得不夠清楚。

A： Maybe I'm not making myself clear. 也許我說得不夠清楚。

B： No, I understand what you said. 不，我明白你的意思。

Tips

■ Do you get what I'm saying? 你聽懂我說的嗎？

■ I don't know if I express myself clearly. 我不知道我是否把我的意思表達清楚了。

■ I failed to explain things properly. 我沒有把事情表達清楚。

⑦ 不，我不是那個意思。我剛剛只是口誤。

A： You mean I am talking nonsense. 你的意思是我在胡說八道。

B： No, I didn't mean that: it was just a slip of the tongue. 不，我不是那個意思。我剛剛只是口誤。

Tips

■ It just slipped out. 只是口誤。

■ I didn't mean it that way. 我原本不是那個意思。

■ I am not talking in that sense. 我談的不是那個意思。

Step 3　實 戰 對 話

① 弄糊塗了

A： Do you understand? 你明白了嗎？

B： You've lost me. 你把我弄糊塗了。

A： I mean it'll be our piece de resistance. 我的意思是這將是我們的傑作。

B： You mean people will be resistant to this new product? 你是說人們會抗拒這種新產品是嗎？

A： No, I say that this will be our great invention. 不，我是說這將會成為我們偉大的發明。

B： I get it now. 現在我明白了。

② 困惑不解

A： Can you clarify that for me? 您可以為我解釋清楚那一點嗎？

B： OK, I will explain it again. Revenues should have been much higher if we don't invest in the ad campaign. 好的，我會再解釋一遍。如果我們沒有投入廣告宣傳的話，營業額會更高。

A： You mean we shouldn't invest in ad. 你的意思是我們不應該投資廣告。

B： No, no, I just tried to explain why the revenues are low now. 不，不，我只是試圖解釋為什麼營業額很低。

A： Come again? 再說一次好嗎？

B： Ad investment made the revenue fewer, but it will bring us more profits in the long run. 廣告投資使得收入減少，但是從長遠來看，它會為我們賺更多的錢。

③ 表述不清

A： I'm sorry if I'm being slow, but I'm not sure I understand. 抱歉，我有點笨，但我不確定我是否明白。

B： Don't worry. I'll explain it to you again. These figures show that the market research worked. 別擔心，我再對你解釋一遍。這些數字說明市場調查起作用了。

A： Oh, I see. What about this pie chart? 哦，我明白了。那這個圓餅圖呢？

B： It indicates the career and age distribution of the consumers. 這個圓餅圖顯示了消費者的職業和年齡分布。

A： After listening to your explanation, I totally understand. 聽了你的解釋後，我完全明白了。

B： Good. Then Let's move to next item. 那就好。那我們繼續下一項議題。

Scene 21　表達建議

Step 1　必備表達

提出	bring up：相當於 put forward、come up with 等。
商談	talk over：相當於 negotiate、exchange views 等。
確信	be convinced：還可以用 make sure 或者 be sure of 來表示。
決定	decision：「做出決定」就是 make a decision。
感謝	be grateful for：還可以用 thank for 或 be obliged to 來代替。
選擇	choice：還可以用 option、selection 等來表示。
立場	stance：相當於 stand、standpoint、position 等。
觀點	opinion：在表達觀點時可以用 in my opinion。
分享	share：常用片語為 share sth. with sb.，表示「與某人分享……」。
滿意的	satisfactory：還可以用 content、pleased 來代替。

Step 2　句句精彩

① 在下次的董事會上我會提出這件事。

A： What do you do about this? 你要怎麼處理這件事呢？

B： I'll bring the matter up at the next meeting of the board of directors. 在下次的董事會上我會提出這件事。

Tips

■ the board of directors 表示「董事會」，而「董事會成員」則是 the member of the board of directors。

■ So what's your suggestion? 那你的建議是什麼呢？

■ I may offer this advice: don't quit your job so early. 我給你的建議是：不要過早辭掉工作。

② 在你做出任何決定之前，我們都需要商談一下。

A： We need to talk it over before you make any decision. 在你做出任何決定之前，

我們都需要商談一下。

B： I don't think It's necessary. 我認為沒有必要。

Tips

The delay allows us to calm down to make the best option. 因為延期，所以我們可以冷靜下來，做出一個最好的決定。

I don't make investment without professional advice. 沒有專業建議，我不做任何投資。

③ 我確信這是一個正確的決定。

A： I'm convinced that It's the right decision. 我確信這是一個正確的決定。

B： I think so. 我也是這麼認為的。

Tips

You should help me make the right decision at the right time. 你應該幫助我在適當的時候做出正確的決定。

It will be one of the best decisions you've made. 這將是你所做的最正確的決定之一。

As I see it, there is no other choice. 依我看，沒有其他選擇。

④ 我很感謝你的意見。

A： I'd be grateful for your opinion. 我很感謝你的意見。

B： Just feel free to tell me when you are in need. 需要時，儘管告訴我。

Tips

片語 feel free to do sth. 的意思是「隨意；儘管」，隱含「不要客氣」的意思。

We really appreciate your advice. 我們非常感謝你的建議。

Your comments on the issues would be greatly appreciated. 非常感謝你提出的建議。

⑤ 對這件事你有什麼想法？

A： What are your thoughts on the matter? 對這件事你有什麼想法？

B： I don't think this plan is workable. 我覺得這個計畫行不通。

Tips

What are your feelings on this proposal? 你對這個提議怎麼看？

Do you have any idea on this plan? 對這個計畫你有什麼看法？

What do you think of that view? 對此觀點你有什麼看法？

⑥ 沒有其他的選擇。

A： I don't think that It's a good idea to negotiate with him. 和他協商不是個好主意。

B： There is no other choice. 沒有其他的選擇。

Tips

- THere's no other way. 別無選擇。
- We have no alternative. 我們別無選擇。
- We have nothing for it but to accept it. 我們只能接受，別無選擇。

⑦ 事情總是這樣。

A： I can't accept that I have to work overtime every day. 每天都得加班，我無法接受。

B： It's always the case. 事情總是這樣。

Tips

- It was not always this way. 過去也不總是這樣。
- Why do they always do that? 為什麼他們總是這樣！

Step 3　實戰對話

① 三思而定

A： I can make the decision by myself. 我可以自己做決定。

B： We need to talk it over before you make any decision. 在你做出任何決定之前，我們都需要商談一下。

A： I don't think so. I have the right to decide. 我可不這樣認為。我有權利做決定。

B： Calm down. You should look before you leap. Or maybe you will regret. 冷靜一下，你應該三思而後行。否則你可能會後悔。

A： Well, I will think it over. Take it easy. I can do it. 那好吧，我會好好考慮的。放心好了，我可以的。

B： OK. I will give you a chance. 好吧，那我就給你一次機會。

② 決定正確

A： I wondered if I was making a right decision. 我不知道我是否做出了正確的決定。

B： I'm convinced that It's the right decision. 我確信這是一個正確的決定。

A： If it is wrong, we will lose a lot. 如果這個決定錯了，我們會損失很多。

B： Believe me, we have discussed it for a long time, and this is the best decision. 相信我，我們已經討論了很長時間，這個是最好的決定。

A： OK, I need a break. 好吧，我需要休息一下。

B： Don't think too much. 別想那麼多了。

③ 感謝建議

A： I'd be grateful for your opinion. 我很感謝你的意見。

B： You are welcome; I just speak my idea out. 別客氣，我只是說出了我的想法。

A： I don't know what to do without you. 沒有你，我真不知道該怎麼辦。

B： You had made a right decision and just didn't have much confidence in it. 你已經做出了正確的決定，只是信心不足而已。

A： Yes, I have failed so many times. 是的，我已經失敗過很多次了。

B： You should believe in yourself. 你應該相信自己。

Scene 22　視訊會議

Step 1　必備表達

花費時間	take the time：在表示「花費時間做某事」時可以用 take the time to do sth.。
麥克風	microphone：相關的「揚聲器」的英文是 speaker。
白板	whiteboard：視訊會議中有時還會用到「投影儀」，對應英文就是 projector。
照相機	camera：video camera 意思為「攝影機」，「網路攝影機」則是 webcam。
大聲	loud：loud speaker 擴音器。
接收	reception：video reception 視訊訊號接收。
影像	image：image processing 影像處理；image size 圖像大小。
耳機	headset：指的是「頭戴式耳機」，另外 earphone 也可表示「耳機」。
伺服器	server：network server 網路伺服器；video server 視訊伺服器。
視訊會議	video conference：conference 表示「會議」通常比較正式。另外，還可以用 meeting 表示。

Step 2　句句精彩

① 感謝你一大早花時間跟我通話。

A： Thanks for taking the time to talk with me this morning. 感謝你一大早花時間跟我通話。

B： It's OK. Let's get down to business now. 沒關係，我們進入正題吧。

Tips

■ 片語 get down to business 的意思是「言歸正傳，進入正題」。

■ We're going to have a video conference with our customers. 我們要和客戶開視訊會議。

Sorry to interrupt you, but I have an important question to ask. Can you see me? 很抱歉打斷你，但是我有一個很重要的問題要問，你能看到我嗎？

② 我聽得很清楚。

A： Can you hear me? 你能聽到我說話嗎？

B： you're coming through loud and clear. 我聽得很清楚。

Tips

come through 在這裡表示「表現，展現」，此外，該片語還有「經歷，電話接通」等意思。

I can see you, but the audio isn't so great. 我能看到你，但是音訊不是很好。

Can you speak loudly? The connection is bad. 你能大點聲嗎？信號很差。

③ 你看見並聽得到我的聲音嗎？

A： Can you see and hear me? 你看見並聽得到我的聲音嗎？

B： Yes, I can. 是的，可以。

Tips

Can you raise the camera a bit? 你能把攝影機調高一點嗎？

Could you kindly adjust the image? 你能調一下畫面嗎？

Can you adjust the volume? I can't hear you clearly. 你能調一下音量嗎？我聽得不是很清楚。

④ 你挪到下一個座位來，麥克風才能對著你。

A： Can you move one seat over so the microphone can reach you? 你挪到下一個座位來，麥克風才能對著你。

B： OK, here? 好的，是這裡嗎？

Tips

片語 seat over 的意思是「坐過來」。

I will adjust microphone volume so that you can hear me. 我調整一下麥克風的音量，這樣你就能聽到了。

Put on your headset and adjust the microphone. 戴上耳機，調整一下麥克風。

⑤ 你們的經理在會議室裡嗎？

A： Is your manager in the meeting room there? 你們的經理在會議室裡嗎？

B： Yes, he is. Would you like to speak to him? 是的，在這裡。你要跟他說話嗎？

Tips

■ Can you point the camera at Johnson? 你能把攝影機對準詹森嗎？

■ Please give Johnson a shot; I want to see his emotion on his face. 請給詹森一個鏡頭，我想看看他臉上的表情。

■ I want to speak to the employee who is in charge of this. 我想和負責此項任務的員工說話。

⑥ 請你把數據寫在白板上好嗎？

A： Can you go ahead and put the figures up on the whiteboard? 請你把數據寫在白板上好嗎？

B： I had sent the figure sheet to you by e-mail. 我已經把數據表發郵件給你了。

Tips

■ Can you work up the figures and send them to me after the meeting? 會後你能把數據資料整理一下傳給我嗎？

■ Can you write some key points on the whiteboard? 你能在白板上把關鍵點列出來嗎？

■ I can't see the whiteboard clearly. Could you change the direction? 我看不清白板，你能換一下位置嗎？

⑦ 我把鏡頭轉給經理愛麗絲。

A： I'd like to know the details of the project. 我想了解一下這個專案的細節。

B： Let me turn the camera over to our manager, Alice. Just wait a moment. 我把鏡頭轉向經理愛麗絲。請稍等。

Tips

■ 片語 turn over 在這裡表示「轉交，移交」，此外，它還可以表示「翻轉」。

■ Do you have anything else to discuss? 你還有什麼要討論的事情嗎？

■ Alice is not here now; I will let her connect you later. 愛麗絲現在不在 我讓她稍後聯絡你。

Step 3　實戰對話

① 視訊會議開始

A： Hello? John? 喂？約翰？

B： I can see you and hear you fine, Nancy. How about over there? 南西，我能清楚接收妳的影像和聲音。妳那邊情況怎麼樣？

A： Great! 很好。

B： Thanks for taking the time to talk with me this morning. 感謝妳一大早花時間跟我通話。

A： This is my job. So since we are all set now, Let's begin. 這是我的工作。既然我們都準備好了，我們就開始吧。

B： OK. I want to finalize the plan. 好的，我想最終確定一下這個企劃。

② 調整影片

A： Can you see and hear me? 你看見並聽得到我的聲音嗎？

B： I can see you, but the audio isn't so great. 我能看到你，但是音訊不是很好。

A： I adjusted the mic; can you hear me now? 我調整了麥克風，現在能聽到了嗎？

B： Come again? I didn't hear you. The reception is bad. 再講一次？我聽不到你，信號不好。

A： I said that could you hear me now? 我是說你現在能聽到了嗎？

B： It's OK now. You're coming through loud and clear. 現在好了。我聽得很清楚，看得很清晰。

③ 寫出數據

A： Can you go ahead and put the figures up on the whiteboard? 請你把數據寫在白板上好嗎？

B： OK, I will list the sales figures on the left side. 好的，我把銷售數據寫在左邊。

A： Good, and the target sales figures on the right. Then we can compare. 很好，然後把目標銷售數據寫在右邊，這樣我們可以進行對比了。

B： OK, wait a moment. 好的，稍等。

A： Wow, the actual sales figures have exceeded our expectation. 哇，實際銷售數據已經超出預期了。

B： Yes, we did a good job. 是的，我們做得不錯。

Scene 23　會議總結

Step 1　必備表達

總結	summarize：相當於 sum up 或 in summary。
重點	main point：表示「重點」的片語還有 key point。
推薦	recommend：在表達「向某人推薦⋯⋯」時可以用 recommend sth. to sb.。
時間不夠了	run short of time：類似表達還有 run out of time，表示「沒有時間了」。
簡言之	in brief：還可以用 in short 或者 in a word 來表達。
回顧	go over：還可用單字 review 來表達此意。
總之	in conclusion：同義表達還有 all in all。
結果	result：常用片語為 as a result，表示「結果是」。
調查	survey：還可以表示為 investigation 或 research。
考慮	consider：其形容詞 considerate 表示「體貼的」，considerable 表示「相當大的」。

Step 2　句句精彩

① 會議結束前，我來總結下重點。

A：So, we can close the meeting. 那麼，我們可以結束會議了。

B：Before we close today's meeting, let me just summarize the main points. 會議結束前，我來總結下重點。

Tips

■ The manager summed up and the meeting was over. 經理做了總結，會議就結束了。

■ Shall I go over the main points? 我們來回顧一下重點好嗎？

■ Before we call it a day, I have something to say. 結束之前，我有話要說。

② 我來快速回顧下今天的重點。

A： Let me quickly go over today's main points. 我來快速回顧下今天的重點。

B： Be all ears. 洗耳恭聽。

Tips

當表示會認真聽對方說話時，中文常說「洗耳恭聽」，對應的英文就是「be all ears.」。

Let's quickly run over our key points. 我們快速瀏覽一下要點。

Let's take a quick look back at what we talked about. 我們快速回顧一下我們所討論的問題。

③ 我們好像已經討論了所有的重點。

A： It looks as though we've covered the main items. 我們好像已經討論了所有的重點。

B： Let me check. 我來核對一下。

Tips

Is there anything else we need to discuss? 還有什麼其他要討論的嗎？

The meeting is focused on the subject of salary, and now we can close it. 會議主要是關於薪水的問題，現在可以結束了。

Do you have anything else to say? 還有什麼要說的嗎？

④ 因此我建議如下策略。

A： I don't think this strategy works. 我覺得這個策略不能奏效。

B： I therefore recommend the following strategy. 因此我建議如下策略。

Tips

work 除了可以表示「工作」，還可以表示「起作用」。

What would you do if you were me? 如果你是我，你會怎麼做？

Do you have any other suggestions? 你還有其他建議嗎？

⑤ 我們快沒有時間了。

A： We're running short of time. 我們快沒有時間了。

B： OK, tHere's one problem left. Let's discuss it quickly. 好的，還剩下一個問題。我們快點討論。

Tips

I think that We're a little bit out of time today; we will talk about this next time. 我想我們快

沒時間了，下次再討論吧。

■ Time is up, but I still want to talk about our management. 時間到了，但是我還是想說一下我們的管理問題。

■ Time is limited, and we will cut the meeting short. 時間緊迫，我們縮短會議。

⑥ 我們改日再討論那個問題。

A： We still have one problem open. 我們還有一個問題沒談。

B： We'll have to leave that to another time. 我們改日再討論那個問題。

Tips

■ open 在這裡用作形容詞，表示「懸而未決的」。

■ We will discuss it in next meeting. 我們下次會議討論。

■ This is the matter which will be further discussed next time. 這個問題下次再繼續討論。

Step 3　實戰對話

① 總結會議

A： Before we close today's meeting, let me just summarize the main points. 會議結束前，我來總結下重點。

B： How time flies! 時間過得真快啊！

A： Yes, we have talked about five points in this meeting. 是的，會議上我們討論了五個問題。

B： New book, the author, royalty on books, printing and layout. 新書、作者、版稅、印刷和版面。

A： Great, hope you can deal with them as soon as possible. 很好，希望你們能盡快處理好。

B： OK. We will give you a report next Monday. 好的，下週一我們會給您一份報告。

② 最後建議

A： I feel that our employees have little enthusiasm about work. 我覺得我們的員工對工作的熱情度不夠。

B： I therefore recommend the following strategy. We should give our employees some freedom. 因此我建議如下策略。我們應該給員工一些自由。

A： Like what? 比如說呢？

B： Like we can allow our employees to modify where and when their work is performed. 比如說我們可以讓員工靈活安排他們的工作時間和地點。

A： We have our regulations. 我們有制度的。

B： They don't come in conflict. 這並不衝突。

③ 結束議程

A： It looks as though We've covered the main items. 我們好像已經討論了所有的重點。

B： Yes, we have four points on the agenda, and all are finished. 是的，議程上我們有四項，都完成了。

A： Does anyone want to say something? 還有人要發言嗎？

B： Nope. 沒有。

A： OK, then I declare the meeting is over. 好吧，那我宣布會議結束。

B： Let's go back to work. 我們回去工作吧。

Scene 24　遺留問題

Step 1　必備表達

簽字	sign：其名詞形式是 signature，表示「簽名」。
簽到表	attendance sheet：attendance「出席，到場」。
忘記	forget：forget to do sth. 表示「忘記去做某事」；forget doing sth. 表示「忘記做過某事」。
提醒	remind：表示「提醒某人做……」要用 remind sb. to do sth.。
注意	pay attention to：注意這裡的 to 是介詞，後面要接名詞。
決定	decision：「做出決定」就是 make a decision。
沒用的	useless：-less 為形容詞尾碼，通常表示否定意義，比如 homeless「無家可歸的」。
忽略	neglect：還可用 ignore 或 be forgetful of 表示「疏忽」。
處理這個問題	address the matter：address 在這裡作動詞，表示「解決，處理」。
回饋	feedback：「資訊回饋」就是 information feedback。

Step 2　句句精彩

① 還有其他事嗎？

A：Any other business? 還有其他事嗎？

B：We need to tie up some loose ends. 我們還有一些收尾工作要做。

Tips

- 片語 tie up 在這裡表示「完成，結束」；loose ends 表示「零散資料；收場」。把這兩個片語放在一起就表示「完成收尾工作」。

- Well, I think that covers everything. Are there any questions? 好的，我覺得所有的議題都討論了，還有什麼問題嗎？

② 你們走之前，要在簽到表上簽字。

A：Before you leave, please make sure to sign the attendance sheet. 你們走之前，要在簽到表上簽字。

B：Oh, yeah, I almost forgot. 哦，是的，我差點忘了。

Tips

This is the sign-in sheet. 這是簽到表。

We will collect the attendance record right after the meeting. 會後我們會回收簽到表。

③ 我差點忘了，我們打算進行員工聚餐。

A：Anything else? 還有其他事嗎？

B：I almost forget to mention that We're planning a staff banquet. 我差點忘了，我們打算進行員工聚餐。

Tips

■ staff banquet 員工聚餐。

I have to remind you again that we have another meeting next week this time. 我不得不再次提醒你們，我們下週同一時間還有一次會議。

As you leave, don't forget to turn off the light. 離開的時候，別忘了關燈。

④ 你們出去時，別忘了把選票放到箱子裡。

A：don't forget to put your ballot in the box on your way out. 你們出去時，別忘了把選票放到箱子裡。

B：No problem. 好的。

Tips

ballot 表示「投票」，此外，還常用 vote 來表達此意，而「投票人」則是 voter。

I'd like to make another point, if That's all right. 如果可以，我想再說一點。

I hope we can bring up a better solution before the end of the meeting. 我希望在會議結束之前我們能找到更好的解決方案。

⑤ 大家能再注意下嗎？

A：Could I have your attention again? 大家能再注意下嗎？

B：Yes, what is it about? 好的，什麼事？

Tips

- Before we wrap up the meeting, I want to say one more point. 結束會議之前 我想再說一點。
- So, We're just about to finish. We have to make a decision. 好了，會議就要結束了，我們必須要做決定了。
- At the end of the meeting, I want to emphasize again. 會議結束之前，我想再強調一下。

⑥ 請大家把廢紙帶走，並把垃圾扔掉。

A： Please take all of your papers with you and throw out any garbage. 請大家把廢紙帶走，並把垃圾扔掉。

B： No problem. 好的。

Tips

- throw out 扔掉；garbage 垃圾。
- The last thing is to clean up the meeting place. 最後一項是打掃會場。
- Please clear up the conference place. 請清理好會場。

⑦ 感謝大家在百忙之中抽出時間來到這裡。

A： At the end of the meeting, again, I want to thank you all for taking time out of your busy schedules to be here today. 在會議最後，我想再次感謝大家在百忙之中抽出時間來到這裡。

B： Sorry to interrupt you, but I have one more question. 抱歉打斷你，但是我還有一個問題。

Tips

- take time out 抽出時間。
- I really appreciate your taking time to attend the meeting.
  非常感謝大家抽出時間來參加會議。
- I want to express my gratitude to you to be here. 我要向各位來參加會議表示感謝。

Step 3　實戰對話

① 簽到表

A： Any other business? 還有其他事嗎？

B： We need to tie up some loose ends. 我們還有一些事情沒有解決。

A： Before you leave, please make sure to sign the attendance sheet. 你們走之前，請在簽到表上簽字。

B： Oh, yeah, I almost forgot. 哦，是的，我差點忘了。

A： I go first. 我先走了。

B： OK. 好的。

② 會議遺漏問題

A： Anything else? 還有事嗎？

B： I almost forget to mention that We're planning a staff banquet. 我差點忘了，我們打算進行員工聚餐。

A： Bravo! 太棒了。

B： It seems to be the most favorite topic today. 好像這是今天最受歡迎的話題。

A： Of course, when should we have the staff banquet? 當然了，我們什麼時候聚餐？

B： Next Friday. 下週五。

③ 清理會場

A： Please take all of your papers with you and throw out any garbage. 請大家把廢報紙帶走，並把垃圾扔掉。

B： OK. 好的。

A： Ah, could you kindly return your chair to the next room? 對了，能把椅子放回隔壁房間嗎？

B： No problem. We will clean up the place. 沒問題，我們會清理好的。

A： Thanks a lot. 多謝。

B： That's OK. 沒問題。

Scene 25　會議結束

Step 1　必備表達

結束	wrap up：表達「結束會議」還可以用 close the meeting。
草稿	draft：還可以用 ground plan 代替。
著手做	go about：還可用 get down to、set about doing、set out to do 表示。
達成協定	get a deal：還可以用 reach an agreement 或 come to an agreement 代替。
著急走	rush off：相當於 go in a hurry。
解決	settle：同義表達還有 solve、work out、figure out。
原諒	forgive：相同含義的詞為 excuse，但是語氣比 forgive 弱。
遺漏	leave out：還可以用 miss 或 omit 代替。
認同	identify：常用片語為：identify as，表示「把……視為……」。
解決方案	solution：find out a solution 表示「找出解決方案」。

Step 2　句句精彩

① 感謝你們來參加今天的會議。

A：I'd like to thank you for coming to the meeting today. 感謝你們來參加今天的會議。

B： We are glad to be here today with you. 今天和您一起開會很高興。

Tips
- I appreciate your suggestions. 非常感謝你們提出的建議。
- Thanks for your participation. 感謝您的參與。

② 我們得結束這次會議了。

A： We have to wrap this meeting up. 我們得結束這次會議了。

B： OK, see you next time. 好的，下次見。

Tips

We have to cut the meeting short. 我們不得不縮短會議。

It's almost the time; Let's give it a close. 時間差不多了，我們要結束了。

Time went by so quickly. We are already at the end of this meeting. 時間過得真快，到了會議結束的時間了。

③ 我想每件事我們都討論過了。

A： I think We've covered everything. 我想每件事我們都討論過了。

B： Yes, we have discussed every issue on the agenda. 是的，議程上的每一項議題我們都討論過了。

Tips

The meeting ended and the problems were solved. 會議結束了，所有的問題都解決了。

If there are no further comments, we will finish. 如果沒有意見的話，我們要結束了。

We are finished ahead of schedule. 我們提前結束議程了。

④ 我會將資訊傳達給相關人員。

A： I'll pass on the info to the right folks. 我會將資訊傳達給相關人員。

B： It is very thoughtful of you. 你真細心。

Tips

在表示「資訊」時，通常會用 information，而 info 其實就是 information 的縮寫。

Our manager will see the meeting minutes. 我們經理會查看會議紀錄。

All content in this meeting are confidential. 會議的所有內容保密。

⑤ 很高興與你交談，但我必須走了。

A： It's been nice talking to you, but I must be going. 很高興與你交談，但我必須走了。

B： OK, see you around. 好的，回頭見。

Tips

I'm very sorry to rush off, but I have to meet someone in five minutes. 很抱歉我急著要走，我約了人 5 分鐘後見面。

Sorry, I've got to go now. 抱歉，我得馬上走。

Sorry, I have an urgent thing to do. 抱歉，我有急事要處理。

6 請原諒，10 分鐘後我有另一個會。

A： Please excuse me, but I have another meeting in ten minutes. 請原諒，10 分鐘後我有另一個會。

B： Then you'd better go now. 那你趕緊走吧。

Tips

- Could I consult something with you about the cost? 我能就成本問題諮詢一下你嗎？
- I'd love to, but I have an emergency to deal with. 我很願意，但是我有一個緊急事件要處理。
- Sorry to cut the meeting short, but we have an emergency here. 很抱歉縮短了會議，但是我們有緊急狀況。

7 會議結束了。

A： The meeting is closed. 會議結束了。

B： Thanks for your hard work. 辛苦了。

Tips

- I guess that will be all for today. 會議就到此結束了。
- Let's bring this to a close for today. 今天就到這裡結束吧。

Step 3 實戰對話

1 會議很成功

A： We're going to have to wrap this up. I'd like to thank you for coming to the meeting today. 我們得結束了。感謝你們來參加今天的會議。

B： We are glad to be here today with you. And this meeting is a success. 今天和您一起開會很高興。今天的會議也很成功。

A： Thank you. 謝謝。

B： You deserve it. 你應該受到這樣的表揚。

A： I hope that next meeting will be as successful as this one. 我希望下次會議也像這次一樣成功。

② 資訊傳達

A： The meeting is over. Hope you can carry out the decisions made in the meeting. 會議結束了，希望你們能夠執行會上的決定。

B： I'll pass on the info to the right folks. 我會將資訊傳達給相關人員。

A： OK, we will have another meeting on Friday. 好的，週五我們會召開另外一次會議。

B： Friday? I am afraid the timing is not good; we all have weekly conference on that day. 週五？恐怕這個時間不太好，我們週五那天都有例會。

A： Then we change the meeting to next Monday. 那麼我們把會議改到下週一吧。

B： OK. 好的。

③ 匆忙離開

A： It's nice to be here in the meeting with you. 和您一起開會真好。

B： It's been nice talking to you, but I must be going. 很高興與你交談，但我必須走了。

A： Sorry, but I have a question to ask you. 抱歉，但是我有一個問題想要問您。

B： Please excuse me, but I have another meeting in ten minutes. 請原諒，10 分鐘後我有另一個會。

A： Oh, sorry, I don't know you are in a hurry. 哦，抱歉，我不知道您著急。

B： It's OK. 沒關係。

Chapter

3

商務談判

Scene 26　即將談判

Step 1　必備表達

談判	negotiation：最常說的「商務談判」就是 business negotiation。
艱難的	tough：還可以用 difficult 或 hard 來代替。
和……談判	negotiate with：也可用 consult with 表示。
代表	representative：其動詞形式是 represent，也可以用 on behalf of... 來表達「代表」。
細節	detail：常和 in 搭配，構成 in detail，意思為「詳細地」。
即將	be about to：還可以用 will 或者 be going to 來代替。
即將來臨	around the corner：同義表達還有 approach。
緊張地	nervously：告訴別人別緊張，可以說「Take it easy.」。
談判中的一方	party：還可以用 side 代替。
參與	participate in：還可以用 take part in 表達。

Step 2　句句精彩

① 你認為該怎樣進行這次談判呢？

A：How would you like to proceed with the negotiations? 你認為該怎樣進行這次談判呢？

B：I think we should first talk about the long-term cooperation. 我認為我們首先應該談論長期合作。

Tips

■ proceed with 進行。

■ We need to know the bottom line. 我們需要知道底線。

■ Be honest in our communication. 真誠溝通。

② 你是不是很期待和他的談判？

A： Are you looking forward to the negotiation with him? 你是不是很期待和他的談判？

B： Yes, I have prepared for the negotiation for a long time. 是的，這次談判我準備很久了。

Tips

look forward to 表示「期待」，注意這裡的 to 是介詞，後面要接名詞或者動名詞。

We can control competitors in the first half. 我們可以在上半場控制住對手。

John will be responsible for the first round of negotiations. 約翰將負責第一回合的談判。

③ 這將會是一場艱難的談判。

A： It's gonna be a tough negotiation. 這將會是一場艱難的談判。

B： I prepared myself for the worst. 我做好了最壞的準備。

Tips

They ask for a slash price. 對方要求大幅度降價。

We hope the negotiation will put an end to the problem of debts. 我們希望這次談判能夠解決欠款問題。

We can't make any concessions this time. 這次我們不能做任何讓步。

④ 我會和代表討論所有細節。

A： I'll discuss everything with the representative. 我會和代表討論所有細節。

B： Every detail can decide whether it is successful or not. 每一個細節都能決定成敗。

Tips

Time and some other details can affect the result of the negotiation. 時間和其他一些細節都可以影響談判的結果。

We can start the talks with the lead time. 我們可以先從交付週期談起。

When you talk about the details, you should pay attention to their expressions. 當他們談論細節時，你應該關注他們的表情。

⑤ 我希望可以多討論價格的問題。

A： I hope we could discuss the price more. 我希望可以多討論價格的問題。

B： Price is the most difficult part to discuss. 價格是最難討論的部分。

Tips

■ Bargaining is the constant theme in every negotiation. 討價還價是每次談判持久不變的主題。

■ The main topic of this talk is about price. 這次談判的主題是價格。

■ We can give you a lot of reasons why we couldn't cut the price. 我們可以給你很多不能降價的理由。

⑥ 當你寫完草稿後我們會仔細檢閱。

A： When you get the draft written up, We'll look it over. 當你寫完草稿後我們會仔細檢閱。

B： OK, I will send it to you later. 好的，我一會兒發給你。

Tips

■ write up 詳細記載；look over 查閱。

■ Here is a copy of the itinerary we have worked out for you. 這是我們為你們擬定的活動排程。

■ We can seek some help from former negotiation cases. 我們可以從以前的談判案例中尋求幫助。

⑦ 他們明天會繼續談判。

A： They will carry on the negotiation tomorrow. 他們明天會繼續談判。

B： OK. We look forward to your good news. 好的。期待你的好消息。

Tips

■ This is only the first round of negotiation. 這僅是第一回合的談判。

■ What is your negotiating strategy for tomorrow? 你明天的談判策略是什麼？

■ I draw up a tentative plan for next round talks. 我為下一輪談判準備了臨時計畫。

Step 3　實戰對話

① 期待談判

A： How would you like to proceed with the negotiations? 你認為該怎樣進行這次談判呢？

B： I think we should make full preparations. And start with John. 我認為我們應該做

好充分的準備。然後從約翰下手。

A： Are you looking forward to the negotiation with him? 你是不是很期待和他的談判？

B： Yes, there is no better opponent than him. 是的，他是很好的對手。

A： We really need to be well prepared. 我們真的需要好好準備。

B： Without any doubt. 這一點毋庸置疑。

② 預測談判過程

A： It's gonna be a tough negotiation. 這將會是一場艱難的談判。

B： Sure it is. We must stand firm during the negotiation. 的確是。我們在談判中一定要堅定立場。

A： John will be responsible for the first round of negotiations. 約翰將負責第一回合的談判。

B： We can control competitors in the first half. 我們可以在上半場控制住對手。

A： Hope so. 希望如此。

B： Fighting! 加油！

③ 鎖定話題

A： I hope we could discuss the price more. 我希望可以多討論價格的問題。

B： Yes, price is primary. After settling down the price, we can talk about other details. 是的，價格是首要的。在價格確定後，我們可以討論一下其他細節。

A： I'll discuss everything with the representative. 我會和代表討論所有細節。

B： OK, what should I do? 我應該做些什麼？

A： Focus on price, and if they interrupt, you need to make them come back on the theme. 鎖定在價格上，如果他們打岔，你得把他們拉回到主題上來。

B： OK. 好的。

Scene 27　開始談判

概述	outline：該詞還可以表示「大綱」。
目標	objective：還可以用 purpose、target、goal 等詞來代替。
開始	get the ball rolling：roll 表示「滾動」，「讓球滾動起來」，隱含意思就是「開始」。
達成	achieve：還可以替換為 reach。
換個話題	change the topic：「話題」也可用 subject 表示。
討論……問題	take up the question of：這裡的 take up 相當於 discuss。
開門見山	come straight to the point：其中 come to the point 表示「直截了當地說」。
立刻	right away：還可以用 immediately 或 at once 表達「立刻，立即」。
合作條件	cooperation condition：「與……合作」可用片語 in cooperation with 表示。
提出	put forward：表示「提出」還可以用 come up with。

Step 2　句句精彩

① 我想概述一下我們的目標。

A：I'd like to outline our objectives. 我想概述一下我們的目標。

B：With some goals, we are sure of success. 有了目標，我們一定會成功。

Tips

■ The aim is to reach agreement with our customers. 目標是與客戶達成一致。

■ What was the original goal of the talks? 談判的最初目標是什麼？

■ We have established a negotiation target. 我們擬定了一個談判目標。

② 那我們先從價格開始談吧。

A： I'd like to get the ball rolling by talking about prices. 那我們先從價格開始談吧。

B： It is a sensitive topic. Let's talk about it later. 這是比較敏感的話題，我們一會兒再談吧。

Tips

At first, we want to talk about the new product. 首先，我們想談一下新產品。

Price is the only topic I want to talk now. 價格現在是我最想談論的話題。

Let's go into price first. 我們開始談論價格吧。

③ 我們想回顧一下上次會議的紀錄。

A： We'd like to review the notes on what We've discussed in the last meeting. 我們想回顧一下上次會議的紀錄。

B： OK. Let's see if there is any problem left. 好的，我們看看是否還有問題遺留。

Tips

Last time we turned to the question of packing. 上次我們談論到包裝的問題。

We discussed about your competitors last time. 上次我們談論了你的競爭對手。

We have talked about it in the last negotiation, but I want to talk it again this time. 我們上次談判談到了，但是這次我還想談。

④ 我們開始吧。

A： Let's get started. 我們開始吧。

B： OK, Let's begin. 好的，開始吧。

Tips

I'd like to begin by extending welcome. 讓我以歡迎開始話題吧。

Let's start off with the price. 讓我們從價格談起吧。

Shall we begin with a review of last time? 我們先回顧上次的內容吧，好嗎？

⑤ 大家都是熟人，我們就開門見山吧。

A： As we are familiar with each other, Let's come straight to the point. 大家都是熟人，我們就開門見山吧。

B： OK. what's the first item? 好的。第一項是什麼？

Tips

- Well, to come straight to the point, could you give us a discount on your new price? 那好，開門見山地說吧，新的價格能不能給個折扣？
- Let's get this straight. 開門見山吧。
- To speak frankly, your product is the same as your competitor's. 實話實說，你們的產品和競爭對手的一樣。

⑥ 我們談下一話題吧。

A： Let's move on to the next topic. 我們談下一話題吧。

B： With pleasure. 好的。

Tips

- I think We've talked enough about that. How about the next one? 我想這個話題談得差不多了，談下一個話題吧。
- This brings us to the next topic. 這就引出了下一個話題。
- The next topic focuses on the leading time. 下一個話題是關於交貨期的。

⑦ 我們討論商品檢驗問題好嗎？

A： Shall we take up the question of inspection? 我們討論商品檢驗問題好嗎？

B： OK, this is the most important topic. 這個是最重要的話題。

Tips

- We care most about the inspection. 我們最關心檢驗問題。
- We found some problems on your products during inspection. 我們在檢驗你們的產品時發現了很多問題。
- Inspection can avoid big loss. 檢驗可以避免大的損失。

Step 3　實戰對話

① 明確目標

A： I'd like to outline our objectives. 我想明確一下我們的目標。

B： The aim of the negotiation is to reach a win-win situation. 談判的目的是要達到雙贏的局面。

A： Yes, That's the objective. 是的，就是這個目的。

B： A win-win situation is the best result. But we both have our positions. 雙贏當然是最好的結果，但是我們雙方都有我們的立場。

A： So we have this negotiation. 所以才有這次談判。

B： You are right. 沒錯。

② 開始話題

A： I'd like to get the ball rolling by talking about prices. 那我們先從價格開始談吧。

B： The price is the key reason why we don't put any orders. 價格是我們不下訂單的主要原因。

A： We have reached agreement on the price last time. 上次我們就價格已經達成了一致。

B： But the market is changing; we have to change, too. 但是市場在變化，我們必須得改變。

A： The price we gave last time is our bottom line. 上次提供的價格已經是我們的底線了。

B： But your competitor offers us a lower price. 但是你們的競爭對手卻給我們報了一個更低的價格。

③ 回顧會議紀錄

A： We'd have to review the notes on what We've discussed in the last meeting. 我們想回顧一下上次會議的紀錄。

B： OK, we can know problems unsolved by doing this. 好，這樣我們可以知道還有哪些問題沒有解決。

A： That is our purpose. 我們就是這個目的。

B： We have solved a lot of issues last time. 上次我們解決了很多問題。

A： Yes, but the type of payment hasn't been determined. 是的，但是付款方式還沒有確定。

B： Well, Let's discuss it now. 嗯，那我們現在討論吧。

Scene 28 談論優劣

Step 1 必備表達

成本	cost：prime cost 是指「首要成本」；first cost 指「最初成本」。
品質	quality：quality control 意思為「品質控制」。
節省開支；走捷徑	cut corners：同義詞組為 take a short cut。
慷慨	generous：be generous with money 表示「在金錢方面慷慨」。
從……中獲益	profit from：相當於 benefit from。
交易	trade：表示「交易」的詞還有 transaction 和 deal 等。
競爭對手	rival：還可以用 competitor 表示。
和……競爭	compete with：compete 的名詞形式為 competition。
名聲	reputation：商業中的「信譽」可以用 credit 表示。
投資於	invest in：相當於 put money into。

Step 2 句句精彩

① 成本很重要，但是品質同樣重要。

A： The cost is important, but so is quality. 成本很重要，但是品質同樣重要。

B： The principle of our company is that quality is above all. 我們公司的宗旨是品質高於一切。

Tips

■ In no case can we lower the quality of products. 在任何情況下，我們都不能降低產品品質。

■ I can assure you that our product is of high quality. 我向您擔保我們的產品品質很好。

■ Our products are attractive in price and quality. 我們的產品物美價廉。

② 他的出價似乎很慷慨。

A： Your competitor provides us a very low price. 你的競爭對手給了我們一個很低

的價格。

B： His offer seems to be very generous. 他的出價似乎很慷慨。

Tips

The price you give can't cover our cost. 你提供的價格都不夠負擔成本。

Our price has already been lower than the prevailing market. 我們的價格已經低於當前的市場價了。

It is impossible to produce this item at this price. 以這個價格根本無法生產這種產品。

③ 他肯定會從這場交易中獲利。

A： You can bet that he'll profit from the deal. 他肯定會從這場交易中獲利。

B： But the price is reasonable. 但是價格很合理。

Tips

You can bet that... 表示「肯定」。

If you do properly, you can raise product quality without too much cost. 如果你做法適當，不需要太高成本你就能提高產品品質。

The deal itself is a success for you. 交易本身對你來說就是成功了。

④ 它容易使用。

A： It is user-friendly. 它容易使用。

B： All the similar products are like this. 所有類似產品都是這樣。

Tips

I mean it really uses easily; even children can handle it. 我的意思是它容易操作，連小孩子都會用。

The product has the advantage of compatibility. 產品的優點是它的相容性。

The key advantage of the product is the reduction of weight. 這個產品的主要優點是減輕了重量。

⑤ 為了和對手競爭，他降低了價格。

A： He has brought down the price in order to compete with his rivals. 為了和對手競爭，他降低了價格。

B： But the price is so attractive to us. 但是對我們來說，這個價格很有吸引力。

Tips

bring down「壓低」，同類片語包括：cut down、go down 等。

■ It is abnormal that the price he gave to you is lower than the cost. 他給你的價格比成本還低，這是不正常的。

■ I think the market needs fair competition. 我認為市場需要公平競爭。

⑥ 首先考慮一下公司的名聲。

A： First of all, consider the reputation of the company. 首先考慮一下公司的名聲。

B： Our company has been established for 20 years, and we really have a good reputation. 我們公司已經成立 20 年了，並且一直有著良好的聲譽。

Tips

■ We want a long term and stable partnership. 我們需要長期、穩定的合作關係。

■ Reputation is one of the most important factors when we choose partners. 名聲是我們選擇合作夥伴時看重的因素。

■ Although the price is high, your reputation is good. 雖然價格很高，但是你們的聲譽很好。

⑦ 我們關注兩個主要的方面。

A： There are two main areas that We'd like to concentrate on. 我們關注兩個主要的方面。

B： Be all ears. 洗耳恭聽。

Tips

■ We want to know your production capacity. 我們想了解你們的生產能力。

■ Do you have the quality certification? 你們有品質認證嗎？

■ Is your production line up to the standard? 你們的生產線符合標準嗎？

Step 3　實 戰 對 話

① 品質重要

A： The cost is important, but so is quality. 成本很重要，但是品質同樣重要。

B： The principle of our company is that quality is above all. 我們公司的宗旨是品質高於一切。

A：That's great. We want to find a partner who can produce high-quality product. 很好，我們要找能夠生產高品質產品的合作夥伴。

B： Our products are attractive in price and of high quality. 我們的產品物美價廉。

A： Can we take a look at some samples? 我們能看一下樣品嗎？

B： Sure. 當然。

② 產品優勢

A： What is the advantage of your product? 你們產品的優勢是什麼？

B： It is user-friendly. 它容易使用。

A： Can you say more about it? 您能詳細說說嗎？

B： I mean it really uses easily; even children can handle it. 我的意思是它容易操作，就連小孩都會用。

A： Really? I want to try. 真的嗎？我想試試。

B： Go ahead. 請吧。

③ 價格戰

A： He has brought down the price in order to compete with his rivals. 為了和對手競爭，他降低了價格。

B： But the price is so attractive to us. 但是對我們來說，這個價格很有吸引力。

A： It is abnormal that the price he gave to you is lower than the cost. 他給你的價格比成本價還低，這是不正常的。

B： Really? I don't know much about the market. 真的嗎？我對市場不是很了解。

A： This price can hurt themselves as well. 這個價格也會損害他們自己的利益。

B： I am a little confused. 我有點糊塗了。

Scene 29　討價還價

Step 1　必備表達

降低	bring down：表示「降低」的動詞有：reduce、lower、drop 等。
費用	fee：charge、price、expense 等都表示「費用」。
降價	lower the fee：相當於 cut price、reduce price。
折扣	discount：「打折」用片語 at a discount 表示。
取決於	depend on：類似的表達法有：up to、lie on、hang on。
數量	size：表示「數量」的詞有：quantity、amount、number 等。
單價	unit price：unit cost 及 price per unit 與此同義。
現金	cash：pay in cash 表示「以現金支付」。
付款	payment：payment term 表示「付款方式」。
討價還價	bargain：bargain on 表示「成交，商定」；這個詞作名詞還有「特價商品」的意思。

Step 2　句句精彩

① 我們來商討一下價錢。

A： Let's get down to the price. 我們來商討一下價錢。

B： OK. Here is our quotation. 好的。這是我們的報價單。

Tips

■ I have to talk with you about your quotation. 我不得不和您談一下報價。

■ Is there room to negotiate the price? 價格還有商談的餘地嗎？

■ We really want to cooperate with you except the price. 除了價格，我們真得很想與你合作。

② 你們可以把費用降低嗎？

A： Can you bring that fee down? 你們可以把費用降低嗎？

B： It's the rock-bottom price. 這是最低價了。

Tips

Can you reduce the price? 你們可以把價格降低嗎？

What can you afford? 你們能接受多少？

Could you kindly tell me your target price? 能告訴我您的目標價格嗎？

③ 讓事情更容易些怎麼樣？

A： How about making things less difficult? 讓事情更容易些怎麼樣？

B： What would you recommend? 你有什麼建議？

Tips

I wonder if you could make it easier. 你們能讓事情簡單些嗎？

Do you think you could try to make things easier? 你覺得你是否可以讓事情更容易些？

We can meet each other halfway. 我們可以各讓一步。

④ 這取決於你的訂購數量。

A： Can you offer a lower price? 你們能提供更低的價格嗎？

B： It depends on the size of the order. 這取決於你的訂購數量。

Tips

■ If you increase your order, we can give you a discount. 如果能夠提高訂單數量，我們將考慮給你一個折扣。

If you can raise the volume, we can offer you a better price. 如果你能增加訂購量，我們能提供一個更優惠的價格。

I want to put this order to you at your lowest price. 我希望以你們最低的價格下訂單。

⑤ 我原希望你們能降到 5 美元左右。

A： I was hoping you could lower the price to around $5. 我原希望你們能降到 5 美元左右。

B： The discount is too much for us to accept. 這折扣太低了，我們沒法接受。

Tips

I'm sorry. Our prices are already discounted. 很抱歉，我們的價格已經是折扣價了。

It is the wholesale price, not the retail price. 這是批發價，不是零售價。

We have provided you with the most favorable price. 我們已經為你提供最優惠的價格了。

⑥ 你們的折扣能提高到 8% 嗎？

A： Could you increase the discount to 8 percent? 你們的折扣能提高到 8% 嗎？

B： We will live with 5%. 我們能接受 5%。

Tips

- Is that your best offer? 這是你們最低的價格嗎？
- Sorry, it is the lowest price we can give. 抱歉，這已經是我們能給的最低價格了。
- If the payment term is 30 days after shipment, then it is ok. 如果貨運 30 天後付款的話就可以。

⑦ 買 100 件的話，你能給我多少折扣？

A： What kind of discount can you give me on a hundred pieces? 買 100 件的話，你能給我多少折扣？

B： I'll give you a 30% discount if you buy 100 pieces. 如果買 100 件，可以打 7 折。

Tips

- Do you give a special discount if we pay in cash? 如果我們付現金，你們能提供特殊折扣嗎？
- 100 pieces is the minimum order quantity and we may not give a discount. 100 件是最小起訂量，我們不提供折扣。
- We can give you 5% discount if you pay the freight. 如果你們付運費的話，我們提供 5% 的折扣。

Step 3　實戰對話

① 商討價格

A： Let's get down to the price. 我們來商討一下價錢。

B： The retail price is 5 dollars. 零售價是 5 美元。

A： Can you bring that fee down? 你們可以把費用降低嗎？

B： It's the rock-bottom price. 這是最低價了。

A： How about that we order more? 如果我們多訂一些呢？

B： It's really the base price. 這真的是底價。

② 訂購數量

A：How about making things less difficult? 讓事情更容易些怎麼樣？

B：What would you suggest? 你有什麼建議？

A：Can you offer a discount if we increase the quantity of the order? 如果我們增加訂貨量，你們能提供折扣嗎？

B：It depends on the size of the order. 這取決於你的訂購數量。

A：The total price for this order will be over million, if you give us a discount. 如果你能給一個折扣的話，這筆訂單的總價將達到百萬以上。

B：I'll talk with our manager. 我會和經理談談。

③ 降價幅度

A：I was hoping you could lower the price to around $5. 我原希望你們能降到 5 美元左右。

B：It is too much for us to accept. 這對我們來說沒法接受。

A：But I'm afraid we can't accept your price now. 但是恐怕我們無法接受你們目前的價格。

B：I'm sorry. Our prices are already discounted. 很抱歉，我們的價格已經是折扣價了。

A：Is that your best offer? 這是你們最低的價格嗎？

B：Yes, it is. 是的，的確是。

Scene 30 條件協商

Step 1　必備表達

代理	agency：sole agency 表示「獨家代理」。
延長	extend：extend business 表示「拓展業務」。
代理期	period of agency：agency agreement 表示「代理協定」。
建議	proposition：該詞用於較為正式的場合，如談判、合約等。
更多的選擇	bigger selection：這裡的 bigger 相當於 much more。
保證	guarantee：相當於 assure。
產品品質	product quality：improve product quality 表示「提高產品品質」。
線上支援	online support：online technical support 表示「線上技術支持」。
隨傳隨到	on call：相當於 on standby，即「待命」。
更多的折扣	deeper discount：deep discount 為固定搭配，表示「高折扣，較大折扣」。

Step 2　句句精彩

① 我們想成為貴公司的獨家代理商。

A：We would like to be the sole agent of your company. 我們想成為貴公司的獨家代理商。

B：You can participate in the bidding. 你可以參加投標。

Tips

■ We have an agent already. 我們已經有代理商了。

■ Welcome, but we have some special requirements. 歡迎，但是我們有一些特殊要求。

■ If you want to be our sole agent, we have to list some terms. 如果你想要成為我們的獨家代理，我們需要列出一些條款。

② 我們想將代理期延長 5 年。

A： We'd like to extend our period of agency by 5 years. 我們想將代理期延長 5 年。

B： I am afraid that we have to raise the commissions. 恐怕我們需要提高佣金了。

Tips

We accept that, but we have to change the payment term. 我們接受這一點，但是我們要更改付款方式。

We can't provide you such a long dealership. 我們無法提供這麼長時間的代理權。

■ We want to be the exclusive distributor for another five years. 我們想再做 5 年的獨家經銷商。

③ 這聽起來是個不錯的建議。

A： It sounds like an interesting proposition. 這聽起來是個不錯的建議。

B： We can talk about it further. 我們可以進一步談談。

Tips

The proposal is so attractive. 這個建議很吸引人。

Our manager shows interest in your idea. 我們經理對你的想法很感興趣。

We can explore the possibility of your proposition. 我們可以就你建議的可能性進行探討。

④ 只要你們保證下單 500 件，我們會考慮提供更多的選擇。

A： We could consider offering a bigger selection as long as you guarantee a 500-piece order. 只要你們保證下單 500 件，我們會考慮提供更多的選擇。

B： What will be the price if we buy 500 units? 購買 500 件的價格是多少？

Tips

There is no room to reduce the price. 沒有降價的空間了。

We give 2% discount if you pay in cash. 如果你們以現金付款，我們可以提供 2% 的折扣。

If you can place order continuously, we can give more discounts. 如果你可以連續下單，我們可以提供更多折扣。

⑤ 如果你們提供品質更好的產品，漲價可以接受。

A： A price hike would be accepted provided you offer product of better quality. 如果你們提供品質更好的產品，漲價可以接受。

B： I assure that the products worth these prices. 我保證這些產品物有所值。

Tips

■ price hike 漲價；provided 作連詞，表示「假如，倘若」，相當於 supposing。

■ We has been providing top quality products. 我們一直提供高品質的產品。

■ Of course we can have further discussion. 當然我們還可以商量。

⑥ 我們當然會提供線上支援。

A： Can you provide online support? 你們可以提供線上支援嗎？

B： We will definitely offer online support. 我們當然會提供線上支援。

Tips

■ Can you provide the drawing for this product? 你能為這款產品提供圖紙嗎？

■ We may need a technician to guide. 我們需要一個技術人員來指導。

■ We hope you sell the product to us only. 我們希望你們把產品只賣給我們。

⑦ 有隨時待命的技術人員很好。

A： It would be a good idea to have technicians on call. 有隨時待命的技術人員很好。

B： I feel the same way. 我也這樣認為。

Tips

■ Your suggestion would be successful if you can perfect it. 如果能完善一下，你的建議會獲得成功。

■ The service with your product will be popular in the market. 這項服務加上你們的產品將會在市場上大受歡迎。

■ We can undertake the cost to shipping. 我們可以承擔運輸費用。

Step 3　實戰對話

① 獨家代理

A： We would like to be the sole agent of your company. 我們想成為貴公司的獨家代理。

B： If you want to be our sole agent, we have to list some terms. 如果你想要成為我們的獨家代理，我們需要列出一些條款。

A： OK, we are here to talk with you. 好的，我們來這裡就是希望與你們協商的。

B： We stress that you can't make fake products. 我們強調不能有假貨。

A： Of course, we won't do this. 當然，我們不會這麼做的。

B： Then we can talk about the payment. 那我們可以談談有關付款的事情。

② 提出建議

A： It sounds like an interesting proposition. 這聽起來是個有趣的建議。

B： We can talk about it further. 我們可以進一步談談。

A： OK, do you mean you can offer a discount? 好的，你的意思是你們可以提供折扣？

B： Yes, but the volume of the order has to be increased. 是的，但是訂購量要增加。

A： What quantity do you want? 你希望我們定多少？

B： Double the order. 現有訂單的雙倍。

③ 額外服務

A： Can you provide online support? 你們可以提供線上支援嗎？

B： We will definitely offer online support. 我們當然會提供線上支援。

A： Is it free of charge? 是免費的嗎？

B： Yes, it is. 是的。

A： Great, then we can accept the price. 太好了，這樣的話，我們可以接受這個價格。

B： OK. We will send you the contract then. 好的。我們隨後會寄出合約。

Scene 31　做出讓步

Step 1　必備表達

達成一致	agree on：agree on the point「同意……」。
運費	shipping cost：同義詞組為：carriage charge；free shipment 可以表示「免運費」。
安裝	installation：installation guide 表示「安裝指導」。
論述	argument：同義詞為 contention。
打折	give a discount：表示「提供 n% 的折扣」可以用 give a n% discount。
支付	pay for：pay 的名詞形式是 payment。
接受	accept：表示接受某種條件時常用，如：accept the price 接受這個價格。
底線	bottom-line：bottom-line price 就是「最低價」的意思。
要求	demand：常用片語為：demand sb. to do sth. 要求某人做某事。
補償	compensate for：同義表述還有：make up for。

Step 2　句句精彩

① 我可以接受。

A：We can offer another 2% discount. 我們可以再提供 2% 的折扣。

B：I can live with it. 我可以接受。

Tips

- I think we could agree with that. 我想我們能夠同意。
- Can we make a compromise here? 我們能做個讓步嗎？
- I would like to make concessions. 我願意做出讓步。

② 既然我們就價格達成了一致，我覺得自己看到勝利的曙光了。

A： Now that we have agreed on a price, I think I can see light at the end of the tunnel. 既然我們就價格達成了一致，我覺得自己看到勝利的曙光了。

B：Yes, I will arrange the formal contract later. 是的，稍後我會安排簽署正式的合約。

Tips

now that 既然。

I am happy that we have reached an agreement finally. 我很高興最終我們達成了一致。

If that is your only condition, I would be happy to concede. 如果這是你的唯一條件，我願意讓步。

③ 我的論述最終說服他同意我的觀點。

A： My arguments at last brought him round to my point of view. 我的論述最終說服他同意我的觀點。

B： Good job. 做得好。

Tips

bring round 說服；同義詞組有：persuade sb.、talk into 等。

You convinced me and I will accept your price. 你說服了我，我接受你的價格。

We all leave the door open. 我們都留了餘地。

④ 我們可以打 8 折。這是我能提供的最低的折扣。

A： We could give a 20% discount. That's the best I can offer. 我們可以打 8 折。這是我能提供的最低的折扣。

B： That sounds good. 這樣很好。

Tips

That's acceptable. 可以接受。

As your wish. 如你所願。

We reach a mutual decision. 我們達成共識了。

⑤ 我們希望你給我們一個折扣。

A： We hope you'd give us a discount. 我們希望你給我們一個折扣。

B： I'll accept to lower one dollar per unit, but That's my bottom line. 我可以接受每件降低 1 美元，但是這是我的底線了。

Tips

- We will accept this price if you pay the installation fees. 如果貴方付安裝費的話，我們就接受這個價格。
- We should split the difference and make it halfway. 我們應該摒棄分歧，各讓一步。
- Sorry, it is already the bedrock price. 抱歉，這已經是最低價了。

⑥ 如果你們同意付所有的運費，我們就可以給你折扣。

A： If you agree to pay for all shipping costs, we could give you a discount. 如果你們同意付所有的運費，我們就可以給你折扣。

B： What kind of offer can you give? 你能提供什麼樣的折扣？

Tips

- Your price is too low. I have to ask our leader. 你的價格太低了，我需要請示一下領導。
- We can get you some discount then. 此外，我們會給你些折扣。

⑦ 對不起，如果由你們來支付安裝費，我們才可以給這個折扣。

A： I'm sorry, but we can't manage the discount unless you pay for the installation. 對不起，如果由你們來支付安裝費，我們才可以給這個折扣。

B： Yes, we are in charge of installation. 是的，我們負責安裝。

Tips

- We can't make it if you give us such a low price. 如果您出這麼低的價格，我們無法接受。
- If it is for export trade, we can give you a discount. 如果是出口的話，我們可以給你一個折扣。
- OK, I will accept this price. 好吧，我會接受這個價格。

Step 3 實戰對話

① 價格妥協

A： We can offer another 2% discount. 我們可以再提供 2% 的折扣。

B： I can live with it. 我可以接受。

A： Now that we have agreed on a price, I think I can see light at the end of the tunnel. 既然我們就價格達成了一致，我覺得自己看到勝利的曙光了。

B： Yes, please arrange the formal contract. 是的，請安排簽署正式的合約。

A： Hope we can cooperate happily. 希望我們合作愉快。

B： We will. 我們會的。

②　說服對方

A： what's the result? 結果怎麼樣？

B： My arguments at last brought him round to my point of view. 我的論述最終說服他同意我的觀點。

A： Good job! 做得好！

B： It's so difficult to persuade them. They asked deep discounts. 說服他們很艱難，他們要求了很高的折扣。

A： Every negotiation is a battle. 每項談判都是一場戰役。

B： I can't agree more. 我完全同意。

③　協商條件

A： We thought you'd give us a discount. 我們希望你給我們一個折扣。

B： If you agree to pay for all shipping costs, we could give you a discount. 如果你們同意付所有的運費，我們就可以給你折扣。

A： What discount can you give? 你能給什麼樣的折扣？

B： How about 5%? 九五折怎麼樣？

A： It's not attractive. We will accept a 7% discount. 這個價格不夠有吸引力。我們接受 7% 的折扣。

B： OK, It's the deal. 好，成交。

Scene 32 意見相同

Step 1 必備表達

同意某人的	agree with sb.：口語中可以用 you bet 或 you said it 對說話人的觀點表示觀點同意。
建議	suggestion：常用片語為 make a suggestion「提出建議」。
問題	problem：可以用 No problem. 表示「沒問題」。
傷害	harm：同義詞有：hurt、damage 等。
只要	as long as：與 so long as 同義，用於引導條件狀語從句。
假設	provided：相當於 if 的用法。
全體一致地	unanimously：相當於 with one mind。
贊成	approve of：「反對」則是 disapprove of。
意見	opinion：同義詞有 view、comment 等。
支持某人	on sb.'s side：等同於 back sb. up。

Step 2 句句精彩

① 這一點我同意。

A： We should give way for long cooperation. 為了長期合作，我們應該各讓一步。

B： I agree with you on that point. 這一點我同意。

Tips

■ That's a good point. 說的對。

■ You said it. 說的對。

■ You bet. 說的對。

② 這個建議不錯。

A： That's a fair suggestion. 這個建議不錯。

B： I am for it. 我贊成。

Tips

The advice did prove sound. 這個建議確實不錯。

The suggestion can fix all our problems up. 這個建議可以解決我們所有的問題。

③ 你說的很有道理。

A： We shouldn't make decision before we learn about the market. 我們不應該還不了解市場就做決定。

B： You have a strong point there. 你說的很有道理。

Tips

I will back you up. 我支持你。

I am in favor of you. 我支持你。

You convinced me to accept your conditions. 你說服我接受你們的條件了。

④ 我看不出那有什麼問題。

A： I don't see any problem with that. 我看不出那有什麼問題。

B： So do I. 我也是。

Tips

I didn't see any harm in that. 我覺得這不要緊。

I have no objection to this. 我同意。

Then we can sign an agreement. 那麼我們就可以簽協議了。

⑤ 我們同意那一點。

A： We agree with that. 我們同意那一點。

B： I am happy that we come to an agreement. 很高興我們達成了一致。

Tips

We reached a consensus on price. 我們就價格達成了一致。

We finally come to a decision. 我們終於定了下來。

I wholeheartedly agree with you. 我完全贊成你的觀點。

⑥ 你說得有道理。

A： You get what you pay. 一分價錢一分貨。

B： I come along with you at that point. 你說得有道理。

Tips

- You have a good point. 你說得有道理。
- It makes sense. 有道理。
- It sounds all reasonable. 有道理。

⑦ 我們非常感興趣。

A： Would you like to see our new products? 你們想看看我們的新產品嗎？

B： We are very interested. 我們非常感興趣。

Tips

- Yes, we are acquiring a taste for it. 是的，我們對此很感興趣。
- Can I have an eye on your new product? 我能看看你們的新產品嗎？
- Would you like to hear our suggestions? 願意聽聽我們的建議嗎？

Step 3　實 戰 對 話

① 觀點相同

A： We should give way for long cooperation. 為了長期合作，我們應該各讓一步。

B： I agree with you on that point. 這一點我同意。

A： So we will accept your price. 所以我們接受了你們的價格。

B： OK, we need a contract, and then we can produce. 好的，我們需要一份合約，然後才能生產。

A：I will send you the formal order as soon as possible. 我會盡快寄給你正式訂單的。

B： OK, thank you. 好的，謝謝。

② 表揚點子

A： That's a fair suggestion. 這個建議不錯。

B： I am for it. 我贊成。

A： It is beneficial for both of us. 這對我們雙方都有好處。

B： Yes, we achieve a win-win situation. 是的，我們達成了雙贏。

A： I will tell my boss to sign the contract with you. 我會告訴我的老闆，和你們簽合約。

B： OK, thank you for your cooperation. 好的，謝謝你們的合作。

③ 有道理

A： Our management can make sure of the quality of the product. 我們的管理可以保證產品品質。

B： I heard you had brought two image inspection machines. 我聽說你們購買了兩台影像檢測儀。

A： Yes, because we thought quality is the most important thing. 是的，因為我們認為品質是最重要的事情。

B： You have a strong point there. 你說得很有道理。

A：All the products will be inspected, so the cost is rising. 所有的產品都會經過檢測，所以成本就提高了。

B： If you can ensure the quality, we can bear the cost. 如果你們能保證品質的話，我們可以承擔費用。

A： I promise we will offer you topquality products. 我保證我們會提供給你品質最好的產品。

B： OK, I will sign the contract with you. 好的，我會和你簽合約。

Scene 33 意見不同

Step 1 必備表達

不同的	different：表示「不同的」的詞還有：diverse、varying、unlike 等。
不同意	disagree：常用片語為 disagree with「與……不同」；同義詞還有 disapprove。
立場	position：同義詞有 standpoint。
妥協	compromise：come to terms with、meet someone halfway 等也能表達同樣的意思。
觀點	perspective：常用搭配為 from the perspective of...；viewpoint 也有同樣的意思。
適用於	work for：同義詞組有 apply to、be applicable to 等。
可接受的	acceptable：常用 be acceptable to 表示「能被……接受」。
想法	idea：類似含義的詞還有 notion、concept 等。
意見衝突	a clash of opinions：表示「意見不合」的詞有：disagreement、dissension 等。
反對	object：object to「反對」，另外這個詞還有「物體、目標」的意思。

Step 2 句句精彩

① 恐怕這和我想的不一樣。

A： We can meet at $5. 我們可以把價格定為 5 美元。

B： I'm afraid I had something different in mind. 恐怕這和我想的不一樣。

Tips

■ Your thoughts didn't agree with mine. 你的想法和我的不一致。

■ Your idea doesn't fit in with mine. 我們想法不一樣。

■ Your thoughts doesn't work with mine. 我們想法不一致。

② 我不這麼看。

A： Your supplier can accept this price. 你們的供應商可以接受這個價格。

B： That's not exactly how I look at it. 我不這麼看。

Tips

I didn't look at it that way. 我不那麼認為。

The price of raw material is lowering, but the exchange rate is lowering, too. 原材料的價格降低了，但是匯率也降低了。

I don't think that way. 我不那麼認為。

③ 恐怕我們不同意你的觀點。

A： I'm afraid we can't agree with you there. 恐怕我們不同意你的觀點。

B： So what's your opinion? 那麼你們的想法是？

Tips

We don't want to make concessions. 我們不想讓步。

I understand your point of view, but I don't share it. 我理解你的觀點，但我並不認同。

I beg to differ from your comments. 對於你的看法，我不敢苟同。

④ 恐怕我們不能接受。

A： Our target price is 50% discount of the current price. 我們的目標價格是目前價格的一半。

B： I'm afraid That's not acceptable to us. 恐怕我們不能接受。

Tips

We can't take the price. 我們不能接受這個價格。

I'd like to work with you, but we can't accept the price. 我很想和貴方合作，但是這個價格我們不能接受。

I am afraid the price you offer is beyond our negotiation limit. 恐怕您的報價已經超過了我們談判的限度。

⑤ 恐怕這對我沒有用。

A： If you give us a discount, we can place a bulk order. 如果你能給我們折扣的話，我們可以大量訂購。

B： I'm afraid that doesn't work for me. 恐怕這對我沒有用。

Tips

■ It doesn't apply to me. 這對我不適用。

■ Your price is not competitive in the market and we can't accept it. 你的價格在市面上沒有競爭力，我們不能接受。

■ Does this sound too far-fetched? 這不是太牽強了嗎？

⑥ 我能用你之前提到的觀點嗎？

A： Can I just pick you up on a point you made earlier? 我能用你之前提到的觀點嗎？

B： It's quite suitable to this situation. 這非常適合這種情況。

Tips

■ Your point is inconsistent. 你的觀點前後矛盾。

■ I want to quote your word here. 在這裡我要引用你的話。

■ If you look at it from our point of view, you can understand that. 如果你從我們的觀點來看，就明白了。

⑦ 我不理解你的觀點。

A： I don't understand where you're coming from. 我不理解你的觀點。

B： I just quoted the data in this magazine. 我只是引用了這本雜誌中的資料。

Tips

■ I don't get it. 我不明白。

■ I don't get the picture. 我不明白。

■ I fail to understand your point. 我不明白你的觀點。

Step 3 實 戰 對 話

① 反駁觀點

A： We can meet at 5$. 我們可以把價格定在 5 美元。

B： I'm afraid I had something different in mind. 恐怕這和我想的不一樣。

A： Why? To be frank, your competitor offers us the same price. 為什麼？坦白講，你的競爭對手報給我們的就是這個價格。

B： The price can't cover the cost. We can't do business at a loss. 這個價格不夠負擔成本，我們不能做虧本生意。

A： But your price is much higher than $5. 但是你們的價格比 5 美元可高多了。

B： We use the high-quality raw material. 我們使用高品質的原材料。

②　無法達成一致

A： Your supplier can accept this price. 你們的供應商可以接受這個價格。

B： That's not exactly how I look at it. 我不這麼看。

A： Can you explain it further? 能進一步解釋一下嗎？

B： OK, I have checked the prevailing price in the market, and I know it is not ac-cpetable. 好的，我調查了市場上的普遍價格，我知道他們無法接受這個價格。

A： Can you change a supplier? 你們能換一家供應商嗎？

B： No, we have cooperated with this supplier for ten years. 不能，我們已經和這家供應商合作 10 年了。

③　提出想法

A： Our target price is 50% discount of the current price. 我們的目標價格是 5 折。

B： I'm afraid That's not acceptable to us. 恐怕我們不能接受。

A： If you give us a discount, we can place a bulk order. 如果你能給我們折扣的話，我們可以大量訂購。

B： I'm afraid that doesn't work for me. 恐怕這對我不適用。

A： Come on, we just want some discounts. 拜託，我們只是想要一些折扣。

B： The discount is so deep.We can't accept it. 這個折扣太高，我們沒法接受。

Scene 34 簽約之前

Step 1 必備表達

協議	agreement：也可以用 deal 表示「協議」。
條款	term：相當於 provision。
條件	condition：同義詞為 circumstance。
合約	contract：sales contract「銷售合約」；contract price「合約價格」。
簽約	sign：同義表達還有 subscribe。
一點一點的	point-by-point：構成方式類似 step-by-step「按部就班的」。
有效	be good for：表示「合約有效」可用形容詞 effective、valid 等。
生效	go into effect：同義詞組還有 in force、in effect 等。
兩份	duplicate：in duplicate 表示「一式兩份」。
三份	triplicate：triplicate form 表示「三聯單」。

Step 2 句句精彩

① 你同意這些交易條款和條件嗎？

A：Do you agree with the terms and conditions? 你同意這些交易條款和條件嗎？

B：Wait a moment, I want to see it again. 稍等，我想再看一遍。

Tips

■ How about considering item 2 and 5 again? 再考慮一下第二條和第五條怎麼樣？

■ I think we should amend some contract terms. 我想我們應該修改一些合約條款。

■ About the payment terms, I have some to say. 關於付款條款，我有話要說。

② 這份合約列出了我們討論過的一切。

A：I want to review the contract. 我想要再看一遍合約。

B：The contract lists everything We've discussed.

這份合約列出了我們討論過的一切。

Tips

Clarity and simplicity are important when drafting a contract. 起草合約時，清晰簡明很重要。

We suggest we should have lawyers draft contracts. 我們建議由律師起草合約。

I use the template to draft the contract. 我用範本來起草合約。

③ 在我們簽合約之前，我們要一點一點詳細看。

A： Before we sign, Let's go point-by-point. 在我們簽合約之前，我們要一點一點詳細看。

B： OK, take your time. 好的，請慢慢看。

Tips

Before the formal contract, we can now sign a pre-contract agreement. 正式簽合約之前，我們可以預先簽一份協議。

Do you have any additional clauses? 有附加條款嗎？

Before we sign this contract, can I confirm something? 在簽署這份合約之前，我能確認一下嗎？

④ 合約的有效期是多久？

A： How long is the contract good for? 合約的有效期是多久？

B： Three-year contract is to our mutual interest and profit. 3 年的合約符合我們的共同利益。

Tips

How long will the contract last? 合約的有效期是多長時間？

The minimum term of this agreement shall be one year. 這份協議的最短有效期是 1 年。

Would you mind if we make a two-year contract? 你是否介意與我們簽訂一份2年的合約？

⑤ 合約什麼時候生效？

A： When does the contract go into effect? 合約什麼時候生效？

B： The contract is effective today. 合約即日生效。

Tips

When does this new contract come into operation? 這份新合約什麼時候生效？

When do the contract come into force? 合約什麼時候生效？

From the signature date of the contract. 從合約簽署日起生效。

⑥ 合約需要一式兩份還是一式三份？

A：Does this contact need to be in duplicate or in triplicate? 合約需要一式兩份還是一式三份？

B：In duplicate. 一式兩份。

Tips

- Any amendment to this contract will become effective. 對合約的修改也會生效。
- This agreement is in duplicate and each of the parties has one copy. 本協議一式兩份，雙方各執一份。
- This contract is in two copies, and will be effective from signing. 本合約一式兩份，自簽署之日起生效。

⑦ 還有什麼問題麼？

A：Any questions? 還有什麼問題麼？

B：Nope. There is no question. 不，沒有問題了。

Tips

- Anything else before we sign the contract? 簽合約之前還有其他問題嗎？
- I think we both agree to these terms. 我想我們雙方都同意了這些條款。
- It's not signed yet, but there is no problem. 合約還沒有簽，但是沒什麼問題了。

Step 3　實戰對話

① 合約條款

A：Do you agree with the terms and conditions? 你同意這些交易條款和條件嗎？

B：Wait a moment, I want to see it through. 稍等，我想仔細看看。

A：Go ahead. 請看吧。

B：About the payment terms, I have something to say. I think we have agreed on 45 days after delivery, not 30 days. 關於付款條款，我有話要說。我想我們已經就發貨後 45 天達成了一致，而不是 30 天。

A：Sorry, I will check it. 抱歉，我看一下。

B：OK. 好的。

② 合約有效期

A： Before we sign, Let's go point-by-point. 在我們簽合約之前，我們要一點一點詳細看。

B： OK, take your time. 好的，請看吧。

A： How long is the contract good for? 合約的有效期是多久？

B： Three years, which is to our mutual interest and profit. 3 年，這符合我們共同的利益。

A： I agree with that. 我同意。

B： Well, please go on. 好的，請繼續。

③ 合約生效

A： When does the contract go into effect? 合約什麼時候生效？

B： The contract is effective today. 合約即日生效。

A： It will be effective as soon as we sign it, right? 我們一簽署馬上就生效，對嗎？

B： Yes, you are right. 是的，你說得對。

A： Then I decide to sign today. 那麼我決定今天簽署。

B： Great! 太好了！

Scene 35 談判期間

Step 1 必備表達

改變	make the change：相當於動詞 modify、alter、transform 等。
要求	ask for：同義詞還有 demand、require 和 request 等。
預期	expectation：還可用 prospect 表示。
終止	terminate：terminate contract 意思為「終止合約」。
範圍	league：除了「聯盟」，這個詞還可以表示「範疇」。
準確的	accurate：相當於 precise。
訂單	order：常用片語有 purchase order，表示「訂貨單」。
律師	attorney：lawyer 泛指律師，deputy 表示「代理人」。
確保	make sure：相當於 make certain、ensure。
估計	pricing estimate：estimate「估計」。

Step 2 句句精彩

① 我們照你們的要求做了修改。

A： We made the changes according to what you asked. 我們照你們的要求做了修改。

B： Great. Can you send me the new version again? 好的。你能把新版本發給我嗎？

Tips

■ Any modification of the contract should be agreed by both parties. 任何對合約的修改都需要經雙方同意。

■ I made some alternations to the terms of the contract. 我對合約的一些條款做了改動。

■ The words in the contract are not accurate. 合約裡的詞用得不準確。

---

② 如果銷售達不到我們的預期，合約即可終止。

A： If sales don't meet our expectations, the contract can be terminated. 如果銷售達不到我們的預期，合約即可終止。

B： We will do according to the contract. 我們會按照合約上寫的做。

Tips

meet one's expectation 滿足......的期望

How would you like to modify it? 你想怎麼修改？

According to the contract, we are entitled to stop the contract. 根據合約 我們有權終止合約。

---

③ 我們需要幾天時間來考慮。

A： If you have no question, we can sign the contract. 如果你沒有什麼問題，我們可以簽合約了。

B： We'll need a few days to consider. 我們需要幾天時間來考慮。

Tips

Would you be willing to sign the contract right now? 您願意馬上簽合約嗎？

I will arrange the time to meet again. 我會安排時間再見面。

I will send a clean contract to you after the modification. 修改後，我重新寄一份合約給您。

---

④ 這不在我的許可權範圍內。

A： I want to add some items here,OK? 我想在此處增加一些條款，行嗎？

B： This is getting out of my league. 這不在我的許可權範圍內。

Tips

out of sb's league 不在某人的權力範圍內；league 在這裡相當於 extent of authority。

■ Sorry, I must consult with my boss. 抱歉，我必須要和我的老闆商量一下。

We want to postpone the signing of the contract. 我們想推遲合約的簽訂。

---

⑤ 你給了我更準確的預估數字，我才能確認訂單。

A： Can you confirm the order? 你能確認一下訂單嗎？

Tips

I can't place an order before you give me a definite price. 在你沒有給出確定價格之前，我不能下單。

Can you confirm the delivery time with me? 你能和我確認一下發貨時間嗎？

We'd like you to give us a week. 我們希望你們給我們一周時間。

■ I find a bit unusual in the contract. 我在合約中發現了一些問題。

⑥ 我們必須先跟老闆談談，再達成一致。

A： We have to change the payment term. 我們要改一下付款方式。

B： I need to talk with my boss before we agree on anything. 我必須先跟老闆談談，再達成一致。

Tips

■ I can't make any promises before I get the permission. 未經許可，我不能做出任何保證。

■ I'm afraid that I can't make a decision now. 恐怕我現在沒法做出決定。

■ My superior has not replied to me by now. 我的上司到現在還沒有答覆我。

⑦ 我們的律師會仔細檢查合約，以確保所有細節無誤。

A： When can I receive the signed contract? 我什麼時候能拿到簽好的合約呢？

B： Our attorneys will look it over to make sure all the details are correct. 我們的律師會仔細檢查合約，以確保所有細節無誤。

Tips

■ We need an attorney to prove the validity of the contract. 我們需要一位律師來證明合約的有效性。

■ Our attorney found a small mistake in the contract. 我們的律師在合約中發現了一處小錯誤。

■ We will sign the contract accompanied by the lawyer. 我們將在律師的陪同下簽署合約。

Step 3　實戰對話

① 修改合約

A： We made the changes according to what you asked. 我們按照你們的要求做出了修改。

B： Great, can you send me the new version? 好的，你能把新版本發給我嗎？

A： OK. I will send the contract to you via e-mail. 好的。我把合約用電子郵件發給你。

B： OK, do you have my e-mail address? 好的，你有我的信箱地址嗎？

A： Yes. And if you have any questions, please feel free to ask me. 有的。如果你有任何問題，儘管問我。

B： OK, thank you. 好的，謝謝。

② 再三考慮

A： If sales don't meet our expectations, the contract can be terminated. 如果銷售達不到我們的預期，合約即可終止。

B： We will do according to the contract. When can we sign the contract? 我們會按照合約上的做。我們什麼時候可以簽合約？

A： We'll need a few days to consider. 我們需要幾天時間來考慮。

B： OK, but we are looking forward to your early reply. 好的，但我們希望您盡快回覆。

A： Sorry for keeping you waiting so long. 抱歉讓你等這麼久。

B： No problem. 沒關係。

③ 請示上級

A： I want to add some items here, OK? 我想在此處增加一些條款，行嗎？

B： This is getting out of my league. 這不在我的許可權範圍內。

A： This is the last point, then we can sign the contract. 這是最後一點，然後我們就可以簽合約了。

B： I need to talk with my boss about this before we agree to anything. 我必須先跟老闆談談，再達成一致。

A： OK, wait for your good news. 好吧，等你的好消息。

B： I will reply to you as soon as possible. 我會盡快答覆你。

Scene 36 簽訂合約

Step 1 必備表達

出差錯	put a foot wrong：相當於 make mistake。
標準合約	normal contract：contract expiration 則指「合約有效期限」。
修改	modify：相當於 amend 或 alter。
餘地	leeway：同義詞為 room；have leeway 表示「留有餘地」。
以書面形式	in writing：片語 agree in writing 表示「書面約定」。
感謝	appreciate：highly appreciate 即「充分肯定」。
合作	cooperation：in cooperation with 表示「與……合作」。
指定日期	indicated date：indicated「指定的，指明的」。
違反	in breach of：與 violate 的意思相近。
取消訂單	cancel the order：cancel「取消」。

Step 2 句句精彩

① 整個談判過程微妙複雜，但他沒出一點差錯。

A： Throughout the delicate negotiations, he never put a foot wrong. 整個談判過程微妙複雜，但他沒出一點差錯。

B： He is cautious and careful. 他細緻謹慎。

Tips

■ You cut a figure in this negotiation. 在這次談判中，你嶄露了頭角。

■ I have to admit that you are an excellent rival. 我不得不承認，你是一位出色的對手。

■ You made a good turning point in this talk. 你在談判中製造了一個出色的轉捩點。

② 這個條款是我們標準合約的一部分。

A： I don't understand this provision. 我不理解這個條款。

B： That provision is part of our normal contract. 這個條款是我們標準合約的一部分。

Tips

We are suggested to use standard contract. 有人建議我們使用標準合約。

Such provisions are the regular part of a construction contract. 這些是建築合約的常規條款。

Can we cancel the item in this contract? 我們能刪除合約裡的這個條款嗎？

③ 你認為這可以修改嗎？

A： Do you think you could modify it? 你認為這可以修改嗎？

B： I don't think so. 我不這樣認為。

Tips

If we change the word here, the whole content in the contract will alter. 如果我們修改了這裡的這個詞，那麼整個合約內容就變了。

I want to amend the number in the contract. 我想改正合約中的這個數字。

The item is included in all our contracts. 這條包含在我們所有的合約之中。

④ 如果你給我們更多的餘地，我們會感覺更好。

A： We'd feel better if you'd give us a little more leeway. 如果你給我們更多的餘地，我們會感覺更好。

B： I will discuss with my manager. 我會和我們經理商量一下。

Tips

We need to allow for unforeseen circumstances. 我們需要為不可預見的情況留餘地。

How about the unpredictable circumstances and needs? 不可預測的情況該怎麼辦？

We should add some exceptional circumstances. 我們應該增加一些特殊情況。

⑤ 我覺得我們應該把這點寫進來。

A： I think we should get this in writing. 我覺得我們應該把這點寫進來。

B： OK, I agree with you. 好吧，我同意。

Tips

I'd like to put all agreements down in black and white. 我想把所有的約定都白紙黑字地寫出來。

Only written in the contract can the items be effective. 只有寫在合約中的條款才可以生效。

Are we anywhere near a contract yet? 我們可以簽合約了嗎？

⑥ 我覺得我們都同意這些條款。

A：I think we both agree to these terms. 我覺得我們都同意這些條款。

B：Yes, you are right. 是的，沒錯。

Tips

- I'm satisfied with this decision. 我對這個決定很滿意。
- It sounds like We've closed the gap. 看來我們已經消除了分歧。
- I'm sure We'll sign a new contract. 我確定我們會簽一份新合約。

⑦ 感謝你們在談判期間的配合。

A：I have appreciated your cooperation throughout the negotiations. 感謝你們在談判期間的配合。

B：Same here. 我也感謝你。

Tips

- I hope We'll be good business partners from now on. 我希望我們從此將成為最好的生意夥伴。
- These negotiations with you turned out to be successful. 與貴方的談判最終非常成功。
- We hope a further cooperation in the future. 希望我們未來能有進一步合作。

Step 3　實戰對話

① 質疑條款

A：I don't understand this provision. 我不理解這個條款。

B：That provision is part of our normal contract.
這個條款是我們標準合約的一部分。

A：But I think that we don't need it. 但是我認為我們並不需要。

B：In fact, it is important to both of us. 事實上，這對我們都很重要。

A：Do you think you could modify it? 你認為這可以修改嗎？

B：I don't think so. 我不這樣認為。

② 留有餘地

A：We'd feel a lot better if you'd give us a little more leeway. 如果你給我們更多的餘

地，我們覺得更好。

B： Sorry, but we can't give you too much leeway. 抱歉，但是我們沒辦法給貴方太多的餘地。

A： How about the unpredictable circumstances and needs? 不可預測的情況該怎麼辦？

B： We have included it in Article 5. 第五條已經包括了。

A： Can you explain it more? 你能再解釋一下嗎？

B： We have explained it. 我們解釋過了。

③ 消除分歧

A： We solved all the problems. 我們解決了所有問題。

B： It sounds like We've settled the differences. 我覺得我們都同意這些條款。

A： I think we both agree to these terms. 看來我們已經消除了分歧。

B： Yes. We will sign the contract tomorrow morning. 是的。我們將在明天上午簽合約。

A： Great! Thank you. 太好了，謝謝。

B： It's a win-win cooperation. 這是個雙贏的合作。

Chapter

4

貿易往來

Scene 37 訂購詢問

Step 1 必備表達

訂購	place an order：order 本身有「訂購」的意思；place 在這裡指「下單」的動作。
庫存	in stock：相當於 merchandise on hand。
無現貨	out of stock：同義詞組為 sell out。
立即出貨	immediate delivery：相當於 prompt delivery。
可用的	available：這裡相當於「有現貨」的意思。
詢問	enquire：常用片語為 enquire about「詢問」。
幾個	a couple of：同義詞還有 few、several。
報價	quote：quoted price 是「報出的價格」；名詞 quotation 則是「報價單」。
最低價	the lowest price：同義詞組為 bottom price。
付得起	affordable：affordable price 意思為「公道的價格」。
報價，報盤	offer：在貿易往來中，賣方向買方報價叫作「報盤」。

Step 2 句句精彩

① 我對你們的產品感興趣，我想知道價格。

A： I'm interested in your products and I'd like to know the prices. 我對你們的產品感興趣，我想知道價格。

B： OK, could you kindly tell me the order quantity? 好的，您能告訴我訂購數量嗎？

Tips

■ We'd like to place an order for your new product. Could you tell me the price? 我很想訂購你們的新產品，能告訴我價格嗎？

■ I want to inquire about the price. 我想詢問一下價格。

■ I received an inquiry from a firm today. 我今天收到了一家公司的詢盤。

② 我想訂購 1000 組晶片。

A：What quantity do you want? 你想要多少？

B：I'd like to place an order for 1,000 chips. 我想訂購 1000 組晶片。

Tips

If your price is reasonable, we will place a trial order for 50 units. 如果價格合適的話，我們想先試訂 50 件。

If you want to order, do it today for the price is changing. 如果你想訂購的話，今天就定吧，因為價格是變化的。

The initial order is subject to a discount of 15%. 第一次下單享受 85 折優惠。

③ 你們還有庫存嗎？

A：Have you got any more in stock? 你們還有庫存嗎？

B：I have checked our system and we have 50,000 pieces in stock. 我查過系統，我們還有 5 萬件庫存。

Tips

Do you have such kind of product in stock? 這類產品有現貨嗎？

Are the products available from stock? 這些產品有現貨嗎？

Sorry, we just have semi-finished products now. 抱歉，現在我們只有半成品。

④ 現在我們沒有這種桌子。

A：Now We're out of the table. 現在我們沒有這種桌子。

B：Then what is the lead time? 那麼交付週期是多久？

Tips

■ The goods you want are no longer in stock. 您想要的商品沒貨了。

The one you want are sold out. 你要的這種賣完了。

Sorry, we are under stock. 抱歉，我們庫存不足。

⑤ 你們的產品能馬上出貨嗎？

A：Are your products available for immediate delivery? 你們的產品能馬上出貨嗎？

B：Yes, they are all ready-made. 是的，都是現成的。

Tips

What is the fastest delivery time? 最快出貨時間是多久？

Have you got any at hand? 你們有現貨嗎？

■ Yes, we offer spot trading. 是的，我們提供現金現貨交易。

⑥ 我們需要加訂杯子，可以嗎？

A： We need to put in an order for more cups, is it OK? 我們需要加訂杯子，可以嗎？

B： How about the delivery time? 什麼時間交貨呢？

Tips

■ We want to renew our order to increase the quantity. 我們想續訂並增加訂購數量。

■ Could we increase the order within the original delivery time? 我們能按原定的交貨時間增加訂量嗎？

■ We need to take a larger quantity. 我們需要加大訂量。

⑦ 我想知道你們公司有沒有彩燈出售。

A： I'd like to know whether your company sells colorful lights. 我想知道你們公司有沒有彩燈出售。

B： Can you tell me the type? 能告訴我型號嗎？

Tips

■ I can send you some pictures to confirm. 我可以給你發一些照片以便確認。

■ Could you produce as the drawing shows? 你們能按照圖紙生產嗎？

■ I hear that you are the sole agent of this product. 我聽說你們是這種產品的獨家代理商。

Step 3　實 戰 對 話

① 詢問價格

A： I'm interested in your products, and I'd like to know the prices. 我對你們的產品感興趣，我想知道價格。

B： OK, could you kindly tell me the order quantity? 好的，你能告訴我訂購數量嗎？

A： I'd like to place an order for 1,000 chips. 我想訂購 1000 組晶片。

B： The initial order is subject to a discount of 15%. 第一次下單享受 85 折優惠。

A： Could you give me more discounts? 能再多給點折扣嗎？

B： I am afraid not. 恐怕不行。

②　詢問庫存

A： Have you got any more in stock? 你們還有庫存嗎？

B： I have checked our system and we have no more in stock. 我查過系統，我們沒有庫存了。

A： Then what is the lead time? 那麼交付週期是多久？

B： What quantity do you want? 你需要多少呢？

A： 200 units. 200 件。

B： So It's about 30 days. 那就是大約 30 天。

③　詢問是否有現貨

A： Are your products available for immediate delivery? 你們的產品能馬上出貨嗎？

B： If you order now, the goods will be prepared for immediate delivery. 如果你現在下單的話，可以立刻交貨。

A： Great! Do you have 500 pieces? 太好了，有 500 件嗎？

B： Yes, we have. 有的。

A： I will put the order right now. 我現在就下訂單。

B： OK. Please fax the order to me. 好的。請把訂單傳真給我吧。

Scene 38　買方詢價與回應

Step 1　必備表達

大概的	rough：表示「大概的意思」，含義相當於 gross。
定價	fixed price：同義表達為 one price，即「固定價格，不二價」。
對……收費	charge for：charge 即有「收費」的意思。
批發	wholesale：可以解釋為 sale by bulk。
大尺寸	large size：表示「尺寸」可以用 size。
豪華的	deluxe：相當於 advanced 或 luxurious。
數量	quantity：quantity of 表示「……的數量」。
每個	apiece：相當於 each。
出價	bid：常用片語為 bid price「投標價格」。
偏高	on the high side：可以用來描述價格，相當於 higher。
報價單	quotation：quotation sheet 也表示「報價單」。

Step 2　句句精彩

① 可以給我個大概的報價嗎？

A： Can you give me a rough idea of the price? 可以給我個大概的報價嗎？

B： $50 per suit. 每套 50 美元。

Tips

■ The machine is quoted $50 per unit. 這種機器的報價為每套 50 美元。

■ The validity of this quotation sheet is a month. 報價單的有效期是一個月。

■ Could you kindly quote on this machine? 你們能報一下這台機器的價格嗎？

② 冷氣的單價是多少？

A： What is the unit price of the air-conditioner? 冷氣的單價是多少？

B： The price is 2,250 yuan. 價格是 2250 元。

Tips

Could you give me a reference price? 能給我一個參考價格嗎？

Do you want the price including tax or not? 你要含稅價還是不含稅價格？

The tax price is a little higher. 含稅價格有點高。

③ 1000 件多少錢？

A：How much for 1,000 units? 1000 件多少錢？

B：We can give you a wholesale price. 我們可以給你批發價。

Tips

It's $350 including the tax. 含稅價格為 350 美元。

To be frank, your price is on the high side. 說實話，你們的價格偏高。

We give 5% discount every 1,000 units. 每 1000 件有 5% 的優惠。

④ 基本款的你們賣多少錢？

A：The price differs from type to type. 不同類型價格不同。

B：How much are you charging for the basic model? 基本款的你們賣多少錢？

Tips

■ basic model 基本款。

How much should we pay for the deluxe version? 豪華版的多少錢？

What about the large-size? 大尺寸的呢？

⑤ 你們的批發價是多少錢？

A：what's your wholesale price? 你們的批發價是多少錢？

B：It's already our wholesale price. 這已經是批發價了。

Tips

I'm afraid that price is beyond my budget. 恐怕這個價格超出了我的預算。

What the price will be if we buy 1,000 units? 如果我們購買 1000 件，價格是多少？

You can get the product at our wholesale price. 你可以以批發價拿到這種產品。

⑥ 你們的報價是離岸價還是到岸價？

A：Do you offer FOB or CIF? 你們的報價是離岸價還是到岸價？

B：Both, it is up to you. 都有，這取決於你。

Tips

■ Do you charge for the freight? 你們會收取運費嗎？

■ It is $18.96, FOB. 離岸價格是 18.96 美元。

■ We can offer both FOB and CIF. 離岸價和到岸價都可以報。

⑦ 只有這個月訂購，單價才是 30 美元。

A： You mean you can give us a discount if we order, right? 你的意思是如果我們下訂單，你就會提供折扣，對嗎？

B： For this month only, the price is $30 a piece. 只有這個月訂購，單價才是30美元。

Tips

■ Yes, we don't offer unit price. We only quote wholesale price. 是的，我們不提供單價，只報批發價。

■ Thanks for your inquiry, but the unit price is fixed price. 謝謝您的詢價，但是單價是固定價格。

■ We give discounts only for this special product. 只有這種特殊產品才有折扣。

Step 3　實戰對話

① 買方詢價

A： Can you give me a rough idea of the price? 可以給我個大概的報價嗎？

B： I can send you a quotation list. 我可以寄報價單給您。

A： I am interested in the air-conditioner. What is the unit price of the air-conditioner? 我對冷氣很感興趣，冷氣的單價是多少？

B： The price is 2,250 yuan. 價格是 2250 元。

A： And the price is negotiable, right? 價格是可以商量的，是嗎？

B： Yes. If you order more than 1,000 units, we can offer a discount. 是的。如果你們訂購超過 1000 件，我們可以提供折扣。

② 詢問價格

A： The price is different from type to type. 不同類型價格不同。

B： How much are you charging for the basic model? 基本款的你們賣多少錢？

A： $350 per unit for the basic one. 基本款每件 350 美元。

B： And how about the deluxe one? 那麼豪華版的呢？

A： It is a little higher, $380. 這個貴一點，380 美元。

B： Umm, let me see. 嗯，讓我想想。

③ 報價方式

A： Do you offer FOB or CIF? 你們的報價是離岸價還是到岸價？

B： I can offer you both. 我們都可以報。

A： what's the CIF price? 到岸價是多少錢？

B： $58 per piece. 每件 58 美元。

A： We will order 2,000 pieces. When will you arrange the insurance? 我們要訂購 2000 件。你們什麼時候辦理保險事宜？

B： As soon as we receive the contract. 拿到合約即可辦理。

Scene 39　報價與回應

Step 1　必備表達

市場價	market price：指通常在市場上出售的價格，一般作參考用。
免費送貨	free delivery：「免運費」還可以用 free shipping 表示。
殺價	drive a hard bargain：相當於 cut price，slash price 等。
直接切入	cut to the chase：同義詞組有 come straight to the point 和 get down to brass 重點 tacks。
貨比三家	shop around：由「到處逛」的含義引申為「貨比三家」；同類表達還有 comparison shopping「對比購物」。
供應商	supplier：同義詞為 provider。
標準價格	standard price：相當於 standard rate。
議價能力	negotiating power：也可以用 bargaining power 表示。
不可議價	no-bargaining：相當於 nonnegotiable。
範圍	scope：常用表達為 with the scope of「在……範圍之內」。

Step 2　句句精彩

① 你覺得一組 100 美元怎麼樣？

A：What do you think about $100 a set? 你覺得一組 100 美元怎麼樣？

B：Your target price is too low to accept. 你的目標價格太低，無法接受。

Tips

■ Could you kindly cut some price? 能不能降低一些價格？

■ Can you bring that price down? 能便宜一些嗎？

■ Can you give me an extra 10% off? 還能再給我打 9 折嗎？

② 市場價大概是 2 萬美元。

A：Market price is around $20,000. 市場價大概是 2 萬美元。

B：But as supplier, your price is a little high. 但是作為供應商，你們的價格有點高。

Tips

> Do you think I can have a discount? 可以給我打折嗎？
> Can I make a counter-offer? 我可以還價嗎？
> Our counter-offer is as follows. 我們的還價如下。

③ 我們出價 10 美元。

A：How much are you willing to pay? 你願意出多少錢？

B：We are prepared to offer $10. 我們出價 10 美元。

Tips

> ■ Your counter-offer is not up to the present market level. 你的反要約不符合目前的市場價格。
> We can not make a business with no profit. 我們不能做賠本生意。
> You are so good at bargaining. 你太能講價了。

④ 恐怕這個報價太高了。

A：I'm afraid that price is too high. 恐怕這個報價太高了。

B：It is the cost price. 這是成本價。

Tips

> The price includes the delivery fee. 這個價格包含運費。
> The price is out of the way. 這個價格太離譜了。
> Your price is not competitive. 你的價格沒有競爭力。

⑤ 如果你能免費送貨，我就將訂單加倍。

A：If you can offer free delivery, I'll double my order. 如果你能免費送貨，我就將訂單加倍。

B：The price we offer has contained the delivery fees. 我們提供的價格已經包含運費了。

Tips

> Could you give me a discount if I pay in cash? 如果我付現金能打折嗎？
> Can we enjoy the free shipping at such a price? 這個價格能享受免運費嗎？
> We can accept the price with a provision. 我們可以有條件地接受這個價格。

⑥ 你太會講價了。

A： If you offer 10% off, I will put the order. 如果你能打 9 折，我就下單。

B： You drive a hard bargain. 你太會討價還價了。

Tips

■ I think you must have shopped around. 我想你已經貨比三家了吧。

■ I really realize your negotiating power. 我真是領教了你的議價能力了。

■ We can't offer the price you requested. 我們沒辦法提供你要求的價格。

⑦ 這已經是最低價了嗎？

A： Is this the best you can do? 這已經是最低價了嗎？

B： Yes, this is the bottom price. 是的，這是最低價了。

Tips

■ Cut to the chase, can you provide the lowest price? 直接說吧，你們能報個最低價嗎？

■ This is our floor price. 這是最低價了。

■ That's the best we can offer. 這是最低價了。

Step 3　實 戰 對 話

① 報價

A： What do you think about $100 a set? 你覺得一組 100 美元怎麼樣？

B： Your target price is too low to accept. 目標價格太低了，無法接受。

A： Come on, your competitor gives us such price for the same product. 算了吧，你們競爭對手有同樣的產品，給的就是這個價格。

B： But I think you have shopped around, right? We are the best. 但是我想你已經貨比三家了，對吧？我們是最好的。

A： I just get used to your product. 我只是習慣了你們的產品而已。

B： For this reason, I will give you another 5% discount. 出於這個原因，我再給你 5% 的折扣吧。

② 商議價格

A： How much are you willing to pay? 你願意出多少錢？

B： We are prepared to offer $10. 我們出價 10 美元。

A： I appreciate your counter-offer but I find it too low to accept. 謝謝你的反要約，但是我覺得太低了無法接受。

B： This is the initial order. If it goes well, we are willing to establish a long-time relationship with you. 這是第一筆訂單。如果一切順利，我們會願意長期和你們合作。

A： This is already the wholesale price no matter how big the order is. 無論訂單多大，這個已經是批發價了。

B： Then is it your lowest price? 那這是你們的最低價嗎？

③ 免費送貨

A： I'm afraid that price is too high. 恐怕這個報價太高了。

B： Please take the cost price into consideration. 請考慮一下成本價。

A： If you can offer free delivery, I'll double my order. 如果你能免費送貨，我就將訂單加倍。

B： Sorry, but we can't provide free delivery. 抱歉，但是我們無法提供免費送貨。

A： Could you give me a discount if I pay in cash? 付現金能打折嗎？

B： Yes. That's acceptable. 可以。這是可以接受的。

175

Scene 40　進一步討論價格

Step 1　必備表達

可協商的	negotiable：price negotiable 表示「價格面議」。
增加	increase：同義詞還有 boost，enhance，gain 等。
有吸引力的	attractive：attractive to 表示「對……有吸引力」。
優惠	favorable：favorable price 表示「優惠價」。
優惠券	coupon：gift coupon 表示「贈券」。
優惠活動	special offer：同義詞組為 special privilege；on special offer 意思為「特別優惠」。
太高	too high：far too high 表示「過高」。
低於	go below：常用片語還有 below the line「在標準線以下」。
高於	go above：go above and beyond 表示「超出」。
折扣期限	discount period：within the discount period 表示「在折扣優惠期內」。

Step 2　句句精彩

① 你能提供的最優惠價格是多少？

A： what's the best you can do? 你能提供的最優惠價格是多少？

B： This is the most favorable price we can offer. 這是我們能提供的最優惠價格。

Tips

■ You will find that we have offered the most competitive price. 你能發現我們已經提供了最具競爭力的價格。

■ Sorry, this is the reserve price. 抱歉，這是最低價了。

■ I want to start the business with you, but we can't sell the products at a loss. 我很想與你們做生意，但是我們不能做賠本買賣。

② 價格不能低於現在的市價。

A： I will accept your offer if you give me 3% more discount. 如果你能再給我 3% 的折扣，我就接受這個價格。

B： We shouldn't go below the current market price. 價格不能低於現在的市價。

Tips

Your competitor is selling the same thing for lower price. 你的競爭對手以更低的價格出售同樣的產品。

I know you sold your products at a lower price. 我知道你們以更低的價格出售過產品。

We can't make ends meet at your price. 以你的價格，我們會賠本的。

③ 你能為我們提供與去年一樣的單價嗎？

A： Can you offer us the same unit price as last year? 你能為我們提供與去年一樣的單價嗎？

B： I am afraid not. The price of raw materials is raising. 恐怕不能。原材料的價格在上漲。

Tips

I will double the order if you can offer me the same price as usual. 如果你們提供與往常一樣的價格，我就增加一倍訂量。

If you can give me the same price as last year, I will renew the contract. 如果你能提供與去年相同的價格，我們就會續約。

④ 如果是現金付款，我們予以 9 折優惠。

A： We give (a) 10% discount if you pay in cash. 如果是現金付款，我們予以 9 折優惠。

B： OK, we agree to pay in cash. 好吧，我們同意以現金付款。

Tips

Can we enjoy some discounts if we pay in cash? 如果現金支付的話，能享受折扣嗎？

Do you have some special offers? 你們有特別優惠嗎？

What special offers can you make for us if we pay in cash? 如果我們用現金支付，你們能提供什麼特別優惠？

⑤ 儘管成本在上升，但是我們的價格保持穩定。

A： In spite of the rising cost, our prices remain stable. 儘管成本在上升，但是我們的

價格保持穩定。

B：But this is a mature product, you could have lowered the cost. 但這個是成熟產品，你們可能已經降低了成本。

Tips

- We have tried our best to hold the price. 我們已經盡最大努力保持價格不變了。
- The exchange rate can affect our prices, too. 匯率也會影響我們的價格。
- We only can promise the validity of the prices for 3 months. 我們只能保證價格在 3 個月內有效。

⑥ 我們可以向您保證品質。

A：We are worried about the quality of the products. 我們擔心產品的品質。

B：We can give you a guarantee on quality. 我們可以向您保證品質。

Tips

- We have advanced production line and quality inspection system. 我們有先進的生產線和質檢系統。
- The products are accompanied with quality testing reports. 這些產品都附有品質檢測報告。
- You can check the products before delivery. 發貨前你可以進行檢測。

⑦ 只有原材料價格不變，我們的報價才有效。

A：Our quotation is valid only if the costs of raw materials don't change. 只有原材料價格不變，我們的報價才有效。

B：But you should keep your quotation stable in a period. 但你們應該在一段時間內保持報價穩定。

Tips

- The quoted prices are valid in 30 days. 報價 30 天內有效。
- Our prices are associated with a lot of factors. 我們的價格與很多因素相關。
- Price is not constant. 價格不是一成不變的。

Step 3　實戰對話

① 最優惠價格

A：What's the best you can do? 你能提供的最優惠價格是多少？

B： This is already the most favorable price we can offer. 這已經是我們能提供的最優惠的價格。

A： I will accept your offer if you give me more discounts. 如果你能再多給我一些折扣，我就接受這個價格。

B： We shouldn't go below the current market price. 價格不應低於目前的市價。

A： Then we can't move on. 那我們就沒辦法繼續了。

B： OK, we only can give you 5%. 好吧，我們只能給 5% 的折扣。

② 保持價格不變

A： Can you offer us the same unit price as last year? 你能為我們提供與去年一樣的單價嗎？

B： I am afraid not. 恐怕不能。

A： If you can give me the same price as last year, I will renew the contract. 如果你能提供與去年相同的價格，我們就會續約。

B： But the situation changes. 但是情況變了。

A： We know your market. The price of raw material has falling down. 我了解你們的市場，原材料的價格已經下降了。

B： But the labor cost and delivery fees haven't. 但是運費沒有降。

③ 品質要求

A： OK, for a long-term cooperation, we will keep the price unchanged. 好吧，為了長期合作，我們保持價格不變。

B： But you should keep your quality, too. 但是也要保證品質。

A： We can give you a guarantee on quality. 我們可以向您保證品質。

B： You have image inspection machines, right? 你們有影像檢測儀，對吧？

A： Yes, we have four sets. 是的，我們有 4 台。

B： It's good that you can use them to check the products. 你們能用機器來檢測產品真是太好了。

Scene 41　敲定價格

Step 1　必備表達

合理的	reasonable：與 favorable 含義相近，後者意思為「優惠的」。
接受	work with：相當於 accept。
可以接受的	agreeable：agreeable 有「欣然同意」的含義。
合理的價格	suitable price：這裡的 suitable 相當於 appropriate。
最近的	latest：同義詞有 current，recent 等。
敲定價格	strike price：常用片語為 at the strike price「以敲定的價格……」。
決定	decide：相當於 determine 或 make up one's mind。
價格變動	price change：等同於 price variation。
成交	make a deal：close a deal 也有同樣的意思。
價格下跌	price falling：相當於 price reduction。

Step 2　句句精彩

① 這個報價聽起來很合理。

A：This offer sounds reasonable. 這個報價聽起來很合理。

B：Could we settle it down? 那我們能確定下來了嗎？

Tips

■ settle down 定下來。

■ I can work with this price. 我能夠接受這個價格。

■ In view of a long-term business relationship, the price is OK. 鑑於長期合作，我們接受這個價格。

② 由於市場價格正在下跌，我們建議你們馬上接受。

A：As the market price is falling, we suggest you accept it immediately. 由於市場價格正在下跌，我們建議你們馬上接受。

B： But we don't think this is the suitable price. 但我們覺得這個價格不合適。

Tips

> If you agree with the price, I will send you the order. 如果你同意這個價格，我會把訂單發給你。

■ We'd better have a quick battle. 我們最好速戰速決。

Let's make decisions to prevent some unexpected problems. 我們定下來吧，以免出現意外問題。

---

③ 我們可以接受 10 件 1000 美元。

A： We can accept $1,000 for 10 units. 我們可以接受 10 件 1000 美元。

B： OK, then we make a deal. 好吧，成交。

Tips

Good, then we two sides reach an agreement. 好的，我們雙方達成一致了。

We adopt this reasonable price. 我們接受這個合理的價格。

This is a wise decision. 這是個明智的決定。

---

④ 每件 20 美元可以接受。

A： What price do you want? 你想要什麼價格？

B： $20 per unit is agreeable. 每件 20 美元可以接受。

Tips

■ The final word, $20. 一錘定音，20 美元。

OK, we set it in a stone. 好的，就這麼定了。

We can accept it this time only. 我們只是這次接受。

---

⑤ 80 美元的價格是合理的。

A： Eighty bucks is suitable. 80 美元的價格是合理的。

B： OK, deal. 好吧，成交。

Tips

All right, we fix on eighty bucks. 好吧，我們定在 80 美元。

Done. 成交。

So, Let's set on it. 好吧，就是這個了。

⑥ 成交。

A： It's a deal. 成交。

B： I am glad to hear that. 聽到這個消息我很高興。

Tips

- Let's strike the deal. 成交。
- Here is the deal! 成交。
- Clinch the deal. 成交。

⑦ 聽起來還算合理。

A： It sounds suitable. 聽起來還算合理。

B： OK, I will arrange the order. 好的，我會準備訂單。

Tips

- The price is reasonable to accept. 價格合理，可以接受。
- Let's make a bargain. 成交。
- OK, I will calculate the volume of business. 好的，我計算一下成交量。

Step 3　實 戰 對 話

① 報價合理

A： This offer sounds reasonable. 這個報價聽起來很合理。

B： Could we settle it down? 那我們能確定下來了嗎？

A： I will ask my manager's advice. 我得問經理的意見。

B： OK, back later. 好的，一會兒見。

A： The price is OK. We will order 500 pieces. 價格沒問題，我們要訂購 500 件。

B： Great. It's very nice to cooperate with you. 太好了。和你們合作很愉快。

② 市場多變

A： As the market price is falling, we suggest you accept it immediately. 由於市場價格正在下跌，我們建議你們馬上接受。

B： OK, this is the suitable price. 好吧，這個價格很合適。

A： Wow, we finally settle it down. 喔，我們終於定下來了。

B： Yes, this is the most acceptable price for you and me. 是的，對你我來說這都是最能接受的價格了。

A： OK, I will send you the order. 好的，我給你發訂單。

B： Thank you. 謝謝。

③ 接受價格

A： What price do you want? 你想要什麼價格？

B： $20 per unit is agreeable. 每件 20 美元可以接受。

A： As your wish, we accept it. 如你所願，我們接受。

B： OK, we set it in a stone. 好的，就這麼定了。

A： At last we can breathe with ease. 我們終於可以鬆口氣了。

B： Yes. Hope we can cooperate happily. 是的。希望我們合作愉快。

Scene 42　訂單內容與裝運方式

Step 1　必備表達

整個訂單	the entire order：entire 表示「完整的」。
包括	comprise：可以直接使用 comprise，也可以用 be comprised of 表示「包括」。
運貨板	pallet：board 也指「板，（尤指）木板」。
集裝箱	container：a container ship 集裝箱貨運船。
冷藏的	refrigerated：refrigerated lorry 冷藏貨車。
運送	deliver：be delivered within 24 hours 在 24 小時內送達。
港口	port：也可用 harbor 來代替。
貨運代表	freight forwarder：freight 貨運；forward 有「發送，寄」的意思，forwarder 指從事這類工作的人，即「運送者」。
物流供應商	logistics provider：logistics 表示「物流」，注意這個單字的最後一個字母 s 並不代表複數形式，是不能丟的。
承運人	carrier：carry 有「運送」的意思，因此 carrier 就是「承運人」的意思。
固定訂購	regular order：regular 表示「經常的」，所以常說的「老顧客」就是 regular customer。

Step 2　句句精彩

① 我有興趣訂購你們的機器。

A： I'm interested in ordering your machine. 我有興趣訂購你們的機器。

B： Great. How many would you like to order? 太好了。您要訂多少？

Tips

■ I'm calling to order your machine. 我打電話來是想訂購你們的機器。

I'd like to make an order for your new printer. 我想訂購你們新出的印表機。

We are very glad to receive the order from you. 我們很高興接到您的訂單。

② 我們訂 100 張桌子。

A： How many tables do you want? 您想要多少張桌子？

B： Let's place an order for 100 tables. 我們訂 100 張桌子。

Tips

■ I'd like to put a rush order on your No.8 computer. 我想緊急訂購你們的 8 號電腦。

Our minimum quantity is 500 sets. 我們的最低訂購量是 500 套。

③ 我們總共需要 200 個盒子。

A： We'll need in total 200 boxes. 我們總共需要 200 個盒子。

B： Sure. What size of the box would you like? 可以。想要多大尺寸的盒子？

Tips

We need the products put in boxes. 我們需要把產品裝箱。

Make sure that you use really strong boxes. 請確定你們的包裝箱是非常結實的那種。

We plan to use cardboard boxes, foamed plastic materials with iron straps for reinforcement.
我們打算用紙板箱、塑膠泡沫材料再加上鐵條來加固。

④ 那些都放在一塊運貨板上嗎？

A： Can all of that fit on one pallet? 那些都放在一塊運貨板上嗎？

B： I'm afraid not. We need two. 恐怕不行，我們需要兩塊板。

Tips

We need ten pallets to put the goods. 我們需要 10 塊運貨板放貨物。

Are 20 boxes enough for the goods? 20 個箱子夠放這些貨了嗎？

Could I put these boxes on the floor? 這些箱子能放在地上嗎？

⑤ 我們的商品都會送到貨櫃區。

A： We'll have everything sent to the container lot. 我們的商品都會送到貨櫃區。

B： I see. I hope we can receive the goods soon. 我知道了。希望我們很快就能收到貨物。

Tips

lot 在這裡表示「(做某用途的) 場地」的意思。

■ We'll send the products directly to your plant. 我們會直接把產品送到你們工廠去。

■ We guarantee you the shipment will be in good condition. 我們保證貨物運抵達後沒有問題。

⑥ 你可以直接跟我們的貨運代表討論細節。

A： I'd like to talk about the shipment. 我想談談貨運問題。

B： You could talk directly to our freight forwarder for details. 你可以直接跟我們的貨運代表討論細節。

Tips

■ Let's discuss the time and method of shipment. 我們討論一下運貨的時間和方式吧。

■ When are you going to ship the order? 您打算什麼時候裝運？

■ How will you ship the goods? 你們怎麼運送這批貨物？

⑦ 我們最快什麼時候能收到貨？

A： When is the earliest we can expect to receive that? 我們最快什麼時候能收到貨？

B： Before June 15th. 6 月 15 日之前。

Tips

■ Can the product be delivered the same day I place the order? 我訂的產品能當天送達嗎？

■ The order is so urgently required that we must ask you to make the earliest possible shipment. 我們急需該訂單的物品，因此要求你方盡可能早出貨。

■ We assure you a delivery of 600 units before July 1st. 我們保證在 7 月 1 日之前交付 600 台。

Step 3　實 戰 對 話

① 接到訂單

A： Hello. Julie, ABC Company. 您好，我是 ABC 公司的朱莉。

B： Hello. It's Daniel Jones from AKK Company.
您好。我是 AKK 公司的丹尼爾·鐘斯。

A： Mr. Jones, what can I do for you? 有什麼可以幫助您的嗎，鐘斯先生？

B： I'm interested in ordering your machine. 我有興趣訂購你們的機器。

A： I'm very glad to receive the order from you. How many would you like to order? 很高興接到您的訂單。您要訂購多少？

B： We'd like to order 15 sets. 我們要訂購 15 台。

②　產品包裝要求

A： We need the products put in boxes. 我們需要將產品裝到盒子裡。

B： All right. How many boxes do you want? 好的。你們需要多少個盒子？

A： We'll need in total 200 boxes. 我們總共需要 200 個盒子。

B： No problem. 沒問題。

A： Make sure that you use really strong boxes. 請確定你們的包裝箱是非常結實的那種。

B： You may rest assured. 您儘管放心。

③　討論運貨問題

A： Let's place an order for 100 tables. 我們訂 100 張桌子。

B： OK. Please send the order via fax. 好的。請把訂單傳真過來吧。

A： Can all of that fit on one pallet? 那些都放在一塊運貨板上嗎？

B： I'm afraid not. At least two pallets are required. 恐怕不行。至少需要兩塊。

A：I got it. When will you fulfill shipment? 我知道了。你們什麼時候能完成裝船呢？

B：As soon as we receive the order, we will send the goods. 一收到訂單我們就會發貨。

Scene 43 確認訂單

訂單	purchase order(PO)：purchase 表示「購買」，又如 purchase price 表示「買價」。
訂單號	PO number：交易時記住訂單號十分重要，這樣查找起來比較方便。
收到	receive：receive the order 接到訂單；receive a letter 收到信件。
確認	make sure：也可用 confirm 來代替。
傳真	fax：fax 既可以做名詞，也可以做動詞。
跟進訂單	follow up on orders：follow up 跟進；注意介詞 on 的使用。
順利到達	arrive safe and sound：sound 完好的，無損傷的。
最近的訂單	recent order：recent 表示「最近的」，比如：in recent days 最近幾日。
發郵件	send an e-mail：表示「收到郵件」就是 receive an e-mail。
確認訂單	confirm an order：confirm 確認，由此衍生的 reconfirm 表示「再次確認」。

Step 2 句句精彩

① 中午前你就該收到我們的訂單了。

A：When are you going to place your order? 您何時下單？

B：You should have a purchase order from us by noon. 中午前你就該收到我們的訂單了。

Tips

■ you'll receive our purchase order before 4 p.m. 下午 4 點前您就會收到我們的訂單了。

■ The purchase order will arrive today. 今天訂單就可以到了。

■ I'll get the purchase order out now. 我這就去下訂單。

② 你們收到我們的訂單了嗎？

A： Have you received our purchase order yet? 你們收到我們的訂單了嗎？

B： Yes. We are dealing with it. 是的，我們正在處理。

Tips

> Has the purchase order been placed? 訂單已經下了了嗎？
>
> Have you received the e-mail about our order? 你收到關於我們訂單的郵件了嗎？
>
> Are you dealing with our purchase order? 你們正在處理我們的訂單嗎？

③ 我打電話確認你們是不是收到了我傳真的訂單。

A： Hello. Can I help you? 您好。您有什麼事？

B： I'm calling to make sure you received my fax for an order. 我打電話確認你們是不是收到了我傳真的訂單。

Tips

> ■ I'm writing this e-mail to make sure you've received my order. 我寫這封郵件是想確認你是否收到了我的訂單。
>
> I'm wondering if you have received the order. 我想知道你們是否收到了訂單。
>
> I faxed a purchase order this morning but didn't receive any reply. 我今天上午傳真了訂單過去，但沒收到任何回覆。

④ 我想再確認下我訂購的貨物的數量。

A： I'd like to double-check the number of goods I ordered. 我想再確認下我訂購的貨物的數量。

B： OK. Could you show me your PO number? 好的。請問您的訂單號是多少？

Tips

> I'd like to reconfirm the number of goods I ordered. 我想再確認下我訂購的貨物的數量。
>
> I'm calling to reconfirm the order I placed. 我打電話來再次確認我下的訂單。

⑤ 我的訂單出什麼問題了？

A： what's happening with my order? 我的訂單出什麼問題了？

B： I'm really sorry to inform you that the goods you ordered is currently out of stock. 真的很抱歉通知您，您訂的東西目前缺貨了。

Tips

■ What's the problem with my order? 我的訂單出什麼問題了？

■ I can't find the purchase order number of the products I ordered in your system. 在你們的系統裡，我找不到我訂購商品的訂單號了。

⑥ 我打電話來跟進你訂購電腦的訂單。

A： I'm calling to follow up on your order of computers. 我打電話來跟進你訂購電腦的訂單。

B： Oh, the goods haven't arrived yet. 哦，貨還沒有到。

Tips

■ I'm calling to inform you that your order has been dealt with. 我打電話來通知您，您的訂單已經被處理過了。

■ Please call me if tHere's something that needs a follow up. 如果有什麼需要跟進的情況，請給我打電話。

⑦ 你訂購的商品是否安全並完好送達？

A： Did your order arrive safe and sound? 你訂購的商品是否安全並完好送達？

B： Yes. We received the goods yesterday. 是的。我們昨天收到貨了。

Tips

■ Have you received your goods yet? 你已經收到貨了嗎？

■ We guarantee you that the goods will be in good condition. 我們保證貨物沒有問題。

■ Your order No. 373 has arrived in Shanghai today. 您的 373 號訂單今天已經抵達上海。

Step 3　實戰對話

① 詢問下單時間

A： Hello. 您好。

B： Hello. Is Mr. Zhang speaking? 您好。是張先生嗎？

A： It's me. May I help you? 是我。可以幫到您什麼嗎？

B： We're very interested in your mobile phone and want to order 100 pcs. 我們對你們的手機很感興趣，想訂購 100 部。

A： Great. When are you going to place your order? 太好了。您何時下單？

B： You should have a purchase order from us by noon. 中午前你就該收到我們的訂單了。

② 確認訂單

A： Have you received our purchase order yet? It's No. 5970. 你們收到我們的訂單了嗎？訂單號是 5970。

B： Please wait a minute...Yes, We've received. 請稍等……是的，我們收到了。

A： That's fine. 我想再確認下我訂購的貨物的數量。

B： It's 5 boxes, isn't it? 是 5 箱，對嗎？

A： It's right. Thank you. 對。謝謝。

B： Don't worry. We'll call you to reconfirm before the shipment. 別擔心。裝運之前我們會再次打電話跟您確認的。

③ 訂單出問題

A： Hello. Can I help you? 您好。您有什麼事？

B： Hello. I'm calling to make sure you received my fax for an order. 您好。我打電話確認你們是不是收到了我傳真的訂單。

A： Sorry, we haven't received your order. 對不起，我們沒收到您的訂單。

B： What's happening with my order? 我的訂單出什麼問題了？

A： There may be something wrong with our fax. I'm so sorry. Would you please send an e-mail? 可能是我們的傳真機壞了。真抱歉。您可以發電子郵件嗎？

B： Fine. I'll send it to you right now. 好吧。我這就發給您。

Scene 44 訂單被取消

Step 1　必備表達

取消訂單	cancel the order：cancel 表示「使作廢，取消」，比如 cancel the contract 表示「撤銷合約」。
暫緩	delay：delay 還可以用來表示飛機的「延誤」。
期望	expect：向對方提要求的時候就可以說：You will be expected to...。
更新	update：regular update 定期更新。
訂單日期	order date：check the order date 確認訂單日期。
回覆	reply：reply 既可作名詞也可作動詞。
因為某些原因	for some reason：some 在這裡指「一定的，特定的」。
平白無故地	for nothing：也可用 for no reason 來代替。
研究	go over：類似意思的單字是 consider，表示「考慮」。
滿足需求	meet the demand：demand 也可以換成 need。

Step 2　句句精彩

① 你要取消訂單？

A： I'm afraid we need to reconsider the order we placed... 恐怕我們需要重新考慮我們下過的訂單……

B： Will you cancel the order? 你要取消訂單？

Tips

■ I am afraid we are canceling our order. 我想我們要取消訂單了。

■ I'm sorry, but I want to cancel my order. 對不起，我想取消我的訂單。

■ Can I cancel my order for 100 computers? 我能取消 100 台電腦的訂單嗎？

② 這張訂單我們需要暫緩至少一兩個月。

A： We're going to need to delay the order by at least a month or two. 這張訂單我們需要暫緩至少一兩個月。

B： May I ask why? 我可以問下為什麼嗎？

Tips

Speaking honestly, we are not going to cancel the order. we just want to delay it. 老實說，我們不是要取消訂單。我們只是想暫緩一下。

Since your inventory is running a little low, we decided to delay the order. 既然你們的庫存不足了，我們決定暫緩訂單。

The goods you want are no longer in stock. Could you please delay the order? 您想要的貨物沒有現貨了。您可以暫緩訂單嗎？

③ 看起來我們沒有想像中那麼快就需要那些車。

A： It doesn't look like We're going to need those cars as soon as we had thought. 看起來我們沒有想像中那麼快就需要那些車。

B： What exactly do you mean? 您到底是什麼意思？

Tips

We're going to need the goods later than we expected. 我們沒有預計中那麼快就需要那批貨。

Our inventory has been consumed a lot slower than we originally hoped. 我們存貨消耗的速度比原本希望的要慢許多。

We have to cancel our order and purchase from another supplier this time. 我們不得不取消訂單，向另一家供應商購買。

④ 事實上，我想跟你談談那筆訂單。

A： Actually, I wanted to talk to you about that order. 事實上，我想跟你談談那筆訂單。

B： Is there any problem with that order? 那筆訂單有什麼問題嗎？

Tips

We decided to go over that order again. 我們決定再研究一下那筆訂單。

We decided to make a little change with the order. 我們決定對訂單做個小小的改動。

Is it convenient for you to talk about the order with me? 你方便和我談下訂單的問題嗎？

⑤ 我會在這個星期結束前給你一個確定的新訂單日期。

A：I'll give you a firm update on the new order date by the end of this week. 我會在這個星期結束前給你一個確定的新訂單日期。

B：I'm looking forward to your order as soon as possible. 我盼望盡快接到您的訂單。

Tips

- We'll confirm a new order date by the end of this month. 我們會在本月底之前確定一個新的訂單日期。
- I'm afraid we need to change the order date. 恐怕我們需要更改訂單日期了。
- I'll give you a final result after We've discussed. 我們討論後會給你個最終結果的。

⑥ 結果就是他們不要這些產品了。

A：Jack called you about the order yesterday. What happened? 傑克昨天打電話給你說訂單的事。怎麼了？

B：The upshot is that they don't want the products. 結果就是他們不要這些產品了。

Tips

- upshot 表示「最後結果」，也可用 final result 或 outcome 來代替。
- They don't want the goods for some reason. 他們由於某些原因不要這批貨了。
- I've tried my best but they decided to cancel the order. 我盡了自己的全力，但他們還是決定取消訂單。

⑦ 我們很遺憾地說，由於貴方不能很快交貨，所以我們不得不取消訂單。

A：Since It's a busy season, the products are expected to be delivered in four to five weeks. 由於現在是旺季，商品需要 4~5 週才能送到。

B：Well, so we regret to say that we have to decline the order since you can't deliver the products very soon. 嗯，那麼我們很遺憾地說，由於貴方不能很快交貨，所以我們不得不取消訂單。

Tips

- Either the delivery is immediate, or We'll have to cancel the order. 若不能立即送貨，我們將取消訂單。
- If the delivery isn't on time, We'll have to cancel the order. 如不能按時送貨，我們將取消訂單。
- Further delays in delivery will result in our canceling our order. 如果貴方再次延誤交貨，我們將取消訂單。

Step 3　實戰對話

① 取消訂單

A： Hello, Bob. It's Jeff speaking. 你好，鮑伯。我是傑夫。

B： Hello, Jeff. 你好，傑夫。

A： I'm calling to confirm the order you placed on June 20th. 我打電話來是想確認你6 月 20 日下的訂單。

B： Actually, I wanted to talk to you about that order. 事實上，我想跟你談談那筆訂單。

A： Oh, what's happening? 哦，怎麼了？

B： I'm afraid there is going to be a change in the order. 恐怕訂單要有變動了。

A： Will you cancel the order? 你要取消訂單？

B： To be honest, yes. 老實說，是的。

② 暫緩訂單

A： Hello, David speaking. 您好，我是大衛。

B： Hello, David. It's Jessica. 大衛，你好。我是潔西卡。

A： May I help you, Jessica? 潔西卡，有什麼事嗎？

B： I'd like to talk about the order of cars. 我想談一下汽車訂單的事。

A： So? 所以？

B： We're going to need to delay the order by at least a month or two. 這張訂單我們需要暫緩至少一兩個月。

A： It doesn't look like We're going to need those cars as soon as we had thought. 看起來我們沒有想像中那麼快就需要那些車。

③ 更新訂單日期

A： I'm afraid that we don't need the goods immediately. 恐怕我們不是馬上就需要那批貨了。

B： So, are you going to cancel the order? 所以，你們要取消訂單？

A： No. We are not planning to cancel the order; what we want to do is just to delay it.

不是的。我們不是要取消訂單，我們只是想暫緩一下。

B：I got it. 我明白了。

A：I'll give you a firm update on the new order date by the end of this week. 我會在這個星期結束前給你一個確定的新訂單日期。

B：OK. I'm looking forward to your order. 好的。期待接到你的訂單。

Scene 45　付款方式

Step 1　必備表達

支票	check：英式英語的寫法是 cheque。
貨到之前	in advance of shipment：in advance of 預先；shipment 運貨。
付款方式	payment terms：payment 付款；terms 表示「條件」，在這裡指「方式」。
貨到付款	cash on delivery：delivery 遞送，交付。
直接匯款	direct deposit：deposit 存款。
付清帳款	pay all the money：pay off 和 pay up 也可以指「付清」。
一次付清	pay in one lump sum：lump 的本義是「堆，塊」，lump sum 是固定搭配，指「一次總付的錢」。
預付款	payment in advance：advance 預先。
信用證	letter of credit：credit 貸款。
匯票	draft：a draft on ICBC 工商銀行提款的匯票。

Step 2　句句精彩

① 我能以支票付款嗎？

A：Can I pay by check? 我能以支票付款嗎？

B：Yes, It's acceptable. 是的，這是我們可接受的。

Tips

■ 為了避免出票人開空頭支票 收款人或持票人可以要求付款行在支票上加蓋「保付」章，以保證到時一定能得到銀行付款，這種加蓋了「保付」章的支票，就叫保付支票。

■ Do you accept cash payment? 你們接受現金付款嗎？

■ Can we use my certified check? 我們可以使用保付支票嗎？

② 你們可以在貨到之前付款嗎？

A： Can you pay in advance of shipment? 你們可以在貨到之前付款嗎？

B： We prefer to pay within 7 workdays when We've received the goods. 我們更希望在收到貨後的 7 個工作日內付款。

Tips

- We would be grateful for prompt payment. 如果立即付款我們會不勝感激。
- You can pay for it when you have received it. 您可以等收到貨再付款。
- Can you tell me when we can expect to receive payment? 你能告訴我什麼時候能收到你的付款嗎？

③ 你們想怎麼完成付款？

A： What kind of payment terms do you prefer? 你們想怎麼完成付款？

B： they're very flexible. It's up to you. 這很靈活的。由你方決定吧。

Tips

- What method of payment do you have in mind? 你想用哪種付款方式？
- In which way do you prefer to pay? 你想要哪種方式付款呢？
- Which way is available for you to accept the payment? 您可以用哪種方式來接受付款？

④ 我們可以直接匯款嗎？

A： Can we pay by direct deposit? 我們可以直接匯款嗎？

B： Sure. Our account number is 9558800200498090657. 當然可以，我們的帳號是 9558800200498090657。

Tips

- I'll send you a check for the full amount within 5 days. 我 5 天內會給你寄一張全額的支票。
- You could wire transfer the payment into our bank account. 你可以電子轉帳到我們的銀行帳戶。
- We accept a certified check or a direct bank remittance. 我們接受保付支票或直接由銀行匯款。

⑤ 我們可以分 3 次付款嗎？

A： Can we pay in three payments? 我們可以分 3 次付款嗎？

B： Yes. But you're required to pay for at least 30% of the total at the end of this month. 可以。不過要求你們這月底至少付全部貨款的 30%。

Tips

I was planning to send you a partial payment at the end of this month. 我打算這個月底先付給你們一部分。

The goods will be paid for in three monthly payments of 50,000 dollars. 貨物將月付 5 萬美元分 3 次付清。

You can purchase the goods in installments over 6 months. 您可以分 6 個月付款購買這批貨。

---

⑥ 我們要求不可撤銷信用證。

A： What are the terms of your payment? 你們對付款有什麼條件？

B： We require payment by irrevocable letter of credit. 我們要求不可撤銷信用證。

Tips

We only accept payment by letter of credit. 我們只接受信用證的付款方式。

I have to ask you to send the full amount of the balance. 我得要求您支付全款。

You need to pay in US dollar. 你需要用美元支付。

---

⑦ 如果你願意以匯票方式付款，我會更願意和你合作。

A： I'd be more willing to work with you if you agree to use demand drafts to pay invoices. 如果你願意以匯票方式付款，我會更願意和你合作。

B： I got it. I'll arrange payment as soon as possible. 我明白了。我會盡快安排付款。

Tips

We give a 10% discount for cash. 如果用現金付款，我們予以 9 折優惠。

We usually offer 2% discount if you pay in cash. 如果你支付現金，我們通常會提供 2% 的折扣。

■ We offer a 10 percent discount if you could pay within one month. 如能一個月內付清貨款，可享受 10% 的折扣。

Step 3　實戰對話

① 要求貨到之前付款

A： Now Let's talk about the terms of payment. 現在我們談談付款方式吧。

B： OK. Do you have any special requests? 好的。你們有什麼特殊要求嗎？

A： Can you pay in advance of shipment? 你們可以在貨到之前付款嗎？

B： Since We're each other's regular clients, yes. 既然我們是彼此的老客戶了，可以。

A： That'll be great. 那太好了。

B： Can I pay by check? 我能以支票付款嗎？

A： Sure, It's acceptable. 當然，這是可以接受的

② 直接匯款

A： What kind of payment terms do you prefer? 你們想怎麼樣完成付款？

B： They're very flexible. It's up to you. 這是很靈活的。由你方決定吧。

A： Can we pay by direct deposit? 我們可以直接匯款嗎？

B： It's OK. 可以。

A： So what's your account number? 那你們的帳號是多少？

B： Our account number is 95588-00200498090657.
我們的帳號是 9558800200498090657。

③ 協商付款方式

A： Let's move on to the next item, the terms of payment. 讓我們進行下一個議題，
付款方式。

B： OK. What would you like? 好的。你們希望怎麼付款？

A： Can we pay in three payments? 我們可以分 3 次付款嗎？

B： I'd be more willing to work with you if you agree to use demand drafts to pay invoices. 如果你願意以匯票方式付款，我會更願意和你合作。

A： I got it. That will be OK. 我明白了。可以的。

B： Thank you so much. Hope we can have a pleasant cooperation. 非常感謝。希望我
們合作愉快。

Scene 46 付款條件

Step 1 必備表達

信用紀錄	credit history：除了「歷史」的含義，history 還有「來歷，經歷」的意思，credit history 就指信用問題上有過的經歷，即「信用紀錄」。
付頭期款	put down：put 20% down 付 20% 的頭期款。
憑提單付款	against the bill of loading：bill of loading 提貨單。
快捷支付	quick payment：快捷支付讓銀行卡用戶無須開通網銀也能方便完成網上付款，只需輸入卡號等資訊就可完成支付。
快速的	speedy：也可用 fast 或 quick 來代替。
信用紀錄好	good credit：have a good credit 有良好的信用紀錄。
信用紀錄差	bad / poor credit：注意 bad 和 poor 都可以表示「不好，壞」。
收到發票時	due on invoice：due 應付的；invoice 發票。
分期付款	installment：pay in installments 以分期付款的方式支付。
見票即付	at sight：at sight 的原意是「一見到……立即」。

Step 2 句句精彩

① 你們能一次付清嗎？

A： Is it possible for you to pay in one lump sum? 你們能一次付清嗎？

B： Well, I have to check with our manager. 嗯，我得和我們經理確認一下。

Tips

■ Upon installation of the equipment, the payment should be fulfilled. 設備一裝好就要完成付款。

■ The total amount must be paid in full upon receipt of the shipping documents. 一收到貨運單據，貨款必須全數付清。

■ We'll be needing payment within 10 days. 我們需要在 10 天內付款。

② 如果你們事先付部分款項，我們或許可以接受分期付款。

A： Do you accept installments? 你們接受分期付款嗎？

B： We might be willing to live with installments if you provide some payment in advance. 如果你們事先付部分款項，我們或許可以接受分期付款。

Tips

■ We accept installments, but 25% of the payment should be paid in advance. 我們接受分期付款，不過你們需要事先支付 25% 的款項。

■ Our terms of payment are as follows: quarterly / monthly / yearly payment. 我們的付款方式如下：季繳、月繳、年繳。

■ We accept neither payment by installments nor deferred payment. 我們既不接受分期付款，也不接受延期付款。

③ 你付 4 成頭期款，然後其他的 6 成在取得提單的 50 天內付清。

A： You put 40 percent down and the other 60 percent in 50 days against the bill of loading. 你付 4 成頭期款，然後其他的 6 成在取得提單的 50 天內付清。

B： It's a deal. 就這麼說定了。

Tips

■ It requires an advance payment of 20% before delivery. 在發貨之前需要先交 20% 的預付款。

■ You can pay the advance, and then the balance is paid off over a period of three months. 你可以先付預付款，然後在 3 個月之內付清餘款。

■ When is the balance due? 什麼時候要付清餘款？

④ 沒有信用紀錄的話，我們就要求預付現金。

A： Without a credit history, we ask for cash in advance. 沒有信用紀錄的話，我們就要求預付現金。

B： We have a good credit. 我們有良好的信用紀錄。

Tips

■ Our terms are cash within 120 days of the date of delivery. 我們的付款條件是交貨後 120 天內支付現金。

■ We accept payment by D / P at sight . 我方接受即期付款交單的付款方式。

■ 即期交單（D / P at Sight）指出口方開具即期匯票，由代收行向進口方提示，進口方見票後即須付款，貨款付清時，進口方取得貨運單據。

(5) 謝謝你快速付款。

A： We've received your goods. And we will pay by check as soon as possible. 我們已經收到你們的貨了。我們會盡快用支票付款的。

B： Thank you for your quick payment. 謝謝你快速付款。

Tips

We expect the payment as soon as possible. 我們希望盡快付款。

you're required to pay for the goods as soon as you receive them. 一接到貨，貴方就需要付款。

We expect to receive payment before the delivery. 我們希望在發貨前就收到貨款。

(6) 我們會在收到貨物後 5 天內付款。

A： When will you pay for it? 你們什麼時候付款？

B： We can pay in full within 5 days of receiving the goods. 我們會在收到貨物後 5 天內付款。

Tips

We will pay in full within 7 days of receipt of the goods. 我們會在收到貨物後7天內付全款。

We can pay 20% in advance and the rest can be paid off after the delivery. 我們可以先付 20%，發貨後再付清餘款。

We can pay for the goods as soon as we receive them. 我們一收到貨物就可以付款了。

(7) 你們可以接受 10 天內付款的條件嗎？

A： Can you accept 10-day payment terms? 你們可以接受 10 天內付款的條件嗎？

B： How about 7 workdays? 7 個工作日內怎麼樣？

Tips

That's acceptable / unacceptable. 這可以／不可以接受。

Our terms of payment are 30-day credit period. It's customary. 我方的付款期是 30 天，這是慣例。

Our invoice requests full payment in 30 days. 我們的發貨單上要求在 30 天內支付全款。

Step 3 實戰對話

① 提出付款要求

A： Is it possible for you to pay in one lump sum? 你們能一次付清嗎？

B： I'm afraid we can't. Could you accept installments? 恐怕我們無法一次付清。你們能接受分期付款嗎？

A： We might be willing to live with installments if you provide some payment in advance. 如果你們事先付部分款項，我們或許可以接受分期付款。

B： 我明白了。那多少你們認為是合適的呢？ I see. How much would be OK for you?

A： We expect 20% payment in advance. 我們希望是預付 20%。

B： No problem. 沒問題。

② 現金分期付款

A： I'm sorry we can't provide a credit history. 很抱歉我們無法提供信用紀錄。

B： Without a credit history, we ask for cash in advance. 沒有信用紀錄的話，我們就要求預付現金。

A： Well, can we pay in installments since It's a large payment? 嗯，因為金額很大，我們可以分期付款嗎？

B： OK. You put 40 percent down and the other 60 percent in 50 days against the bill of loading. 好吧。你付 4 成頭期款，然後其他的 6 成在取得提單的 50 天內付清。

A： It sounds reasonable. 這聽起來很合理。

B： Deal. 說定了。

③ 收貨後付款

A： Hello, Peter. I'm calling to inform you that we have delivered the goods. 彼得，你好。我打電話來是通知你我們已經發貨了。

B： Great. We can pay in full within 5 days of receiving the goods. 太好了。我們會在收到貨物後 5 天內付款。

A： I got it. We'll be appreciated if you can fulfill payment as soon as possible. 知道了。

如果你方能盡快付款，我們將不勝感激。

B： And we will pay by check. Would that be OK for you? 我們會用支票付款。你們

覺得可以嗎？

A： Sure. 當然。

B： Then We're looking forward to your goods. 那我們就等著你們的貨。

Scene 47　付款出現問題

Step 1　必備表達

發票	invoice：make out an invoice 開發票。
包含	contain：contain the shipment fee 含運費。
另函寄送	separate cover：separate 分開的；cover 在這裡相當於 envelope「信封」。
到期的	due：become / fall due 到期。
帳款	account：on account 可以指「記帳；賒帳」，還有「作為預付的部分款項」的意思。
不足的	insufficient：insufficient for sth. ……不足。
帳戶餘額	account balance：account 帳戶；balance 餘額。
逾期的	overdue：overdue bill 逾期未付的帳單。
拖欠	default：default on sth. 未付……的款。
匯寄	remit：remit sth. to sb. 給某人匯寄……（如款項、支票等）。

Step 2　句句精彩

① 可以給我開張發票嗎？

A： May I have an invoice please? 可以給我開張發票嗎？

B： Of course, you'll receive it with the goods. 當然，發票會和貨物一起到達。

Tips

- Do I need to provide a receipt or an invoice for the goods? 貨物需要提供收據或發票嗎？
- I'd like a receipt for the payment. 我要一張該款項的收據。
- We trust that you will check your records before sending out invoices. 謹希望貴方在寄送發票之前能核查紀錄。

② 發票已經另函寄送。

A： Will you please send the invoice? 你可以寄發票過來嗎？

B： Why not? The invoice has been sent under separate cover. 當然可以。發票已經另函寄送。

Tips

I will give you an invoice. 我會給你開一張發票。

The invoice has been made out. 發票已經開出了。

The total value of the invoice will be 6,790 yuan, including tax and delivery. 發票總值為 6790 元，包含稅款和運費。

③ 你的最後付款期限是下個月 1 號。

A： Your payment is due on the 1st of next month. 你的最後付款期限是下個月 1 號。

B： I see. Thank you for reminding me. 知道了。謝謝提醒。

Tips

The deadline of the balance due is July 15th. 餘款的截止日期是 7 月 15 日。

Please pay out the balance by next Friday. 請在下週五前付清餘款。

When is the pay period over? 付款截止到什麼時候？

④ 今天，2013 年 6 月 1 日，你的帳款已付清。

A： As of today, June 1, 2013, your account is up to date. 今天，2013 年 6 月 1 日，你的帳款已付清。

B： Thank you for the information. 謝謝你的通知。

Tips

you've paid off the debt before the due dates. 規定日期之前你已經還清欠款了。

I'm very glad to inform you that you have paid up all the money. 我很高興地通知您，您已經付清了所有欠款。

⑤ 銀行通知我們你的帳戶餘額不足。

A： The bank informed us that there were insufficient funds in your account. 銀行通知我們你的帳戶餘額不足。

B： I'll check it. 我會去查的。

Tips

- The bank informed us that you have drawn all the balance in this account. 銀行通知我們你已經把這個帳戶裡的餘額取光了。
- Payment on deferred terms is unacceptable to us. So be sure that there're always sufficient funds in your account. 我們不接受延期付款。所以請確保你的帳戶裡有足夠的錢。
- You need to check your bank balance right away. 你需要馬上核對帳戶餘額。

⑥ 到 6 月 18 日，我們都沒收到錢。

A： The payment was due on June 11, 2013. But as of June 18, we have not received payment. 付款的最後期限是 2013 年 6 月 11 日，但到 6 月 18 日，我們都沒收到錢。

B： I'm so sorry but tHere's a problem with our capital. 真抱歉，我們在資金上出了點問題。

Tips

- We haven't received payment after the due date. 規定日期之後我們沒有收到錢。
- If you don't settle your account within 3 days, we will be forced to prosecute. 如果你方 3 天內不能結清欠款，我們將不得不起訴。

⑦ 提醒您，您有一筆 1 萬美元的款項已於 2013 年 5 月 1 日到期未付。

A： This is a reminder that your account balance of $10,000 was overdue as of May 1, 2013. 提醒您，您有一筆 1 萬美元的款項已於 2013 年 5 月 1 日到期未付。

B： Oh, I'm very sorry. I'll pay it off today. 哦，真對不起。我今天就付清。

Tips

- We regret to inform you that the payment, which should have been paid off by July 18th, is now considerably overdue. 我們很遺憾地通知您，本該在 7 月 18 日付清的款項現在已經超期未付。
- You're required to remit the payment into our bank account by May 1st. 你方需要於 5 月 1 日前匯款到我們的銀行帳戶。
- You need to pay for it by the end of this month and we accept a bank remittance. 你需要本月底前付款，我們接受銀行匯款。

Step 3　實戰對話

① 發票另寄

A： Hello, Bob. I'm calling to tell you we have received the goods without its invoice. 你好，鮑伯。我打電話來告訴你我們已經收到貨了，但是沒有發票。

B： Oh, I've known the mistake. It seems like somebody forgot to send the invoice. 哦，我知道這個錯誤。似乎是有人忘了寄發票。

A： Will you please send the invoice? 你可以寄發票過來嗎？

B： Sure. The invoice has been sent under separate cover. 當然。發票已經另函寄送。

A： Oh, I see. Thank you. 哦，我知道了。謝謝。

B： you're welcome. Please inform me when you receive the invoice. 別客氣。你收到發票後請通知我。

② 提醒付款最後期限

A： Hello, is it Mr. Jack Smith of ABC Company? 你好，是 ABC 公司的傑克·史密斯先生嗎？

B： Speaking. 我就是。

A： The bank informed us that there were insufficient funds in your account. 銀行通知我們你的帳戶餘額不足。

B： Oh, thank you for the reminding. I'll check it soon. 哦，謝謝提醒。我會盡快核實的。

A： Your payment is due on the 1st of next month. 你的最後付款期限是下個月 1 號。

B： I see. I'll deposit enough money as soon as possible. 知道了。我會盡快存足夠的錢進去的。

③ 通知帳款已付清

A： Hello. What can I do for you? 你好，請問有什麼事？

B： Hello, is it Mr. Wang Ning speaking? 你好，是王寧先生嗎？

A： Yes. Who is it? 是的，你是哪位？

B： Jeff speaking. I'm calling to inform you, as of today, June 1, 2013, your account is up to date. 我是傑夫。我打電話來通知你，今天，2013 年 6 月 1 日，你的帳款已付清。

A： Oh, thank you for the information. 哦，謝謝你通知我。

B： you're welcome. 別客氣。

Scene 48 公司業績

Step 1 必備表達

業績	performance：performance 既可以指一個集體在市場中取得的成績，也可以指個人在職場中的表現。
商業環境	business environment：environment 也可用 circumstance 來代替。
利潤	profit：make a profit 營利。
價值	value：gain in value 增值；drop in value 貶值。
股份	share：share value 股票價值。
股票	stock：stock market 股票市場。
市場占有率	share of the market：share 一份。
成長	grow：也可用 go up 來代替。
下降	drop：也可用 fall 或 go down 來代替。
恢復	recovery：recovery from 從……中恢復。

Step 2 句句精彩

① 更好的業績取決於商業環境。

A： We have had a good performance last quarter and hope to achieve a better performance this quarter. 我們上一季度業績不錯，希望這季度能有更好的業績。

B： Better performance depends on your business environment. Come on! 更好的業績取決於商業環境。加油吧！

Tips

■ Successful marketing is a very key factor in better performance. 成功的行銷是取得更好業績的一個非常重要的因素。

■ How would you describe the company's performance in 2013? 你覺得 2013 年公司的業績怎麼樣？

■ I think 2014 is going to be a fantastic year for us. 我覺得 2014 年將會是我們大放異彩的一年。

② 今年公司營利 700 萬美元。

A：This year, the company made a profit of 7 million dollars. 今年公司營利 700 萬美元。

B：Thanks to everyone's efforts. 多虧了每個人的努力。

Tips

■ Our profit reaches 5 million dollars last year. 去年利潤達到了 500 萬美元。

■ The total sales volume claims a record high of 50 million yuan. 總銷售額達到了創紀錄的 5000 萬元。

■ We netted one million dollars from this deal. 我們從這筆交易中淨賺 100 萬美金。

③ 每股增值 15%。

A：I've heard the share values have risen. 我聽說股票漲了。

B：Yes. THere's a 15% increase in value per share. 是的。每股增值 15%。

Tips

■ Our share value has doubled over the past three years. 過去 3 年來我們的股票價值翻倍了。

■ The shares have appreciated in value. 股票增值了。

■ Our share index went up 2 points yesterday. 我們的股票指數昨天上升了 2 個點。

④ 每股的股票值 50 美元。

A：The stock is now worth $50 per share. 每股的股票值 50 美元。

B：It is higher than last week. 比上週高了。

Tips

■ This $1 share is now worth $2. 這個 1 美元的股份現在值 2 美元。

■ I bought 1,000 yuan's worth of shares. 我買了價值 1000 元的股票。

■ The value dropped to 1.75 yuan per share early last month, with a slight recovery at the end of last month. 每股的價值曾下降到 1.75 元，上個月月底稍有所回升。

⑤ 我們的投資成長了 20%。

A：We made a twenty percent increase on investment. 我們的投資成長了 20%。

B：And we made a big profit because of that. 因此我們也贏得很多利潤。

Tips

Last quarter our sales rose by 7%. 上一季度我們的銷售額成長了 7%。

Last year we saw an annual growth of 6.1% in net profit. 去年我們純利潤年成長 6.1%。

Our marketing went quite well last year. 去年我們行銷做得不錯。

⑥ 目前，你們的市場占有率有多少？

A： what's your share of the existing market? 目前，你們的市場占有率有多少？

B： About 25%. 大約 25%。

Tips

existing 目前的。

We serve clients in more than 20 countries. 我們的客戶遍及 20 多個國家。

We opened over 100 retail shops in the whole country. 我們在全國開了超過 100 家零售店。

⑦ 整體市場也在成長。

A： Our sales are increasing. 我們的銷售額在成長。

B： The total market is growing as well. 市場總體也在成長。

Tips

■ Everything is going the way we expect it to go. 所有事情都在向我們預期的方向發展。

We are confident that our company will continue to grow. 我們相信公司會繼續發展。

We see solid improvements in marketing this year. 今年我們看到在市場行銷方面我們取得了實實在在的進步。

Step 3 實 戰 對 話

① 取得良好業績

A： Big news! 重大新聞！

B： what's up? 怎麼了？

A： This year, the company made a profit of 7 million dollars. 今年，公司營利 700 萬美元。

B： Good job! Thanks to everyone's efforts. 幹得漂亮啊！多虧了每個人的努力。

A： Yeah, I do hope we can achieve a better performance next year. 是啊，真心希望明年能有更好的業績。

B： Better performance depends on your business environment. Come on! 更好的業績取決於商業環境。加油吧！

② 股票增值

A： Hi, Bob, have you heard the news that our shares has appreciated in value? 嗨，鮑伯，我們的股票增值了，你聽說了嗎？

B： Really? 真的？

A： Yes. There's a 15% increase in value per share. 是的。每股增值 15%。

B： Amazing! Then how much is it worth now? 太棒了！那現在值多少錢？

A： The stock is now worth $50 per share. 每股的股票值 50 美元。

B： It's really good news. 真是個好消息啊。

③ 投資與利潤並漲

A： We have made a great progress last year. 去年我們進步不小。

B： Yes. We made a twenty percent increase on investment. 是的。我們的投資成長了 20%。

A： And we made a big profit because of that. 因此我們也贏得很多利潤。

B： You're right. Last year we saw an annual growth of 6.1% in net profit. 你說得對。去年我們純利潤年成長 6.1%。

A： This year Let's work harder to achieve a better performance. 今年我們要更努力，以取得更好的成績。

B： I believe we can make it. 我相信我們能成功的。

市場行銷

Scene 49 門市推銷

Step 1 必備表達

介紹	show：show 在推銷中常指「介紹」，比如：show the features of the product 介紹一下產品的特點。
預算	budget：推銷商品時往往要詢問顧客大概想買什麼價位的，也就是 budget「預算」有多少。
範圍	range：a range of 各種的。
計畫	plan：plan to do sth. 計劃做某事。
大約	around：也可用 about 來代替。
禮物	gift：推銷時經常要送顧客一些小禮物，即：gift；有時也會送 coupon「優惠券」或者 sample「試用包」。
特別的	special：goods on special offer 特價貨。
完美的	perfect：表達讚美時不要總是用 good、great 等，如果非常滿意也可以用 perfect 來加強語氣。
推銷	promote：promote 的名詞形式 promotion 也很常用，表示「推銷活動」。
廣告商品	advertisement product：advertisement 廣告。

Step 2 句句精彩

① 我能為您介紹嗎？

A： Good morning, sir. May I show you something? 早上好，先生。我能為您介紹嗎？

B： No, thanks. I'm just looking around. 不用了，謝謝。我只是隨便看看。

Tips

■ Which one would you like? 您喜歡哪一款？

What stuff do you want to buy? 您想買什麼東西？

Let me show you its specialty. 讓我介紹下它的獨特之處。

② 你的預算是多少？

A： what's your budget? 你的預算是多少？

B： It ranges from 200 yuan to 300 yuan. 200 到 300 元。

Tips

How much is your budget for it? 你對它的預算是多少？

How much is affordable to you? 你能承受多少錢？

How much is OK for you? 對你來說多少錢合適？

③ 這個本週特價。

A： This is on sale this week. It's only 5 yuan. 這個本週特價。才 5 元錢。

B： Well, I'll take two. 哦，那我要兩個。

Tips

We offer a special discount. 我們會有特別折扣。

Its original price is 100 yuan while the present price is 88 yuan. 原價 100 元，現價 88 元。

■ 50 dollars is its wholesale price and the retail price is 60 dollars. 50 元是批發價，零售價是 60 元。

④ 推銷員每銷售一件產品可以得到 50 美元的抽成。

A： A salesman will get a $50 commission for every piece he sold. 推銷員每銷售一件產品可以得到 50 美元的抽成。

B： It's a good deal. 這是個不錯的買賣。

Tips

推銷員通常按業績來抽成，專業的說法就是「佣金」，即 commission。

You can earn around 1,000 yuan commission in this deal. 在這次交易中你可以賺大約 1000 元的佣金。

They work for the company on commission. 他們以賺佣金的方式為公司工作。

⑤ 一組訓練有素的推銷員是必要的。

A： How do you plan to promote your new product? 你們打算怎麼推銷你們的新產品？

B：A group of well-trained salesmen are necessary. 一組訓練有素的推銷員是必要的。

Tips

■ well-trained 表示「訓練有素的」，也就是說業務水準很高。

■ It will be perfect if the salesmen have a good performance. 如果推銷員們能有好的表現就完美了。

■ The salesmen need a training course before the promotion. 促銷活動開始前推銷員們需要參加培訓課程。

⑥ 他們討論過如何推銷這款產品。

A：The product sells not very well. 這款產品銷售得不是很好。

B：They had discussed how to promote the product. But their plan doesn't work. 他們討論過如何推銷這款產品。但是他們的計畫沒有奏效。

Tips

■ They have made a marketing plan for selling the product. 他們為銷售商品做了行銷企劃。

■ They're making every effort to sell this advertisement product now. 現在他們正盡全力銷售這款廣告商品。

■ They plan to do a special promotion of their new product. 他們計劃為新產品辦一次促銷活動。

⑦ 我們可以發傳單給顧客。

A：We can distribute leaflets to the customers. 我們可以給顧客發傳單。

B：It's a good idea. 好主意。

Tips

■ We can send some gifts to the customers. 我們可以送些禮物給顧客。

■ Customers can get coupons of the product in the newspaper. 顧客可以從報紙上得到產品的優惠券。

■ We'd better prepare some samples for the customers. 我們可以為顧客準備些試用品。

Step 3　實戰對話

① 推銷商品

A：Welcome, Madam. May I show you something? 歡迎您，女士。我能為您介紹

嗎？

B： I'm looking for a dress. 我想買條裙子。

A： What's your budget? 你的預算是多少？

B： About 200 yuan. 200 元左右。

A： Let me see... How about this one? This is on sale this week. 讓我看看……這件怎麼樣？這個本週特價。

B： Oh, how much is it? 哦，多少錢？

A： It costs you only 228 yuan. 這個只要 228 元。

B： May I try it on? 我可以試穿嗎？

A： Of course. 當然可以。

②　選擇推銷員

A： How can we promote our new product? 我們該怎麼推銷我們的新產品呢？

B： A group of well-trained salesmen are necessary. 一組訓練有素的推銷員是必要的。

A： Exactly. What incentives could we offer for them? 沒錯。我們能為他們提供什麼獎勵呢？

B： A salesman will get a $50 commission for every piece he sold. 推銷員每銷售一件產品可以得到 50 美元的佣金。

A： It's great. I suggest you giving them a training course before the promotion. 很不錯。我建議在促銷活動開始前為他們提供培訓課程。

B： Good point. 好主意。

③　產品推銷得很好

A： The product sells very well! Jack's team did a good job! 這款產品賣得非常好！傑克的團隊幹得漂亮！

B： Yeah! They had discussed how to promote the product. 是啊！他們討論過如何推銷這款產品。

A： It seems that their promotion plan works. 看起來他們的推銷計畫奏效了。

B： They have made every effort to promote the product. 他們盡了全力來推銷產品。

A： They work very hard. 他們工作很賣力。

B： No pains, no gains. 一分耕耘，一分收穫。

Scene 50　討論促銷方案

Step 1　必 備 表 達

主攻	hit：hit 的原意是「擊中」，也可以作名詞，表示「成功」。
時機	timing：比如 Timing is important. 時機很重要。
目標	target：也可以用 aim 來代替。
贊助	sponsor：sponsored by 由……贊助。
突然增加	explode：也可以用 increase suddenly 來代替。
保持	maintain：也可用 keep 來代替。
界定	define：define... as... 為……下定義為……
縮小	narrow down：narrow 在這裡作動詞 還有「窄的 小的」的意思。
水準	level：high level 高水準。
效果	effect：effect on sth. 對……的效果。

Step 2　句 句 精 彩

① 我們將主攻新生。時機剛好！

A：The new term will start next Monday. 新學期將在下週一開始。

B：We'll hit new students. Good timing! 我們將主攻新生。時機剛好！

Tips

- ■ Our target customer is the young. 我們的目標顧客是年輕群體。
- ■ We're aiming at college students. 我們的目標是大學生。
- ■ The product is very popular with parents. 這款產品很受家長們的歡迎。

② 你的銷售目標是什麼？

A：What is your target? 你的銷售目標是什麼？

B：I plan to target at the young market. 我計畫把目標定在年輕人的市場。

Tips

What is your aim? 你的目標是什麼？

What market will you target? 你將針對什麼市場？

what's your plan? 你有什麼計畫？

③ 我們可以贊助像是音樂會之類的活動。

A： We could sponsor an event like a concert. 我們可以贊助像是音樂會之類的活動。

B： Yeah, we can put our samples on the seats. 是的，我們可以把樣品放在座位上。

Tips

We are the official sponsor of this football game. 我們是這場足球賽的官方贊助商。

We have attracted a lot of young people through our sponsorship of youth educational programs. 透過贊助青年教育專案，我們吸引了很多年輕人。

We can provide financial support for this event. 我們可以為這項活動提供資金支持。

④ 我們需要可以促進銷售的活動。

A： We need a promotion that will gear up sales. 我們需要可以促進銷售的活動。

B： We must make a good preparation. 我們必須做好準備。

Tips

gear up 促進。

We need promotion campaigns through which consumers can be well aware of our products. 我們需要透過促銷活動讓消費者認可我們的產品。

The promotion of the new product is very successful. 新產品的促銷活動很成功。

⑤ 我們必須界定我們的目標顧客。

A： It's necessary for us to focus on a certain market. 我們有必要把目標放在特定的市場。

B： You're right. We have to define our target customer. 你說得沒錯。我們必須界定我們的目標顧客。

Tips

At first, we need to know who our target customer is. 首先，我們需要知道誰是我們的目標客戶。

We have to narrow down the target customer. 我們必須縮小目標客戶群。

We'd better focus on young consumers. 我們最好把重點放在年輕消費者上。

⑥ 別想一網打盡。

A： Don't try to be everything to everyone. 別想一網打盡。

B： I got your point. 我明白你的意思。

Tips

- You should have specific aims. 你應該有些具體的目標。
- One specific use is enough. 有一種特定的用途就足夠了。
- Less is more. 物以稀為貴。

⑦ 我希望保持一定熱度的促銷活動。

A： Our promotion is quite a hit. 我們的促銷活動十分成功。

B：I hope to maintain a certain level of excitement. 我希望保持一定熱度的促銷活動。

Tips

- We decided to conduct a well-prepared promotion. 我們決定舉辦一次準備周全的促銷活動。
- I think we should start a large-scale promotion soon. 我覺得我們應該立刻開始大規模的促銷活動。
- We need a strong ad campaign. 我們需要有力的廣告宣傳。

Step 3　實 戰 對 話

① 討論銷售目標

A： What is your target? 什麼是你的銷售目標？

B： I decided to target at the young market. 我決定把目標定在年輕人的市場。

A： Do you mean college students? The new term will start next Monday. 你的意思是大學生嗎？新學期將在下週一開始。

B： OK! We'll hit new students. Good timing! 好啊！我們將主攻新生。時機剛好！

A： Hope it will make a hit. 希望能獲得成功。

B： I hope so! 我也希望！

② 討論促銷活動

A： We need a promotion that will gear up sales. 我們需要可以促進銷售的活動。

B： You are right. Successful promotion matter. 你說得對。成功的促銷很重要。

A： We could sponsor an event like a concert. 我們可以贊助像是音樂會之類的活動。

B： Good idea. Our target consumer is just young people. 好主意。我們的目標客戶正好是年輕人。

A： Yeah, we can hand out our samples before the show. 是的，我們可以在演出開始前發放試用品。

B： That can attract a lot of people to use our product. 這樣可以吸引很多人來使用我們的產品。

③ 討論目標顧客

A： It's necessary for us to focus on a certain market. 我們有必要把目標集中在特定的市場。

B： You're right. We have to define our target customer. 你說的沒錯。我們必須界定我們的目標顧客。

A： Don't try to be everything to everyone. 別想一網打盡。

B： I got your point. 我明白你的意思。

A： So we should narrow down the target market. 所以我們應該縮小目標市場。

B： I think the product is perfect for college students. 我認為這款產品非常適合大學生。

Scene 51　各類促銷方案

Step 1　必備表達

四件一組的	four-piece：piece 一件；促銷活動中經常是幾件商品捆綁銷售。
超值組合	value package：有時幾件商品搭配在一起銷售會比較便宜，package 的原意是「包裹」，這裡可以理解為「打包銷售」。又比如 package deal 表示「一攬子交易」。
回饋金	rebate：我們常說「滿 ×× 元減 ×× 元」，這裡減去的錢就是 rebate。
會員資格	membership：membership card 會員卡。
無息的	interest-free：interest 利息；-free 是一種構詞成分，表示「無，免除」，比如：duty-free 免稅的。
選擇	option：也可用 choice 來代替。
換購	trade in：trade sth. in for sth. 以……換……。
長期的	long-standing：也可用 long-term 來代替。
限時	limited time：offer... for a limited time 限時提供。
補償	compensation：compensation for... 對……的補償。

Step 2　句句精彩

1 只要 50 美元，你就能擁有香水套組 4 瓶裝。

A： For the price of $50, you can have the four-piece fragrance set. 只要 50 美元，你就能擁有香水套組 4 瓶裝。

B： Then I'll buy one set. 那我買一套。

Tips

■ set 在這裡是「一套，一組」的意思。

■ The value package costs you only 46 dollars. 這個超值組合只要 46 美元。

■ If you buy three pieces, I will give you a 10% discount. 如果您買 3 個，我可以幫您打 9 折。

② 消費每滿 400 美元，就享受 20% 的現金回饋。

A： You will receive 20 percent cash back for every $400 you spend. 消費每滿 400 美元，就享受 20% 的現金回饋。

B： So you mean I can get a $80 rebate if I spend $400? 所以你的意思是如果我消費 400 美元，就可以得到 80 美元的回饋金了？

Tips

You can save some money with coupons. 您可以使用優惠券來省一些錢。

We offer quantity discounts for larger orders. 我們為大批量訂購提供折扣。

This kind of product is priced at 12 yuan each for quantities up to 100. 如果數量達到100件，這種產品每件 12 元。

③ 消費 6000 美元就能享有會員資格。

A： How can I be your member? 我怎樣才能成為你們的會員？

B： Your $6,000 purchase qualifies you for membership. 消費 6000 美元就能享有會員資格。

Tips

■ We want to offer you a free trial membership. 我們想為您提供一次免費入會的試用機會。

You can join our fitness club at the introductory price of 800 yuan. 您可以以 800 元的推廣價加入我們的健身俱樂部。

It includes unlimited access to all our promotions. 這包括無限制參加我們所有的促銷活動。

④ 如果你想多省點錢，可以現在全都付清。

A： If you want to save a little more money, you could pay in full now. 如果你想多省點錢，可以現在全都付清。

B： How much will I save then? 那我可以多省多少錢？

Tips

We offer a rebate of 5 dollars for early settlement of the bill. 盡早結帳立減 5 元。

You can pay in installments, interest-free. 你可以無息分期付款。

Would you like to save more money? There are some great men's shirts on sale now. 您想多省點錢嗎？有些很棒的男式襯衣正在特價銷售。

---

⑤ 我們為長期顧客提供送貨優惠。

A： Welcome you back at any time. We have a delivery special for long-standing cus-tomers. 歡迎您隨時再來光臨。我們為長期顧客提供送貨優惠。

B： I see. Thank you. 我明白了。謝謝。

Tips

■ We are offering a 10% discount for long-standing customers now. 我們現在為長期顧客提供 9 折優惠。

■ We are offering a cash rebate for our regular customers now. 我們現在給老顧客現金回饋。

■ We will provide coupons and giveaways for our regular customers this weekend. 本週末我們會為老顧客提供優惠券和贈品。

---

⑥ 我們限時提供免費住宿本飯店一晚。

A： For a limited time, We're offering one free night in our hotel. 我們限時提供免費住宿本飯店一晚。

B： When is the limited time? 限時是指什麼時間？

Tips

■ There is an option for regular customers to reserve a double room in our hotel at a special price. 老顧客可以選擇以特價預訂我們飯店的雙人房。

■ We have a clearance sale from June 20th to July 20th. 我們從 6 月 20 號到 7 月 20 號進行清倉大拍賣。

■ The big sale is from May to June. 折扣季從 5 月到 6 月。

---

⑦ 買一送一。

A： How much is it? 這個多少錢？

B： It's 50 yuan. Buy one, get one free. 50 元。買一送一。

Tips

■ You can trade in your used sofa for a brand-new one. 你可以把沙發以舊換新。

■ This product is a promotional item only during these three days. 這種產品只在這 3 天促銷。

■ We will hold an end-of-season sale. 我們會舉辦季末大減價。

Step 3 實戰對話

① 買套裝得優惠

A： It smells good. How much is this bottle of perfume? 真香啊。這瓶香水多少錢？

B： 15 dollars. 15 美元。

A： It's a little expensive. 有點貴啊。

B： For the price of $50, you can have the four-piece fragrance set. 只要 50 美元，你就能擁有香水套組 4 瓶裝。

A： Wow, It's a little cheaper then. 哇，這就便宜點了。

B： Yes. It is a real bargain. 是的，真的很划算。

② 加入會員

A： Hello, Miss. I felt you would wish to know about our promotional offer. 小姐，妳好。我覺得妳會想知道我們現在的促銷活動。

B： What kind of promotion? 什麼促銷？

A： Your $6,000 purchase qualifies you for membership. Then you can get a 10% off every time you buy stuff. 消費 6000 美元就享有會員資格。然後你每次買東西都可以享受 10% 的折扣。

B： $6,000 dollars...Can I pay in installments? 6000 美元……可以分期付嗎？

A： If you want to save a little more money, you could pay in full now. 如果你想多省點錢，可以現在全都付清。

B： I'll think about it. 我考慮考慮吧。

③ 各種特別優惠

A： Excuse me, I'd like to buy a purse. 打擾一下，我想買個錢包。

B： Well, I highly recommend this one. 嗯，我強烈推薦這一款。

A： How much is it? 多少錢？

B： It's 300 yuan. Buy one, get one free. 300 元。買一送一。

A： That will be great. I can give my friend a purse as a gift as well. 那太好了。我還可以送給我朋友一個當做禮物。

B： Yes. Which color do you like? 是的。您想要什麼顏色的？

A： The black one and the yellow one. 黑的和黃的。

B： OK. And we have a delivery special for long-standing customers. So welcome you back at any time. 好的。而且我們為長期顧客提供送貨優惠。所以歡迎您隨時再來光臨。

A： I got it. Thank you. 我明白了。謝謝。

Scene 52　市場調查前期準備

Step 1　必備表達

電訪	telephone survey：打電話對目標客戶進行的訪問叫作電訪，進行電話訪問時要注意電話用語和平時說話的區別。
問卷	questionnaire：complete the questionnaire 填寫問卷。
網路調查	web survey：網路調查的形式包括線上回答問題、回覆郵件中的調查問卷等。
街頭訪問	face-to-face interview：face-to-face 面對面的。
參與	take part in：也可用 participate in 或 join in 來代替。
資料	data：也可用 statistics 來代替。
活動	campaign：an advertising campaign 廣告宣傳活動。
刺激	motivate：常用來指激發某人的興趣。
目標年齡層	target demographic：demographic 的原意是「人口統計的」。
特別地	specifically：specific 特別的、特定的。

Step 2　句句精彩

① 你們想用哪種方式進行調查？

A：What method do you want to use for the research? 你們想用哪種方式進行調查？

B：I prefer questionnaire. 我覺得問卷調查比較好。

Tips

■ We hope a good response from the telephone survey. 我們期待電話調查有好的反響。

■ We sent people to the large retailers in person. 我們派人親自走訪各大型零售店。

■ We plan to do a face-to-face interview in the shopping mall. 我們打算在購物中心做面對面的訪問。

② 我們要召集多大的焦點族群？

A： How large will the focus group be? 我們要召集多大的焦點族群？

B： We will focus on the young group. 我們會把重點放在年輕族群。

Tips

- Who will be our interviewee of the market survey? 誰會是我們這次市場調查的受訪者？
- We should pay special attention to old people when We're doing the survey. 在做調查時我們要特別關注老年族群。
- This product agrees with many people. 這種產品適合大多數人。

③ 我們鎖定的目標市場是什麼？

A： what's the target market We're looking at? 我們鎖定的目標市場是什麼？

B： Our target market is among the students. 我們的目標市場在學生間。

Tips

- Middle school students are the target. 中學生是我們的目標。
- We will target at the market of college students. 我們會鎖定大學生這個市場。
- We'd better maximize the exposure of our product to our target market. 我們應該針對目標市場盡可能增加產品曝光度。

④ 我們的目標年齡層是幾歲？

A： Who is our target demographic? 我們的目標年齡層是幾歲？

B： The product targets at female people of 20 to 30 years old. 這種產品針對 20 到 30 歲的女性。

Tips

- We focus on people aged between 20 and 35. 我們的目標群體是年齡在 20 到 35 歲之間的人。
- The students in middle school, namely children aged between 11 and 13 years, are our target customers. 讀中學的學生，也就是 11 到 13 歲的孩子，是我們的目標客戶。（編按：美國中等教育與臺灣國高中的學制並不相同，11 到 13 歲為中學，14 到 18 歲為高中。）
- Our product targets at middle-aged man. 我們的產品針對中年男性。

⑤ 這個週末前，我們會設計好資訊收集表。

A： Have you get prepared for your market survey? 你們的市場調查做完準備工作了嗎？

B： We'll have data collection forms designed by the end of this week. 這個週末前，我們會設計好資訊收集表。

Tips

We have designed a questionnaire. 我們設計了一張問卷調查表。

The questionnaires have been handed out. 調查表已經分發出去了。

We decided to gather more information from various sources. 我們決定從各種管道收集更多的資訊。

⑥ 這次活動我們將特別針對 30 歲以下的女性。

A： For this campaign, We'll specifically target women under the age of 30. 這次活動我們將特別針對 30 歲以下的女性。

B： It's a huge group. 這是個很大的族群。

Tips

Only students will have access to this promotion campaign. 這次促銷活動只有學生可以參加。

We plan to hold a campaign especially for girls between 15 and 25 years. 我們打算為 15 到 25 歲的女孩特別舉辦一次活動。

■ Everyone can take part in this campaign. 人人都可以參加這次活動。

⑦ 我們需要解消費者購物的動機。

A： We need to understand what motivates consumers to make a purchase. 我們需要了解消費者購物的動機。

B： I think that includes many factors. 我認為會包括很多因素。

Tips

We need to understand who will be interested in our products. 我們需要了解什麼人會對我們的產品感興趣。

We should be concerned about the consumers' shopping habits. 我們需要關注消費者的購物習慣。

We must know how to meet the target audience's needs. 我們必須了解如何滿足目標消費族群的需求。

Step 3　實戰對話

① 調查鎖定目標市場

A： I heard you're preparing for a market research. What method do you want to use for the research? 我聽說你在準備做市場調查。你們想用哪種方式進行調查？

B： I prefer questionnaire. 我覺得問卷調查比較好。

A： I think so. What's the target market We're looking at? 我也覺得。我們鎖定的目標市場是什麼？

B： We will target at the market of college students. 我們會鎖定在大學生這個市場。

A： I see. I suggest you doing the survey just in campus. 我明白了。我建議你就在校園裡做調查。

B： You're right. I have planned to. 你說的沒錯。我已經計劃這樣做了。

② 鎖定焦點族群

A： Jack, I'd like to talk about the market survey with you. 傑克，我想和你談談市場調查的事。

B： Sure. 好啊。

A： In your opinion, how large will the focus group be? 在你看來，我們要召集多大的焦點群體？

B： The product targets at female people of 20 to 30 years old. So We'd better focus on them. 這種產品針對 20 到 30 歲的女性。所以我們應該集中精力在她們身上。

A： That makes sense. 有道理。

B： I think paying attention to a certain group is more effective than to everyone. 我認為把注意力集中在特定族群比廣泛撒網要有效得多。

③ 鎖定目標年齡層

A： Who is our target demographic? 我們的目標年齡層是幾歲？

B： Our product is specifically for young girls. 我們的產品是特別針對年輕女性的。

A： Yeah. The promotion campaign will be launched next month. 嗯。促銷活動下月就要開始了。

B： Yes. So for this campaign, We'll specifically target women under the age of 30. 是啊。所以這次活動我們將特別針對 30 歲以下的女性。

A： I got your point. 我明白你的意思。

B： I do hope the campaign will make a hit with them. 真希望這次活動能夠受到她們的歡迎。

Scene 53　市場調查

Step 1　必備表達

進行調查	conduct a survey：conduct 也可用 do 或者 carry out 來代替。
介意	mind：mind doing sth. 介意做某事。
忠誠的	loyal：be loyal to 對……忠誠。
與……相比	stack up against：也可用 compare with 來代替。
競爭者	competitor：也可用 rival 來代替。
決定性因素	deciding factor：decide 表示「做決定」，其現在分詞 deciding 可以作形容詞表示「決定性的」。
禮券	gift certificate：certificate 證明書。
超值優惠券	valuable coupon：valuable 很有價值的；coupon 優惠券。
騰出	spare：spare the time 騰出時間。
習慣	habit：have the habit of doing sth. 有做某事的習慣。

Step 2　句句精彩

① 我們正在進行一項調查。你有時間嗎？

A：We're conducting a survey. Could you spare a few minutes? 我們正在進行一項調查。你有時間嗎？

B：OK. What is the survey about? 好的。調查是關於什麼的？

Tips

■ I would like you to spare me several minutes and fill in this form. 我想占用您幾分鐘的時間，請您填一下這個表格。

■ We're making a market research and I hope you could help me fill in it. 我們正在做一份市場調查，我希望您能填一下。

■ I'm carrying out a survey on behalf of NEC Market Research Department. 我代表 NEC 市場調研部進行一次調查。

② 我來電是想問您幾個購物方面的問題。

A： Hello. I'm calling to ask you a few questions about shopping. 你好。我來電是想問您幾個購物方面的問題。

B： OK, go ahead. 好的，請說吧。

Tips

I'm calling to ask you to answer a few questions for me on the clothing market. 我來電是想讓你幫我回答一些有關服裝市場的問題。

I'm calling on behalf of our company, Times Mobile Phone Company. 我代表我們公司——時代手機公司來電。

We'd like to conduct a phone interview with you. 我們將向您進行電話訪問。

③ 你可以告訴我你用哪個牌子的潤膚乳嗎？

A： Would you mind telling me what brand of skin cream you use? 你可以告訴我你用哪個牌子的潤膚乳嗎？

B： Dove is my favorite. 我最愛多芬。

Tips

I'd like to know which brand of TV is in your house. 我想了解一下你家電視機是什麼牌子的。

Have you ever used skin cream of our brand? 你用過我們牌子的潤膚乳嗎？

A and B, which one do you prefer? A 和 B，你喜歡哪個？

④ 你最喜歡這個產品的哪一點？

A： What do you like most about this product? 你最喜歡這個產品的哪一點？

B： It's of high quality. 它的品質很好。

Tips

Could you name one or two features of the product you like? 你可以說出一兩個你喜歡的這個產品的特色嗎？

Why do you choose to use this product? 你為什麼選擇使用該產品？

Why are you so loyal to this brand? 你為什麼如此青睞這個品牌？

⑤ 你用這個品牌多久了？

A： How long have you been enjoying this brand? 你用這個品牌多久了？

B： Let me see. Over three years. 讓我想想。超過 3 年了。

Tips

■ It's over ten years for you to choose this brand. Why? 你選擇這個品牌已經超過 10 年了，為什麼呢？

■ How often do you change a brand? 你多久會換一個品牌來用？

■ Why have you used this mobile phone for over six years? 你為什麼用這款手機用了 6 年？

⑥ 你覺得這個品牌和其競爭者比較之下，表現如何？

A： How do you think this brand stacks up against its competitors? 你覺得這個品牌和其競爭者比較之下，表現如何？

B： It can rank top 3. 它可以排到前 3 名。

Tips

■ Do you think this product can compete with its rivals? 你認為這個產品可以和它的對手競爭嗎？

■ I rank this brand very highly. 我對這個品牌的評價很高。

■ In my opinion, this product ranks top 1 among its competitors. 在我看來，這個產品在它的競爭對手中可以脫穎而出。

⑦ 你覺得品質和價格，哪個更重要？

A：what's more important to you, quality or price? 你覺得品質和價格，哪個更重要？

B： Quality, of course. 當然是品質。

Tips

■ What is your shopping habit, a high-quality one or a cheap one? 你的購物習慣是怎樣的，選品質好的還是便宜的？

■ Which one do you prefer, a fashionable one or a useful one? 時尚的和實用的，你更喜歡哪種？

■ What is the deciding factor do you think for a consumer to buy a product? 你認為對於一個顧客來說什麼會是購買一件商品的決定性因素？

Step 3　實戰對話

① 調查某類商品的市場

A：Excuse me, Miss. Could you do me a favor? 小姐，打擾一下。可以幫我個忙嗎？

B： What can I do for you? 你有什麼事嗎？

A： We're conducting a survey. Could you spare a few minutes? 我們正在進行一項調查。你有時間嗎？

B： All right, just a few minutes. 好的，就幾分鐘啊。

A： Would you mind telling me what brand of skin cream you use? 你可以告訴我你用哪個牌子的潤膚乳嗎？

B： Ah...Dove. 啊……多芬。

A： I see. We produce skin cream, too. Here is a sample for you. 我知道了。我們也生產潤膚乳。這是送您的樣品。

B： Thank you. 謝謝。

A： I hope you can have a try at our product. 希望您也可以試試我們的產品。

② 電話訪問

A： Hello. 你好。

B： Hello. I'm calling to ask you a few questions about where you shop. 你好。我來電是想問幾個你在購物方面的問題。

A： Oh, I often go shopping in Xidan business area. 哦，我經常在西單商圈買東西。

B： I see. What's more important to you, quality or price? 我知道了。你覺得品質和價格，哪個更重要？

A： High quality at low price, of course. 當然是物美價廉最好了。

B： I got your point. Thank you. May I have your e-mail address? We'll send a valuable coupon to you. 我明白你的意思。謝謝了。可以告訴我你的郵寄地址嗎？我們會發給你一張超值優惠券。

③ 針對產品的調查

A： Good afternoon, Madam. I saw you buying this product. 女士，下午好。我看到妳買了這個產品。

B： Yeah. what's up? 是的。怎麼了？

A： Actually We're conducting a survey now. So could you answer me a few questions? 事實上我們在進行市場調查。所以可以回答我幾個問題嗎？

B： Fine. 好啊。

A： What do you like most about this product? 妳最喜歡這個產品的哪一點？

B： It's of high quality. 它的品質很好。

A： Anything more? 還有別的嗎？

B： It costs me not much money. 價錢也便宜。

Scene 54　分析調查

Step 1　必備表達

報告	report：report on 關於……的報告。
調查	investigation：也可用 inquire 來代替。
分析	analysis：analysis 的動詞形式是 analyze，也很常用。
正面回應	favorable response：favorable 肯定的，支持的；response 反應。
接受	acceptance：動詞形式是 accept。
厭惡	put off：也可用 dislike 來代替，另外這個片語還有「延後」的意思。
大約的	approximate：也可用 about 或者 around 來代替。
回應	respond：respond to 對……的回應。
介紹	referral：也可用 introduction 來代替。
延長期限	renew：renew a subscription 續訂。

Step 2　句句精彩

① 這是我們調查結果的報告。

A： This is the report on the findings of our investigation. 這是我們調查結果的報告。

B： I'll have a careful look. 我會仔細看看的。

Tips

■ The report on customer's shopping habit has been finished. 關於顧客購物習慣的報告已經完成了。

■ We've just carried out a survey of consumers. 我們剛剛完成了消費者方面的市場調查。

■ I'm here today to give you the results of these months' survey. 我今天來這裡向大家報告這幾個月的調查結果。

② 在我們的目標市場的人群中，有 37% 的人給予正面回應。

A： We got a 37 percent favorable response rate from members of our target market. 在我們的目標市場的人群中，有 37% 的人給予正面回應。

B： We should work harder. 我們要更努力了。

Tips

- Almost 85% of the customers are satisfied with our products' performance. 有近 85% 的消費者對我們的產品性能表示滿意。

- According to surveys, 55% of the target customers have expressed their interest in our product. 根據調查，55% 的目標客戶對我們的產品表示有興趣。

- 67% of our customers said that they would renew the subscription of our service. 67% 的顧客表示會續訂我們的服務。

③ 這個產品將被更大的市場所接受。

A： After only one month, the product has already been popular with young consumers. 僅僅一個月時間，這個產品就受到年輕消費者的歡迎了。

B： The product will find acceptance in a wider market. 這個產品將被更大的市場所接受。

Tips

- Our market report shows that tHere's quite a demand for our products. 根據市場報告，我們的產品有它的需求。

- The report shows that the market is on the upgrade. 報告說明市場正在看漲。

- Though We're in market slump, this product increases our market share. 儘管我們現在市場不景氣，但是這個產品還是提高了我們的市場占有率。

④ 消費者似乎不太喜歡這種口味。

A： The customers were a little put off by this kind of flavor. 消費者似乎不太喜歡這種口味。

B： Then I suggest we should not produce this kind of flavor any longer. 那我建議我們不要再生產這種口味的了。

Tips

- The market report shows that the customers have little interest in this product. 市場報告顯示顧客對這個產品的興趣不大。

- We found that only 14% of the people would buy it. 我們發現只有 14% 的人會買它。

20% of the customers don't accept this kind of product. 20% 的客戶不接受這種產品。

⑤ 對這個產品的大致需求仍不清楚。

A： It's still not clear what the approximate level of demand is for the product. 對這個產品的大致需求仍不清楚。

B： We'd better make a further investigation. 我們最好進行進一步的調查。

Tips

We haven't found out what the customers really need. 我們還沒找出客戶真正需要的是什麼。

It's still not clear which group of people that this product is targeting at. 還不清楚這個產品的目標客戶群。

What's the demand of our target market? 我們目標市場的需求是什麼？

⑥ 從問卷調查中，我們發現年輕人喜歡去大型購物中心購物。

A： We find out from the questionnaire that young people like to shop in large shopping malls. 從問卷調查中，我們發現年輕人喜歡去大型購物中心購物。

B： So we can do our promotions there. 所以我們可以在那裡做促銷活動。

Tips

We checked over the questionnaires, and found it turns out that young people prefer fashionable products. 我們研究了調查問卷，發現事實證明年輕人喜歡時尚的產品。

The market report says that middle-aged women prefer products of good quality than fashionable ones. 市場報告顯示，比起時尚產品，中年女性更注重產品的品質。

The survey shows that promotion campaigns will attract a lot of people when they're held in shopping malls. 調查顯示，促銷活動在購物中心舉辦會吸引很多人。

⑦ 調查顯示，將近一半的新客戶是透過介紹來的。

A： Our research shows that almost half of our new clients are from referrals. 調查顯示，將近一半的新客戶是透過介紹來的。

B： It means our product enjoys a wide acceptance among consumers. 這意味著我們的產品在消費者中的接受度很廣。

Tips

Most of our customers are attracted by our advertisement and promotion campaigns. 大多數的客戶是被我們的廣告和促銷活動吸引的。

- Nearly half of the new customers get the information of our products from TV advertisement. 近一半的新顧客是從電視廣告中了解到我們產品資訊的。
- 35% of the clients know our brand from the Internet. 35% 的客戶是從網上了解到我們的品牌的。

Step 3　實 戰 對 話

① 調查報告出爐

A： Good morning, manager Wang. This is the report on the findings of our investigation. 王經理，早上好。這是我們調查結果的報告。

B： Great. What did you find out from the report? 太好了。你從報告中發現了什麼？

A： We did a research on our target market and got some data. 我們對目標市場做了研究，得到一些資料。

B： For example? 比如呢？

A： In terms of our products, we got a 37 percent favorable response rate from members of our target market. 就我們的產品而言，在我們的目標市場的人群中，有 37% 的人給予正面回應。

B： It's not very high, to be honest. Well, I'll have a careful look at the report later. 實話講，這不是很高。好了，我稍後會仔細看看報告的。

② 市場接受度

A： David, have you finished the market survey? 大衛，你完成市場調查了嗎？

B： Yes, here is the report. 是的，這是報告。

A： Great. Let me see. 太好了。我看看。

B： According to surveys, 65% of the target customers have expressed their interest in our product. 根據調查，65% 的目標客戶對我們的產品表示有興趣。

A： Brilliant. I believe the product will find acceptance in a wider market. 太棒了。我相信這個產品將獲得更大的市場接受。

B： As long as we work harder, we will make it. 只要我們更加努力，我們會做到的。

③ 產品不被市場接受

A： Our new ice cream doesn't sell very well. Did you do a survey to find the reason? 我們的新款霜淇淋賣得不太好。你有沒有做調查找找原因呢？

B： Yes, only 14% of the people said that they would buy it. 是的，只有 14% 的人表示會買它。

A： It's a shame. what's wrong? 太遺憾了。出什麼問題了？

B： The customers were a little put off by this kind of flavor. 消費者似乎不太喜歡這種口味。

A： What's the customers' demand? 那消費者的需求是什麼？

B： It's still not clear what the approximate level of demand is for the product. 對這個產品的大致需求仍不清楚。

Scene 55　廣告訴求

Step 1　必備表達

廣告	advertisement：報紙上的「廣告專版」就是 advertisement page。
革命性的	revolutionary：revolutionary influence 革命性的影響。
投資計畫	investment plan：investment 表示「投資」，investment in 就是「對……的投資」。
強調	highlight：也可用 emphasize 來代替。
加快	quicken：quick「快的」加上表示「使……」的詞根 -en，即 quicken，就是「使……快」的意思。
展現	demonstrate：也可用 show 或者 present 來代替。
特色	feature：也可用 characteristic 來代替。
以……為基礎	base on：也可用 take... as the base 來代替。
競爭	competition：competition between/with 和……的競爭。
集中	concentrate on：也可用 focus on 來代替。

Step 2　句句精彩

①　我想把這個廣告登在《中國日報》上。

A：It will be the most revolutionary investment plan on the market. 這將是市場上最具革命性的投資計畫。

B：I want to put this advertisement in China Daily. 我想把這個廣告登在《中國日報》上。

Tips

■ We're putting full-page ads in the Sunday edition of the newspapers. 我們會在報紙的周日版登全頁廣告。

■ We plan to take out full-page ads with two large magazines. 我們計畫在兩家大型雜誌上刊登全版廣告。

We could use print advertising, for example, newspapers, business journals and magazines.
我們可以使用平面廣告來宣傳，比如報紙、商業週刊和雜誌。

② 我們想要強調它卓越的性能。

A：Have you gotten any ideas on the advertising of the product? 你們對產品的廣告有什麼想法嗎？

B：We want to highlight its excellent performance. 我們想要強調它卓越的性能。

Tips

The fashionable design is the focus of this product promotion. 時尚的設計是這次產品促銷的重點。

This kind of beverage product is well-known for natural ingredients. 這種飲品以天然成分而著稱。

The strong point of this new laptop is portable. 這台新款筆記型電腦的最大優點是便攜性。

③ 我們會展現它對整個家庭的幫助。

A：We'll demonstrate its usefulness for the entire family. 我們會展現它對整個家庭的幫助。

B：It's a good point. 這是個很好的賣點。

Tips

We'll demonstrate how to use it in a very easy way. 我們會展示使用它是如何的方便。

This product is designed for students. 這個產品是為學生設計的。

The product will be sold specifically to young people, so We'll need to appeal directly to them. 產品主要面向年輕人出售，所以我們要直接迎合他們的訴求。

④ 我們將呈現它容易使用的新特色。

A：We'll present its new user-friendly features. 我們將呈現它容易使用的新特色。

B：That matters. 這點很重要。

Tips

It's designed with special attention to ergonomics. 它是特別針對人體工學而設計的。

The product we sell is refreshing, enjoyable and of the highest quality. 我們銷售的產品會使人耳目一新、感覺愉悅，並且品質很高。

Our product can be enjoyed, at any time, as part of a healthy and active lifestyle. 作為一種健康和積極的生活方式，我們的產品可以隨時被享用。

⑤ 我們會展示它比其他的產品更寬敞。

A： what's the difference between your product and its competitors? 你的產品和競爭者的有什麼不同？

B： We'll show how much more roominess it has than others. 我們會展示該產品比其他的產品更寬敞。

Tips

- We'll show how faster the machine runs than others. 我們會展示這台機器比其他的機器運行得更快。
- In terms of after-sales, we have an advantage. 在售後服務方面我們有優勢。
- This is our newly improved product, which have more functions than the first models. 這是我們新改良的產品，它比第一代的功能更多。

⑥ 我們的廣告活動以食品的低脂肪含量為基礎。

A： I've heard you held an advertising campaign for the new product. 我聽說你們為新產品舉辦了廣告活動。

B： Yes. Our advertising campaign is based on the food's low fat content. 是的。我們的廣告活動以食品的低脂肪含量為基礎。

Tips

- We will take the concept of healthy life style as the base of this promotion campaign. 我們會把本次促銷活動的基礎定為健康的生活方式這個概念。
- We concentrate on the safety of the car. 我們會把重點放在汽車的安全性上。
- We hit our customers with the modern factor. 我們以時尚元素來打動消費者。

⑦ 電視廣告詳細敘述了這個概念。

A： The product brings a new way of spending people's spare time. 這個產品為人們度過閒置時間帶來了一種新的方式。

B： The TV commercial detailed the concept. 電視廣告詳細敘述了這個概念。

Tips

- The commercial shows the concept of a healthy life. 這個廣告展示了健康生活的概念。
- The TV advertisement expressed the idea. 電視廣告表達了這個想法。
- We'll have ten retailers running demonstrations at the branches. 我們會有 10 家零售商在分店做現場展示。

Step 3　實戰對話

① 策劃刊登廣告

A： Our product will be released this summer. 我們的產品這個夏季就要發布了。

B： Yes, I'm considering putting an advertisement. 是的，我在考慮登廣告。

A： In which media? 在什麼媒體上？

B： I want to put this advertisement in China Daily. 我想把這個廣告登在《中國日報》上。

A： It has a very large circulation. Which feature of the product will you highlight? 它的發行量很大。你們想要強調產品的哪個特點？

B： We want to highlight its excellent performance. 我們想要強調它卓越的性能。

② 展示產品優勢

A： How would you like to advertise the new car? 你想怎麼替新車做廣告？

B： We'll demonstrate its usefulness for the entire family. 我們會展現它對整個家庭的幫助。

A： Could you explain it? 可以解釋一下嗎？

B： We'll show how much more roominess it has than others. 我們會展示它比其他車更寬敞。

A： I got your point. So the car can take more people or stuff. 我明白你的意思了。所以車就可以載更多人或者東西了。

B： Exactly. 正是。

③ 展現產品特色

A： what's your idea on the advertising? 你對廣告有什麼看法？

B： We'll present its new user-friendly features. 我們將呈現它容易使用的新特色。

A： User-friendly? 容易使用？

B： Yes. It's designed with special attention to ergonomics. 是的。它是特別針對人體工學而設計的。

A： That sounds great. 這聽起來很棒。

B： The TV commercial detailed the concept. 電視廣告詳細敘述了這個概念。

Scene 56　廣告主題與廣告手法

Step 1　必備表達

主題	theme：也可用 subject 來代替。
標誌	logo：一個公司的標誌就是一個特別設計出來的商標，可以幫助消費者記住這個品牌，比如蘋果公司的 logo 就是一個缺了一角的蘋果。
商標	trademark：trademark 可簡寫為 TM，產品的名字、標誌或者特別設計都可以作為商標，受法律保護，不得仿冒。
標語	slogan：也就是廣告語，一般是一句簡短的口號，比如 Nike 的廣告語就是「Just do it.」。
強化	reinforce：也可用 strengthen 來代替。
品牌認同度	brand recognition：recognition 認同，認可。
看板廣告	billboard ad：billboard 也可用 hoarding 來代替；ads 是 advertisement 的簡寫。
橫幅廣告	banner ad：可以指橫幅廣告，也可以指網路上的通欄廣告。
海報	poster：post a poster 張貼海報；poster 的同義詞是 placard。
傳單	flyer：也可用 leaflet 或 handbill 來代替。

Step 2　句句精彩

① 我們把「全球商業生活模式」當作我們廣告的主題。

A：What's your idea on the advertisement? 關於廣告你們有什麼想法？

B：We've chosen 「global business lifestyle」 as our advertising theme. 我們把「全球商業生活模式」作為我們廣告的主題。

Tips

■ We decided to use 「living in a healthy way」 as the theme of the commercial. 我們決定把「健

康生活」作為廣告的主題。

The main idea of our advertising is to make people's life simple. 我們廣告的主要思想就是讓人們的生活變得簡單。

The commercial is expected to express the concept of environmental protection. 這個廣告希望表達出環保的理念。

② 我們商標中的蘋果代表產品對健康有益。

A：What's the meaning of the apple on your logo? 你們商標上的蘋果有什麼寓意嗎？

B： We use the apple on our logo to represent our product's health benefits. 我們商標中的蘋果代表產品對健康有益。

Tips

I think there should be a star on our logo since We're named Red Star Company. 我認為我們的商標中應該有顆星星，因為我們就叫做紅星公司。

In my opinion, we just take the snowman as our logo. 要我看，我們就把雪人作為我們的標誌。

Our logo, a leopard, represents the speed of our browser. 我們的標誌，豹子，代表了我們瀏覽器的速度。

③ 我們將用星星作為商標。

A： A star will be our trademark. 我們將用星星作為商標。

B： It's attractive. 這很吸引人。

Tips

Our boss has decided to use the sun as our trademark. 我們老闆決定用太陽作為我們的商標。

■ We use the pattern of coffee beans with the word「COSTA COFFEE」as our trademark. 我們用咖啡豆的圖案加上「COSTA COFFEE」的文字作為我們的商標。

This is a best-known trademark. 這是最著名的商標。

④ 我們的廣告語是「全力以赴」。

A： Our slogan is 「Try your best」. 我們的廣告語是「全力以赴」。

B： You want to express a positive attitude, don't you? 你們想表達一種積極的態度，是嗎？

Tips

The company's slogan is「Cheers」. 這家公司的廣告語是「乾杯」。

■ The slogan「Keeping walking」is to encourage people to be positive. 廣告語「一直向前走」是想鼓勵人們積極一些。

⑤ 網路廣告會強化品牌認同度。

A： We use Internet ads to publicize our brand. 我們使用網路廣告來推廣品牌。

B： Great idea. Internet ads will reinforce brand recognition. 好主意。網路廣告會強化品牌認同度。

Tips

■ Successful commercial will enhance the reputation of the company. 成功的廣告可以提高公司的聲譽。

■ Advertisements in supermarkets and department stores will help increase sales. 在超市和百貨公司的廣告可以幫助增加銷量。

■ An interesting TV commercial will increase the interest of the audience in the product. 一則有趣的電視廣告可以增加觀眾對產品的興趣。

⑥ 報紙廣告會提供產品的細節。

A： Newspaper ads will provide product details. 報紙廣告會提供產品的細節。

B： I say we should choose a large-circulation newspaper. 我認為我們應該選擇一家發行量大的報紙。

Tips

■ Detailed information of a product can be put on a newspaper. 產品的詳細資訊可以登在報紙上。

■ TV commercials will show the product's features in a vivid way. 電視廣告可以形象地展示產品的特點。

■ Attractive posters will raise people's interest in the product. 吸引人的海報可以提高人們對產品的興趣。

⑦ 我們的電視廣告將結合看板廣告。

A： Where would you like to do the advertising? 你要在哪裡做廣告？

B： Our commercials will combine with our billboard ads. 我們的電視廣告將結合看板廣告。

Tips

■ We're doing focused advertising on network TV. 我們在網路電視上投放目標明確的廣告。

■ We use TV and radio to publicize the product. 我們透過電視和廣播來宣傳產品。

■ We should focus on the big financial magazines. 我們應該集中在大型金融類雜誌。

Step 3　實戰對話

① 廣告主題

A： What's your idea on the advertisement? 關於廣告你們有什麼想法？

B： We've chosen "global business lifestyle" as our advertising theme. 我們把「全球商業生活模式」作為我們廣告的主題。

A： That sounds good. How to publicize this concept? 這聽起來不錯。怎麼推廣這個概念呢？

B： We decided to use Internet ads. 我們決定使用網路廣告。

A： Agreed. Internet ads will reinforce brand recognition. 同意。網路廣告會強化品牌認同度。

B： Exactly. 說得沒錯。

② 產品商標

A： Hey, our logo has been designed. 嗨，我們的商標設計出來了。

B： Let me have a look. Oh, what's the meaning of the apple on the logo? 讓我看看。哦，你們商標上的蘋果有什麼寓意嗎？

A： We use the apple on our logo to represent our products health benefits. 我們商標中的蘋果代表產品對健康有益。

B： Yeah, people are paying more attention to health now. 對啊，人們現在越來越關注健康了。

A： You're right. 沒錯。

B： Where are you going to put the advertisement? 你們打算在哪裡投放廣告？

A： Newspapers. Newspaper...newspaper ads will provide product details. 報紙。報紙……報紙廣告會提供產品的細節。

B： That's the advantage of paper media. 這是紙質媒體的優勢。

③ 廣告投放

A： Have you decided what will be your trademark? 你們決定好用什麼做商標了嗎？

B： Yes. A star will be our trademark. 是的。我們將用星星作為商標。

A：I see. Where would you like to do the advertising? 明白了。你們要在哪裡做廣告？

B： On TV. 在電視上。

A： Any other ways? 還有其他途徑嗎？

B： Our commercials will combine with our billboard ads. 我們的電視廣告將結合看板廣告。

Scene 57　廣告時程

Step 1　必備表達

上市時間	release date：release 發布，發表。
播出	air：air 除了表示「空氣」之意外，還可以作動詞表示「（透過電台或電視台）播出」。
同時地	simultaneously：也可用 at the same time 來代替。
推出	come out：也可用 release 或者 launch 來代替，不過要說 the product comes out 或者 release / launch the product，注意主動被動關係。
刊登	run：run 強調的是持續一段時間的刊登。
雜誌	magazine：commercial magazine 商業雜誌。
網路廣告	Internet ads：ads 是 advertisements 的簡寫。
每天	daily：a daily newspaper 日報；daily 也可以直接做名詞表示「日報」。
彈出廣告	pop up ads：pop up 出現。
到期	expire：也就是 come to an end 的意思。

Step 2　句句精彩

① 平面廣告會在電視廣告之後發表。

A： Have you finished preparing the print ads? 你們準備好平面廣告了嗎？

B： Yes. Print ads will be released after television ads. 是的。平面廣告會在電視廣告之後發表。

Tips

■ Television advertisement will be released after billboard advertisement. 電視廣告會在看板廣告之後發表。

■ The print ad in Business Weekly will be released on July 1st. 平面廣告將於 7 月 1 日在《商業週刊》上發表。

■ When is the release date of the TV commercial? 電視廣告什麼時候發表？

② 我們會在產品上市當天播放第一個廣告。

A： We'll air the first commercial the day our product goes on the market. 我們會在產品上市當天播放第一個廣告。

B： I'll say we need a warm-up. How about a week before the release of the product? 我認為我們需要做個預熱。產品上市前一個星期怎麼樣？

Tips

■ The first advertisement will come out the same day our product goes on the market. 第一個廣告會在產品上市的同一天出現。

■ We'll air the TV commercial at the same time the product is launched. 我們會在產品上市的同時播放電視廣告。

■ The product and its ads will be released simultaneously. 產品和其廣告將同時發表。

③ 我們會在產品推出前一個月刊登平面廣告。

A： The product will be put out in two months. 產品兩個月內就要上市了。

B： Yeah. We'll publish print ads one month before we put out our product. 是啊。我們會在產品推出前一個月刊登平面廣告。

Tips

■ The print ads of our product will be published before we release the TV commercial. 我們產品的平面廣告會在我們發表電視廣告之前刊登。

■ We'll release print ads first, and two weeks later, We'll launch our new product. 我們會先發布平面廣告，兩週後，我們再發表新產品。

■ The posters and billboard ads will come out a week before we put out the product. 我們會在產品推出前一週就推出海報和看板廣告的。

④ 它什麼時候播出？

A： When will it be aired? 它什麼時候播出？

B： It will be aired next Monday. 下週一播出。

Tips

■ When will the ads come out? 廣告什麼時候播出來？

When will the TV commercial be released? 電視廣告什麼時候播出？

When will the posters be posted? 海報什麼時候貼出來？

⑤ 我們會在新產品推出一個星期後，播放這個電視廣告。

A： When will the commercial be on air? 電視廣告要在什麼時候播出？

B： We'll broadcast the commercial a week after the new product comes out. 我們會在新產品推出一個星期後，播放這個電視廣告。

Tips

We'll release the Internet ads after the new product is launched. 我們會在新產品發表後推出網路廣告。

We'll broadcast the ad after the posters are posted. 我們會在海報貼出之後再播出廣告。

The commercial is due for release next week. 廣告預計在下週發布。

⑥ 每天都在報紙打廣告。

A： Newspaper ads will run daily. 每天都在報紙打廣告。

B： That will cause a huge influence. 那會產生很大的影響力的。

Tips

Newspaper ads will run every day from June to July. 從6月到7月每天都會在報紙打廣告。

Pop up ads will run daily on the Internet. 彈出廣告在網路上每天都有。

TV commercial will run every hour. 電視廣告每小時都會播放。

⑦ 雜誌和網路廣告將刊登到下個月。

A： When will the ads expire? 廣告什麼時候到期？

B： Magazine and Internet ads will run until next month. 雜誌和網路廣告將刊登到下個月。

Tips

The commercial is planned to run until the end of next month. 電視廣告計劃播放到下月底。

Newspaper ads will run until August 20th. 報紙廣告會刊登到8月20號。

The ads in the commercial magazine will run until this season ends. 在商業雜誌上的廣告會刊登到這一季度結束。

Step 3　實戰對話

① 廣告發布時間

A： Our product is coming out. How about the commercial? 我們的產品快要發表了。廣告怎麼樣了？

B： We'll air the first commercial the day our product goes on the market. 我們會在產品上市當天播放第一個廣告。

A： I see. How about print ads? 知道了。平面廣告呢？

B： Print ads will be released after television ads. 平面廣告會在電視廣告之後發布。

A： On which newspapers or magazines? 在哪家報紙或者雜誌上呢？

B： Business Weekly. 在《商業週刊》上。

② 提前推出廣告

A： The product will be put out in two months. 產品兩個月後就要上市了。

B： Yeah. We'll publish print ads one month before we put out our product. 是啊。我們會在產品推出前一個月刊登平面廣告。

A： I've heard you have also prepared a TV commercial. 我聽說你們還準備了電視廣告。

B： Yes. The TV commercial will be released after we publish the print ads. 是的。電視廣告會在我們刊登平面廣告之後發布。

A： I hope the well-prepared advertising will be a help to the product promotion. 我希望準備充分的廣告會對產品推廣有幫助。

B： I believe it will. 我相信會的。

③ 廣告播出時間

A： Bob, I have seen the commercial. Amazing! 鮑伯，我看到你們的廣告了。太棒了！

B： Thank you. The product is going to be launched soon. Everything is ready! 謝謝。產品馬上就要發表了。一切就緒了！

A： Good job. When will it be aired? 幹得好。它什麼時候播出？

B： We'll broadcast the commercial a week after the new product comes out. 我們會在新產品推出一個星期後，播放這個電視廣告。

A： I believe it will be a hit. 我相信它會取得很大成功的。

B： I hope so! 希望如此！

Scene 58　新品發表

Step 1　必備表達

上市，發表	launch：launch a new product 發表新產品。
發表	release：與 launch 的意思相近，還可以指發行電影、書、唱片等。
市場計畫	marketing plan：marketing 行銷，促銷。
企劃案	proposal：submit a proposal 提交企劃案。
競爭優勢	competitive advantage：competitive 有競爭力的；advantage 也可用 strength 來代替。
占優勢的	superior：be superior to 比……占優勢。
銷量預期	target sales volume：target 目標；sales 銷售量；volume 量。
開發	develop：develop a new product 開發新產品。
研究	research: 一家公司內常見的 R&D Dpt.，就是 Research and Development Department「研發部」的簡寫。
嶄新的	brand-new：反義詞是 used「用過的，二手的」。

Step 2　句句精彩

① 我們正在規劃產品的上市企劃。

A： The product is about to be launched. 產品快要上市了。

B： Yeah. We're working on the launch plan now. 是啊。我們正在規劃產品的上市企劃。

Tips

■ We're preparing the launch plan. 我們正在準備上市企劃。

■ We're making a launch plan of the new product. 我們正在做新產品的上市企劃。

■ We're working on launching new products. 我們正在做發表新產品的工作。

② 新產品預計下個月發表。

A： You have developed a new product, right? 你們開發了一個新產品，是嗎？

B： Right. The new product is due for release next month. 對。新產品預計下個月發表。

Tips

The product is prepared to be launched on July 10th. 新產品打算於 7 月 10 號發表。

We'll hold the new product release this Friday. 我們會在本週五舉辦新品發表會。

We have just released our new product. 我們的新產品剛剛發表。

③ 在產品推出之前，我們需要一個詳細的行銷企劃。

A： Before we release the product, we need to have a detailed marketing plan. 在產品推出之前，我們需要一個詳細的行銷企劃。

B： Exactly. Marketing is very important. 沒錯，行銷是非常重要的。

Tips

You'd better write a detailed marketing plan. 你最好寫一份詳盡的行銷企劃。

Why don't you write a launch plan? 你為什麼不寫一份上市企劃？

I have done some tactical planning already. 我已經完成一些策略計畫。

④ 我相信這個企劃會很有效。

A： I've read your marketing plan already. I'm sure this plan is going to be effective. 我已經讀過你的行銷企劃了。我相信這個企劃會很有效。

B： Thank you for your appreciation. 謝謝你的誇獎。

Tips

It sounds like an effective plan. 這聽起來是個有效的計畫。

I think this marketing plan is worth considering. 我認為這個行銷企劃值得考慮。

We hope the marketing plan will work. 我們希望行銷企劃能夠奏效。

⑤ 很高興經過幾個月的努力，我們已經開發出具有競爭優勢的產品。

A： After months of work, I'm so glad We've developed a product with competitive advantages. 很高興經過幾個月的努力，我們已經開發出具有競爭優勢的產品。

B： Yeah, We've all tried our best. 是啊，我們都盡力了。

Tips

■ I feel really happy to announce that our new product line has been launched. 我很高興地宣布我們發表了新的產品線。

■ This is our most newly released product. 這是我們最新推出的產品。

■ I'd like to introduce a new brand product to you. 我想給你介紹一種新牌子的產品。

⑥ 這款新產品要勝於其他產品。

A：This new product is superior to other products. 這款新產品要勝於其他產品。

B：Could you show me its advantages in detail? 你能向我具體展示一下它的優勢嗎？

Tips

■ Our products have a competitive advantage. 我們的產品有競爭優勢。

■ Our products' technology is more advanced than other products' . 我們產品的技術比其他產品的要先進。

■ Our product meets the needs of the market. 我們的產品符合市場需求。

⑦ 你對此款新產品的預期銷量是？

A：What is your target sales volume for this new product? 你對此款新產品的預期銷量是？

B：Well, we expect more than ten million yuan. 嗯，我們希望超過 1000 萬元吧。

Tips

■ We don't set any specific number, but I hope it could sell 200,000 pieces. 我們沒有設定具體數字，但我希望它能賣到 20 萬件。

■ I expect our sales of this product can be better than anyone before. 我希望這個產品的銷量比之前的都要好。

■ I expect We're going to have a great season. 我期待著我們這一季將會大豐收。

Step 3　實戰對話

① 產品終要上市

A：The new product is due for release next month. 新產品預計下個月發表。

B：To be honest, I feel a little nervous about that. You know, We've spent two years on it. 說實話，我有點緊張。你知道，我們為此花了兩年時間。

A： Yeah,We're working on the launch plan now. 是啊，我們正在規劃產品的上市企劃。

B： That should be well-prepared. 應該要好好準備準備。

A： No pains, no gains. I believe we can make it. 一分耕耘，一分收穫。我相信我們能成功。

B： Yes, we can! 是的，我們能！

② 制定市場計畫

A： The product is about to be released. 產品快要上市了。

B： Before we release the product, we need to have a detailed marketing plan. 在產品推出之前，我們需要一個詳細的行銷企劃。

A： You got it. We should have a good preparation. 你說得對。我們應該好好準備一下。

B： What is your target sales volume for this new product? 你對此款新產品的預期銷量是多少？

A：I have no idea. Well, at least five million yuan. 我也不知道。嗯，至少500萬元吧。

B： I hope it can be more than that. 我希望比這更多。

③ 期待企劃奏效

A： After months of work, I'm so glad We've developed a product with competitive advantages. 很高興經過幾個月的努力，我們已經開發出具有競爭優勢的產品。

B： Yeah. I have made a marketing plan for it. 是啊。我為它制定了一個行銷企劃。

A： Let me see... Great, great. I'm sure this plan is going to be effective. 我看看……很棒，很棒。我相信這個企劃會很有效。

B： Thank you. Some updates have been made for the product. And that is highlighted in the plan. 謝謝。我們對這款產品進行了升級。企劃裡強調的就是這個。

A： Impressive. 讓人印象很深刻。

B： We expect the sales volumes of more than ten million yuan. 我們希望銷量超過1000萬元。

Scene 59 客服回饋

Step 1 必備表達

嚴格的	strict：strict regulation 嚴格的規章制度。
品質管制	quality control：control 表示「管理，控制」，比如 in control 指「掌管，控制」；out of control 指「失去控制」。
客服人員	customer service staff：customer service 客戶服務；staff 員工，職員。
耐心的	patient：patient with 對……有耐心。
盡快	ASAP：ASAP 是 as soon as possible 的縮寫。
滿足	meet：也可用 satisfy 來代替。
需求	demand：也可用 need 來代替。
讓人滿意的	satisfying：形容事物讓人滿意用 satisfying，形容人很滿意或滿足用 satisfied。
對待	treat：treat sb. with 以……方式對待某人。
解決問題	solve the problem：solve 表示「解決」，也可用 handle 或者 settle 來表示這個意思。

Step 2 句句精彩

① 到目前為止，顧客對我們的服務品質評價甚高。

A： Have you received any complaints about our customer service? 你們收到過關於我們客戶服務方面的投訴嗎？

B： So far, our service has been very well-received by our customers. 到目前為止，顧客對我們的服務品質評價甚高。

Tips

■ Our customers speak highly of our service. 顧客對我們的服務評價很高。

Our customers are satisfied with our service. 顧客對我們的服務很滿意。

We haven't received any complaints about our service. 我們還沒有收到關於我們服務方面的投訴。

② 我們公司的品質管制很嚴格，因為我們得讓顧客滿意。

A： Our company is strict with quality control because we want to make our customers happy. 我們公司的品質管理很嚴格，因為我們想讓顧客滿意。

B： Impressive. 非常不錯。

Tips

In order to satisfy our clients, we pay much attention to quality control. 為了使我們的客戶滿意，我們特別注重品質管控。

We have great customer service staff who can deal with complaints on the phone very well. 我們有非常棒的客服人員，能夠很好地處理電話投訴。

I suggest we arrange for more training to improve our service. 我建議我們再多安排些培訓來提高我們的服務。

③ 感謝您如此耐心等待。

A： Ms Cooper, thanks for being so patient. We'll send someone to repair your mobile phone soon. 庫伯女士，感謝您如此耐心等待。我們很快就會派人去為您修手機的。

B： I see. Thank you so much. 我知道了。非常感謝。

Tips

I'm sorry for keeping you waiting so long. 很抱歉讓您久等了。

Pleased to be of any help to you. 很高興為您服務。

You are always welcome to call again. 隨時歡迎您再次來電。

④ 我們必須盡快解決這個問題。

A： One of our clients called to tell me that his printer couldn't work. 我們的一個客戶打電話來告訴我說他的印表機無法工作了。

B： We've got to get this fixed ASAP. 我們必須盡快解決這個問題。

Tips

I'll deal with it as soon as possible. 我會盡快處理的。

Let me handle the problem. 讓我來解決這個問題吧。

■ We have already settled this problem. 我們已經把這個問題搞定了。

⑤ 您對我們的服務有什麼問題嗎？

A： Did you have any problems with our service? 您對我們的服務有什麼問題嗎？

B： None. I'm very satisfied. 沒有。我很滿意。

Tips

■ Are you satisfied with our customer's service? 您對我們的客戶服務還滿意嗎？

■ I'm sorry to hear that. what's the problem? 真抱歉，出什麼問題了？

■ I make this call to apologize for our customer's service. 我打電話來是為我們的客戶服務向您道歉。

⑥ 顧客永遠是對的，我們要盡量滿足他們的要求。

A： Customers are always right; we should try our best to meet their demands. 顧客永遠是對的，我們要盡量滿足他們的要求。

B： Exactly. We should treat them with patience. 沒錯。我們應該耐心對待他們。

Tips

■ Our aim is to make the customers satisfied. 我們的目標是讓顧客滿意。

■ As a customer service staff, you should always keep your customer on your mind. 身為客服人員，你應該始終把客戶放在心上。

■ Our manager always tells us to do our best to serve the customers. 經理經常告訴我們要盡力服務好顧客。

⑦ 感謝來電。

A： Thank you for having my problem solved. Bye. 謝謝你幫我解決了問題。再見。

B： My pleasure. Thanks for calling. Bye. 別客氣。感謝來電。再見。

Tips

■ It's been an honor to assist you today. 很榮幸今天能為您服務。

■ Your advice is valuable to us. 您的建議對於我們來說很有價值。

■ Just give me a call if tHere's anything you need. 如果您有什麼需要，就儘管打電話給我。

Step 3　實戰對話

① 客戶服務令人滿意

A： Have you received any complaints about our customer service? 你們收到過關於我們客戶服務方面的投訴嗎？

B： So far, our service has been very wellreceived by our customers. 到目前為止，顧客對我們的服務品質評價甚高。

A： How can you make it? 你們是怎麼做到的？

B： Our company is strict with quality control because we want to make our customers happy. 我們公司的品質管制很嚴格，因為我們想讓顧客滿意。

A： I see. You made great effort. 我明白了。你們付出了很大的努力。

B： And we have great customer service staffs who always keep the customers on their mind. 而且我們有非常棒的客服人員，能夠很好地處理電話投訴。

② 接到客戶投訴

A： Hello. 您好。

B： Hello. Is this the Customer Service Department of ABC Company? 你好。是 ABC 公司的客戶服務部嗎？

A： Yes. Did you have any problems with our service? 是的。您對我們的服務有什麼疑問嗎？

B： The computer I bought is broken. 我買的電腦壞了。

A： I'm so sorry to hear that. Let me see if there can be a technician to deal with that this afternoon. 聽到此事我很抱歉。讓我看看能不能派位技術人員今天下午去處理這個問題。

B： OK. Thank you. 好的。謝謝。

A： Hello, sir. Thanks for being so patient. We'll send someone to your place this afternoon. 您好，先生。感謝您如此耐心等待。我們今天下午會派人去您那裡的。

B： That would be good. I'll wait at home. 那太好了。我就在家等著了。

③ 積極處理投訴

A： Jim, I received a complaint from a client. 吉姆，我接到了一個客戶投訴。

B： What happened? 怎麼了？

A： He said he couldn't log in our system because tHere's a bug. 他說他無法登入我們的系統，因為有一個程式錯誤。

B： Oh. We've got to get this fixed ASAP. 哦。我們必須盡快解決這個問題。

A： Yes. The customer is always right; we should try our best to meet their demands. 是的。顧客永遠是對的，我們要盡量滿足他們的要求。

B： don't worry. I'll deal with it as soon as possible. 別擔心。我會盡快處理的。

Scene 60　商 務 簡 報

Step 1　必 備 表 達

圖表	chart：常見的三種圖表是 bar chart「柱狀圖」、pie chart「圓餅圖」和 graph「曲線圖」。
市場的走勢	tendency of the market：upward tendency 上升的趨勢。
顯著變化	significant change：significant 強調的是因為重大、有意義而明顯。
巔峰時期	peak period：peak 的本義是「山峰」，引申表示「頂峰，巔峰」。
達到	reach：reach the target 達成目標。
認識	recognize：也可用 know 來代替。
品牌	brand：brand image 品牌形象。
結論	conclude：conclude sth. with sth. 以⋯⋯為⋯⋯做結尾。
消費者滿意指數	customer satisfaction index：satisfaction 滿意；index 指數。
連續的	consecutive：consecutive 強調的是「連續不斷的、緊連著的」意思，相似意思的單字還有 successive。

Step 2　句 句 精 彩

① 請看下一張圖表。

A：If you are clear about this, please take a look at the next illustration. 如果這個你明白了，請看下一張圖表。

B：All right. 好的。

Tips

■ illustration 的意思是「圖示」，其動詞形式 illustrate 表示「（用圖表等）說明」。

■ I've prepared a bar chart and a graph for you. 我為大家準備了一張柱狀圖和一張線形圖。

■ Let's move on to the next page. 讓我們來看下一頁。

② 這張表描述了市場的走勢。

A： What does this chart show? 這張圖表顯示的是什麼？

B： This chart shows the tendency of the market. 這張表描述了市場的走勢。

Tips

- This chart shows the sales volumes of the past five years. 這張圖表顯示了過去 5 年的銷售量。

- Significant changes can be observed on this chart. 從這張表上可以觀察到顯著的變化。

- We can find from this diagram that this product had a ready market. 我們可以從這張圖表來看出這個產品占領了現有市場。

③ 在巔峰時期，我們的銷售成長了 15%。

A： During the peak period, our sales rise by 15%. 在巔峰時期，我們的銷售成長了 15%。

B： Impressive. Have you analyzed the reason? 很不錯。你們分析為什麼了嗎？

Tips

- We're above sales target by about 7 percent this year. 這一年度我們超出銷售目標大約 7%。

- We hit a peak in export business in January. 我們的出口業務在 1 月達到了高峰。

- Sales on the product were steady for the past six months. 這個產品過去半年的銷量穩定。

④ 去年我們的利潤達到了 10 億美元。

A： Our profit reaches one billion dollars last year. 去年我們的利潤達到了 10 億美元。

B： what's the target of this year? 今年的目標是什麼呢？

Tips

- This year, our company made a profit of $10 million. 今年我們公司營利 1000 萬美元。

- Our sales topped 50 million last year. 去年我們的銷售額達到了 5000 萬。

- Our net profit increased by 5% or so every single month. 我們的純利潤每月成長 5% 左右。

⑤ 根據最新的調查，我們品牌的大眾認知度達到了 55%。

A： How's our brand promotion going? 我們的品牌推廣進行得怎麼樣了？

B： According to recent survey, 55% people are able to recognize our brand. 根據最新的調查，我們品牌的大眾認知度達到了 55%。

Tips

If we combine the two graphs, we may conclude that the brand recognition has been increased by 13 percent. 如果我們將這兩個曲線圖結合起來，得出的結論是我們品牌的大眾認知度提升了 13%。

■ After a vigorous new advertising campaign, our brand recognition has been increased. 經過新一輪的強勢廣告推廣活動，我們品牌的大眾認知度提升了。

Now, more and more customers are learning about our brand by word of mouth. 現在，越來越多的消費者透過口口相傳知道了我們的品牌。

⑥ 消費者滿意指數提升至 93%。

A： Customer satisfaction index rises to 93%. 消費者滿意指數提升至 93%。

B： We're making a progress. 我們一直在進步。

Tips

More and more customers show their satisfaction with our products and service. 越來越多的消費者表示對我們公司的產品和服務滿意。

Clients are satisfied with both the price and quality of our products. 客戶對我們產品的價格和品質都很滿意。

The customers are very satisfied with the quality of our products. 消費者對我們產品的品質很滿意。

⑦ 我們的整體銷量已經連續兩個季度大幅下滑。

A： Our sales plunged for the second consecutive season. 我們的整體銷量已經連續兩個季度大幅下滑。

B： We've got to do something. 我們需要做點什麼了。

Tips

Sales of the products fell for the third straight month. 產品銷量連續下跌了 3 個月。

Sales dropped to 3 million, with a slight recovery at the end of last month. 銷量下跌到300萬，上月底稍有回升。

There is no market for the product anymore. 這個產品不再有市場了。

Step 3 實戰對話

① 看圖說話

A： OK. I see your point. 好的。我明白你的意思了。

B： Great. Please take a look at the next illustration. 好。請看下一張圖表。

A： What does this chart show? 這張圖表顯示的是什麼？

B： This chart shows the tendency of the market. 這張表描述了市場的走勢。

A： A steady growth. 平穩的成長。

B： Exactly. So we shouldn't lose heart. 正是。所以我們不應該喪失信心。

② 利潤成長

A： Our profit reaches 1 billion dollars last year. 去年我們的利潤達到了 10 億美元。

B： It is the highest record ever. 這是歷史最高紀錄。

A： Yes. Look at this chart. During the peak period, our sales rise by 15%. 是的。看這張圖表。在巔峰時期，我們的銷售成長了 15%。

B： Brilliant. what's the target of this year? 太棒了。今年的目標是什麼呢？

A： I expect the profit of 1.2 billion dollars this year. 我希望今年利潤能達到 12 億美元。

B： Hope we can make it. 希望我們能夠做到。

③ 認知度與滿意率

A： According to recent survey, 55% people are able to recognize our brand. 根據最新的調查，我們品牌的大眾認知度達到了 55%。

B： Now, more and more customers are learning about our brand by word of mouth. 現在，越來越多的消費者透過口口相傳知道了我們的品牌。

A： It's due to the good quality of our products. 這歸功於我們產品良好的品質。

B： Yes. At the same time, customer Satisfaction Index rises to 93%. 是的。同時，消費者滿意率提升至 93%。

A： We're making a progress. 我們在進步。

B： Next we target at increasing the customer satisfaction rate to 95%. 下一步我們的目標是將消費者滿意率提升至 95%。

商務英語必備指南

作　　　者：金利 主編

發 行 人：黃振庭

出 版 者：崧博出版事業有限公司

發 行 者：崧燁文化事業有限公司

E - m a i l：sonbookservice@gmail.com

粉 絲 頁：https://www.facebook.com/sonbookss/

網　　　址：https://sonbook.net/

地　　　址：台北市中正區重慶南路一段六十一號八樓
815 室

Rm. 815, 8F., No.61, Sec. 1, Chongqing S. Rd.,
Zhongzheng Dist., Taipei City 100, Taiwan (R.O.C)

電　　　話：(02)2370-3310

傳　　　真：(02) 2388-1990

總 經 銷：紅螞蟻圖書有限公司

地　　　址：台北市內湖區舊宗路二段 121 巷 19 號

電　　　話：02-2795-3656

傳　　　真：02-2795-4100

印　　　刷：京峯彩色印刷有限公司（京峰數位）

國家圖書館出版品預行編目資料

商務英語必備指南 / 金利主編 . -- 第一
版 . -- 臺北市：崧博出版：崧燁文化發
行 , 2020.10

　面；　公分

POD 版

ISBN 978-957-735-996-4(平裝)

1. 商業英文 2. 讀本

805.18　　109015794

官網

臉書

定　　　價：360 元

發行日期：2020 年 10 月第一版

◎本書以 POD 印製